Also available from Hudson Lin and Carina Press

Hard Sell

Also available from Hudson Lin

Three Months to Forever
Lessons for a Lifetime
Fly With Me
Inside Darkness
Stepping Out in Faith

Between the Tension Series

Between the Push and Pull
Embracing the Tension

Coffee House Shorts

Take Me Home
Ipso Facto ILU
My Name on Her Lips

Going Public contains the following subjects that some readers may find difficult:

Drug trafficking
Fraud
Police arrests
Incarceration
Hospitalization

GOING PUBLIC

HUDSON LIN

carina
press

carina press®

Recycling programs for this product may not exist in your area.

ISBN-13: 978-1-335-50016-8

Going Public

Copyright © 2022 by Hudson Lin

For questions and comments about the quality of this book, please contact us at CustomerService@Harlequin.com.

Carina Press
22 Adelaide St. West, 41st Floor
Toronto, Ontario M5H 4E3, Canada
www.CarinaPress.com

Printed in U.S.A.

Dear Reader,

The world of high finance is often composed of shades of gray where good people engage in sometimes questionable activities or support less than ideal conduct. Money can drive people to do things they would normally never consider doing otherwise.

I have never personally encountered drugs or drug trafficking during my time working in the finance industry. But investments that harm the environment, discriminate against low income communities, and purposefully circumvent government regulations are commonplace. I wrote *Going Public* to explore what happens when good people are incentivized to do bad things.

If you'd like to connect with me, you can find me on Instagram, Twitter, and Facebook under the handle @HudsonLinWrites or through my website at HudsonLin.com.

Happy reading!

Lin

GOING PUBLIC

Chapter One

It was a dance Elvin did pretty much every day. A stack of dry cleaning balanced on one arm, a tray of Tim Hortons coffees in the other hand, dodging a stream of office workers speed walking through Toronto's financial district. Elvin jogged across Lakeshore—careful not to spill any precious liquid gold—and slipped down a small side street.

The entrance to Ray's condo building was discreet. Not one of those flashy things popping up all over the city announcing the status of its residents to passersby. No, Ray and his neighbors had no interest in publicizing their wealth. That was how much money they had.

Elvin used his elbow to hit the automatic door button and slipped inside.

"Mr. Goh, good morning!" the security desk attendant greeted him.

"Good morning, Mohammad!" Elvin set his tray of coffees on the counter and wiggled one cup loose. "Here you go. Large double double."

"Aw, Mr. Goh. You didn't have to do that." Mohammad and his co-workers rotated through the night shift and Elvin had made a point to memorize their schedule. It wouldn't do to bring the wrong coffee order for the hardworking staff who stayed up all night manning the desk.

"Don't worry. I'm charging it to the boss." Elvin winked before heading to the elevators, Mohammad's laugh ringing behind him.

The doors opened immediately, like the elevator had been waiting there for him. Then it shot up the building so fast Elvin's ears popped on the way.

The condo was mostly quiet when Elvin stepped inside, save for the sound of water running from the primary suite. Good, Ray was up already. Which would make the morning much less awkward for Elvin.

He toed his shoes off and went into the large open-plan living space. Kitchen on the right and living room on the left. A dining table the size of a boat in between. Everything glistened white, from the tiled floors to the walls that reached for the double-height ceilings to the leather-upholstered furnishings.

If something wasn't white, it was transparent. Like the multilevel coffee table or the glass-topped dining table or the crystal chandelier that hung from the ceiling, guaranteed to inflict serious damage if it fell on anyone. Also crystal clear were the floor-to-ceiling windows that provided a view of Lake Ontario, glistening green blue in the early morning sun.

Elvin set down the tray of coffees on the large marble island in the kitchen—white, of course—and took the dry cleaning to the primary suite that made up one entire wing of the condo. Everything in here was white too, though punctuated with clothes tossed haphazardly over chairs and couches and the floor. How the hell Ray managed to go through so many clothes over the course of one weekend, Elvin would never know.

Elvin pulled open the sliding doors of the dressing room, which was probably bigger than the whole of his basement apartment, and put away the dry cleaning. Arms free, he made a circuit of the bedroom, picking up discarded clothing and dropping it into the laundry basket for Ray's housekeeper to deal with. With all the clothes cleared from it, the bed sat in pride of place in the room, pristine with hospital corners.

Had Ray not slept in it all weekend? Elvin shook his head as he paused outside the en suite bathroom. The door was ajar and steam billowed from the crack.

"Hey! I'm here!" he called out.

"I'll be out in a minute!" Ray answered from inside, the sound muffled by the rushing water.

Elvin let himself out of Ray's bedroom with a smile on his face. It was silly and stupid, but he couldn't help it. The casualness of their standard weekday morning exchange was often the highlight of Elvin's day. But then, he often felt that way whenever he worked with Ray. The ease of their relationship was unlike anything Elvin had experienced before—with friends, with family and with the odd ex-boyfriend.

His smile disappeared as he stopped by the kitchen island on his way to the other wing of the condo, made up of guest bedrooms. He had to pop his head into two empty rooms before finding what he was looking for. A rumpled bed with a distinctly human-shaped lump still wrapped up in the duvet. What kind of one-night stand would Elvin find this morning? He'd seen it all—men, women, trans and non-binary folks; light skinned, dark skinned and every shade in between; big folks, petite folks, folks with hair color more varied than the rainbow. Ray wasn't particular when it came to whom he took to bed. He could find something attractive in just about anyone he came across.

Today, as he set the coffee on the nightstand, Elvin found himself staring down at a tousled head of short blond hair. The guy had a baby face, accentuated by the duvet pulled all the way up to his chin. Cozy.

"Hey." He leaned over, grabbed the guy by the shoulder and gave him a firm shake. "Wake up."

The blond groaned and tried to hide under the duvet, which only reminded Elvin of his siblings when he tried to get them up in time for school.

"Hey, kid." He tried again. This time he grabbed the edge of the duvet and pulled it off the bed. "Time to get up and go. Don't you have school or something?"

Exposed to the cool air, the blond curled into the fetal position—completely naked. He presented a long expanse of pale-skinned back and a round ass that could be considered a bubble butt. Elvin examined the sight before him, tilting his head in case it would look more appealing from a different angle. Nope—it didn't work for him. Not that he'd expected it to. Most nudity didn't and he would never fully understand how people got so caught up in images of others undressed.

Whatever. He'd come to terms with his own demisexuality a while ago and Monday morning was not the time to be rehashing it. He picked up the coffee, walked around the bed and shoved the hot cup into the hands of the naked blond. "Take this. Drink."

Thankful, he took the cup and sat up. "Who *are* you?" he asked as he rubbed his eyes.

"It doesn't matter." Elvin pointed to the en suite bathroom. "Wash up and then you can leave."

"Where's Ray?"

Elvin sighed with a pinch of sympathy for the guy. He really had no clue, did he? "Sorry buddy, he's moved on."

Elvin left him looking morose in the middle of the bed and went back to the kitchen. He wiggled the last coffee cup free from its tray and took a sip of the steaming brew, more sugar than coffee. Then he set it aside to start on Ray's standard morning drink—a homemade cappuccino, fresh from the industrial espresso machine imported from Italy. Elvin ran an affectionate hand along its glossy surface before embarking on the ritual of grinding coffee beans and

steaming milk. According to Ray, Elvin made the best cappuccino in the city, a title that Elvin did not take lightly.

By the time he'd poured the palm leaf design onto the
top of the brimming cappuccino mug, Ray was sauntering
into the main room. His feet were bare, his black hair was
still wet, his tie was draped around the back of his neck
and he held his suit jacket in one hand.

"Mmm." He moaned as he took a seat at the kitchen island. Elvin placed the cappuccino in front of him and Ray
lifted it to his nose. He took a deep breath with his eyes
closed and Elvin grinned at Ray's obvious appreciation.

This was why he woke up extra early in the mornings
and trekked all the way to Ray's condo, even when it
wasn't a part of his job description. He couldn't quite remember how it'd all started, but he'd come to cherish this
time when it was just him and Ray in the intimacy of the
kitchen, getting ready for a day of work. There was no one
else there to interrupt them and he had Ray all to himself.

Well, no one except the leftover hookups from the night
before. Appearing right on cue, the skinny blond materialized at the end of the kitchen island and looked uncer-
tainly between Elvin and Ray. "Uh, hi."

Ray's expression lit up like he was pleasantly surprised
to find the blond still around. "Hey." He set his cup down
and slipped from his stool. "Good morning. Did you sleep
well?" Ray's smile oozed charm, enough to soften the blow
and make the guy feel special before he was kicked out.

Elvin didn't bother following them to the door, but
rather pulled out his laptop and set up a makeshift desk

on the kitchen island. He'd already checked both his and Ray's inboxes that morning, sorting through items that needed immediate responses and ones that could wait. He navigated to a folder he kept updated with all the emails that Ray would have to address personally—everything else Elvin would take care of for him.

When Ray came back alone, Elvin pointed to the laptop. "You've got emails to review."

Ray pouted. Full on pouted. And Elvin had to dig deep for his stern big brother expression. "Don't give me that. Do your emails or you're not getting any breakfast sausage."

Ray gave him a mock gasp. "No! Don't take away my breakfast sausage!"

Elvin pinned him with a knowing look, then shifted his gaze to the laptop. "Emails. Then breakfast sausage."

That brought out a chuckle from Ray, who obediently took his seat behind the laptop while sipping his cappuccino. Elvin turned to the giant fridge to pull out the necessary ingredients. Eggs, hash browns, tomatoes, sausage—the appliance was kept fully stocked with every conceivable breakfast food item by Ray's personal cook. On the lower shelves and in the freezer were prepared meals that could be heated in the oven or by a quick *ding* in the microwave.

"Why is this in here?"

Elvin glanced over his shoulder to find Ray frowning at the computer screen. "Why is what in where?"

"A meeting with Ming in my schedule."

He'd been expecting this. "You can't avoid him forever."

Ray turned his frown toward Elvin. "Why not?"

"Oh come on." Elvin went back to tending the eggs in the skillet. "A meeting with Ming isn't the worst thing in the world. Besides, remember Joanna's directive for all senior partners to take a more active role in courting investors?"

It was always safe to invoke Joanna's name. As founder and CEO of Jade Harbour, Joanna was someone no one messed with—not even Ray. She could turn the largest, most brutal man into a simpering fool with one glare. Packed conference rooms fell deadly silent whenever she walked in. She ruled with an iron fist that both terrified and garnered worship from her employees.

Ray dropped his head backward in defeat. "Ugh."

"I don't know why you always get so worked up about this. You're great with investors. They can't resist your charm."

"I don't get worked up." Ray crossed his arms defensively, which was a telltale sign that he was lying through his teeth.

The truth was, Ray was a natural at investor relations. He knew it, Joanna knew it, and unfortunately for Ray, Ming knew it too. As the Head of Investor Relations, Ming was responsible for getting the rich and wealthy to invest in Jade Harbour's portfolio companies. It involved a lot of schmoozing with influential people and flattering those with already inflated egos. It was something Ming was good at, and something that drove almost everyone else at Jade Harbour nuts. Ray especially—just because he was good at investor relations didn't mean he had to like it.

"Besides," Ray continued. "I already know what Ming wants to talk about."

"Which is?" Elvin pulled a plate from the cabinet and carefully arranged the food on it.

"Phoenix Family Trust. What else?" From the tone of Ray's voice, one would have thought that he'd been asked to dive into the nearest dumpster for pennies.

Phoenix Family Trust was a conglomerate of the wealthiest families in Hong Kong, who pooled their assets to create greater returns on their investments. It also happened to be managed by Ray's father.

Elvin ran a clean towel around the edges of the plate before setting it carefully in front of Ray, along with a full set of utensils. "You don't know that. Maybe Ming wants to talk about something else."

"How much do you want to bet on that?" Ray unfurled his napkin and laid it across his lap.

"Nothing." Elvin grabbed another plate for himself and piled the remaining food on it. "Gambling's more your thing than mine."

"Hmm." Ray lifted the fork and knife and cut into the perfectly fried over-easy eggs with an elegance that felt overblown for something as simple as breakfast. He created a perfect bite-sized morsel of food before lifting it to his mouth.

Elvin watched from the other side of the island, his hip braced against the counter and his own plate in hand. He wiggled the edge of his fork through the egg, stabbed at as many things as he could get onto the tines, and shoveled the whole lot between his lips.

Ray met his gaze as they both chewed. There was a tiny crinkle at the edges of Ray's eyes, hinting at his amusement, and Elvin felt little compunction in returning it. Ray was an only child raised in prep schools. Elvin was the eldest of six and had acted like a third parent to his younger siblings from the time he could hold a baby bottle by himself. For Ray, meal times were an affair to be enjoyed. For Elvin, they were war zones defined by scarcity—if you didn't fight for your share, you went hungry.

They'd had heated discussions about this particular difference numerous times in the past. Ray nagging Elvin to take a seat and slow down for fear of choking on his food. Elvin showing Ray his already empty plate with a shrug; no need to sit down when there was nothing left to eat.

He loaded the dirty dishes into the dishwasher as Ray continued eating. By the time Ray was finished, the kitchen was spotless and Elvin had stashed his laptop away.

"Ready to go?" he asked, giving the kitchen a once-over for anything he might have missed.

Ray stood and stretched. "Ready when you are."

Ray's version of ready meant another twenty minutes of gathering his things from rooms across the condo. His socks and shoes were in the bedroom. His laptop was on the coffee table. His sunglasses were…it had taken a full ten minutes to find them under the bed of the guest bedroom.

By the time they made it to Jade Harbour, the weekly Monday morning investment meeting was about to start. The largest conference room in the office was filled to overflowing. Around the large conference table were all the senior investment and operational professionals. Behind them were their junior staff, sitting in office chairs that had been rolled in from elsewhere. The perimeter of the room was lined with cushioned benches, where all other support staff sat. The unlucky late ones took up standing positions by the doors.

At least Ray and Elvin were the lucky late ones.

Ray strolled in and claimed the last empty chair at the table. Elvin slipped into a narrow spot on the bench next to Mike, Jade Harbour's legal counsel.

"Nice of you to grace us with your presence," Mike whispered to him.

Elvin rolled his eyes. "Monday morning."

"Now that we're all here," Joanna looked pointedly at Ray, "let's get started."

She spoke from the front of the room, where she sat with her long legs crossed, hands steepled by her chin. She sat a little back from the conference table, where she'd placed a giant binder. It contained the most up-to-date information on all Jade Harbour investments and potential investments, everything from monthly financial statements, budget to actual reporting, key performance indicators, supply and demand analysis, down to the most recent hiring decisions at each portfolio company. Elvin had no doubt that she had every word on every page memorized. She was one of those people.

A couple junior investment professionals stood and opened a presentation on the TV that spanned nearly one entire wall. They launched into a progress report on a portfolio company that Elvin wasn't familiar with. All he knew was that Ray wasn't working on that company, which meant it wasn't relevant to him.

Zoning out, Elvin gazed around the room, taking in his coworkers. Some of them were listening intently. Others looked about as engaged as he was. Everyone was dressed immaculately in well-tailored suits or dresses, not one hair out of place. After years at the company, Elvin had mostly gotten used to this world where a single watch could cost twice as much as his parents' car, where thousand-dollar handbags were never more than a season old. But there were times when he marvelled at it all. So different from his working-class upbringing, where hand-me-downs were considered new.

His gaze landed on Ray, the epitome of this world. Elvin wasn't exactly sure how wealthy Ray's family was. He'd looked it up at one point and the Chao family's net worth had been so high that the number had meant nothing to Elvin. It was well-known in the company that Ray didn't *need* this job at Jade Harbour. His family had more money than he could realistically spend in one lifetime. But he still worked—and worked fairly hard—like it was some sort of pet project, something to occupy his time. This was usually spoken of with more than a hint of derision, which Elvin was quick to squelch whenever he could. So what if Ray didn't need to work? He was here and Jade Harbour was lucky to have him. Ray had saved Jade Harbour from unexpected losses and public humiliation, and he had cleaned up other people's messes more times than Elvin could count. Rather than scolding him for being late, they should be thanking him for showing up at all.

"Ray?"

All heads turned to him and Elvin scrambled to figure out what they were talking about. On the TV screen was a chart labelled with the name of a portfolio company that Ray had helped out with a while ago.

"I've got it handled." Ray sat low in his chair, leaning to one side with an elbow propped on the armrest like it was the only thing keeping him upright. "They've got more than enough dirty laundry that I'm sure they don't want aired. A couple phone calls should be enough to get them on board with our plan."

"Good." Joanna turned to the young woman standing at the front of the room. "Anything else?"

"Nothing else." The young woman took her seat.

"What's next?"

"Caron Paper." A young man took control of the TV screen and brought up the next set of slides. "As you can see from this graph here, we're in a good place to take the company public. It is ahead of our original investment schedule, but with the current market conditions, an initial public offering would give us a generous return on investment."

The young man clutched the remote control in his hands

and stared wide-eyed at Joanna. Despite how full the room was, it was eerily silent. An occasional flutter of paper, or squeak of an office chair, but otherwise, the loudest sound was the hum of the building's air-conditioning system.

Joanna studied the TV screen, her expression inscrutable. Listing a company on the stock market was a massive undertaking and usually took months and months of preparation. To make such a recommendation ahead of the anticipated schedule was ballsy. If they pulled it off, it could be the most profitable deal in Jade Harbour's history. But if they didn't, bankruptcy wouldn't be out of the question.

Without turning, Joanna spoke. "Ray, I want a top-to-bottom audit. Leave no stone unturned. If there's even one dust bunny in Caron's closet, I want it dissected. If they get a clean bill from you, then we can talk about an IPO."

"You got it," Ray responded immediately before shooting a quick look at Elvin.

Elvin gave him a slight nod in response. They were on the job.

Chapter Two

"Ray, my man!" Ming stood in the middle of Ray's office with his arms held out like he was presenting himself for Ray's inspection.

From behind his desk, Ray sighed. "Hello, Ming."

Ray liked to think he got along with everyone, or at least most people. But there was something about Ming that annoyed the hell out of him. He was too friendly, too familiar. Like he wanted to be best friends just a little too desperately.

"I finally managed to get on your calendar!" Ming grinned like he'd won the lottery as he helped himself to one of the guest chairs.

Ray gave him a tight smile and nodded. "Yep."

"You're a busy guy!"

Not nearly as busy as he should be, given Ming was in his office. "Yep."

"Whew." Ming shook his head like landing a meeting with Ray had taken a physical toll on him. "I really had to work that assistant of yours. He's a tough cookie to get through." He pointed over his shoulder with his thumb in the direction of Elvin's desk outside Ray's office.

"You mean Elvin? He has a name."

"Yeah, yeah, Elvin, I know his name." Ming chuckled as if Ray's comment was ridiculous. "Of course I know Elvin. He's got good taste."

Ray's eyebrows shot up. What the hell did Ming know about Elvin's tastes? "Excuse me?"

"You know, musical theater!" Ming wiggled his fingers in a poor imitation of jazz hands. "We've been chatting about the shows coming through Toronto this season!"

Musical theater. Right. It was one of Elvin's rare hobbies, about the only thing he talked about aside from work and family. Ray hadn't realized Ming was a fan as well. How often had they been chatting, exactly, and why hadn't Elvin mentioned anything about it to him? Hrm.

Ming was still talking. Something about some show Ray had never heard of. He raised a hand to stop him. "What did you want to talk about?"

Ming sat there with his mouth gaping like he'd stalled his engine. Ray forced himself to take a slow breath so he wouldn't reach across his desk and shake the life out of him.

"Yes, right!" Ming shifted forward in his seat. "I wanted to touch base about Phoenix Family Trust."

He *knew* it! Elvin owed him. Ray ran a hand over his face to stifle a groan. "No."

Ming opened his mouth and closed it again with a confused look. "What?"

"No," Ray said louder in case Ming hadn't heard him the first time. "We've tried this before and it didn't work. Why do you think it will this time?"

"Because it's been years since we've pitched them! The market has changed! We've got a stronger track record!" Ming's hands got more animated with every sentence.

"So set up the meeting yourself." Ray pushed back his chair to stand. "You have their contact information. What do you need me for?"

"Oh, come on, Ray. They're much more likely to respond to you than they are to me."

Ray paced around the room, stretching his arms over his head. Talking about PFT always made him antsy and restless. "I don't know why you think that. I'm not exactly a welcomed entity over there."

"Why not?"

Ray rolled his eyes. He wasn't about to detail his complicated family history to Ming of all people. "I'm just not."

"But why?"

Ray spun toward Ming, not entirely sure what he was hearing. Was Ming seriously pressing this point? "Because!"

"Okay! Okay!" Ming settled back into the chair like he planned to be there for a while.

Ray planted his hands on his hips. "Anything else I can help you with?"

"Are you sure there's no one there you can ask for a meeting? As a favor? For me?"

As if Ming was anyone Ray wanted to do favors for. The dude didn't understand the word *no*. But if it would get him off Ray's back... Ray sighed. "I can try to make a couple calls."

Ming jumped up. "Great! I knew I could count on you!" He came over and clapped a hand on Ray's shoulder before shaking it a little too forcefully. "We're going to make a great team, buddy. Just you wait and see."

Ming headed toward the door, spinning halfway so he was walking backward. "You and me, Ray!" He shot finger guns at Ray. "Joanna's going to be stoked."

Ray let out an audible groan as Ming left. What the hell had he gotten himself into?

Elvin poked his head in. "You still alive?"

"Barely." Ray flopped onto the long couch on the far side of his office. He stuck out an arm and pointed in Elvin's general direction. "I win our bet. Ming wouldn't stop going on about PFT."

"Would it really be so bad to reach out? It's not like you have to talk to your father."

His father. Ugh. That was the real problem. Once upon a time, Ray had been groomed to take over management of the trust. But he'd ruined all his father's plans when he insisted on joining Jade Harbour instead. It was still a sore spot for the family and Ray had been all but disowned for wanting to work for someone else.

A number of Ray's relatives held senior positions within

the trust. All good people who knew what they were doing, but every single one of them had gotten to where they were because of their last name. Nepotism wasn't only alive and well, it was considered a fucking virtue, and Ray didn't want anything to do with it.

"I know." He ran through the short list of cousins and uncles he could call. Who wouldn't give him too hard a time for missing the family reunion the year before? Or try to ask for an IOU in return? There was no way he'd be able to avoid a lecture on filial piety, giving back to the family and carrying on their good name. He let out a frustrated groan and shot to his feet so fast that his head spun a little.

"You okay?"

"Yeah. I'm great."

"You don't look great." Elvin looked like he was trying really hard to hold back a laugh.

Ray shot him a glare. "I need to get out of here." He shook out his limbs, trying to throw off the feeling of insects crawling across his skin. "I need a swim."

Elvin nodded. "I'll cover for you if anyone asks where you are."

"Thanks." Trust Elvin to always know exactly what to say at exactly the right time.

Ray grabbed his suit jacket from the coat hanger and slipped it on. "Stop by later and catch me up on anything I missed, okay?"

"Sure."

"Great." Ray stopped at the door. "And for the love of god, don't put Ming on my calendar again."

Elvin chuckled and shrugged. "I'll do my best."

Ray headed for the elevator. Few people, including Elvin, understood the weird dynamic between Ray and his family. Hell, he didn't fully understand it himself. His parents hadn't been around for most of his childhood, happy to shuffle him from boarding school to vacation resort and back again depending on the time of year. They'd paid for him to have music lessons and language classes. His closet was always full of the latest high-end fashions; his garage with luxury cars. There wasn't a single thing he'd wanted that they didn't buy for him, so they were baffled when he refused to join the family trust like all his relatives did.

He stepped out onto the sidewalk outside Jade Harbour's office building and found his driver waiting for him by the curb. Elvin must have given him a heads-up that Ray was on his way down.

"Home, Mr. Chao?" The driver opened the car door as Ray approached.

"Yes, thank you."

What do you mean you want to join a private equity company no one has ever heard of? Ray could still hear the incredulity in his father's voice when he'd broken the news. It wasn't like Ray wanted to become a monk in some remote monastery. Hell, his father might actually prefer that over the prospect of Ray working anywhere other than PFT.

He'd met Joanna while completing his MBA. His family had sent him as a representative to some fundraising event and over the course of the evening, Joanna had enthralled him with her take-no-prisoners attitude. Then a few months later, he ran into her at a restaurant where she was meeting an executive of a struggling portfolio company. She'd invited Ray to sit down with them and by the time he'd finished his drink, he'd managed to come up with three viable solutions to their problems.

She'd called him with a job offer the next day. Nothing fancy. No corner office or unlimited expense account. Jade Harbour had been in the early stages of its growth at the time. But the chance to build something from nothing was too enticing to give up. PFT was established, well-known, stable. He'd be taking over an organization that already ran on autopilot. What was the fun in that? Jade Harbour was an opportunity to see what he could do without the safety net of his family's wealth and status.

The car pulled up in front of Ray's building and stopped. "Thanks," Ray called to the driver before letting himself out.

What was so wrong with wanting to do his own thing? To see if he had the chops to make it on the basis of his abilities rather than the name he'd been born with? He'd never gotten a satisfactory answer from his father, and after a while they'd settled into an uncomfortable stalemate on the subject. The less they interacted, the better.

Ray scrolled through his phone as the elevator spat him out into his condo. He found the number he was looking for and hit dial. After a couple rings, it went to voicemail. Thank the fucking lord.

"Hey, Ginny. It's Ray. I need to talk to you about something. Call me back."

Chapter Three

"Hello?" Elvin called out, his voice echoing in the cavernous room. There was no response. Ray had better not have skipped out on him. He hadn't replied to the texts Elvin had sent before he left the office.

He sighed, toed off his shoes and went to drop his things on the kitchen island. Ray's suit jacket and tie lay across the back of the couch, so at least he'd been through here sometime during the afternoon.

Elvin headed to the stairs off the main entrance, taking them two at a time until he arrived at the landing that led to the rooftop pool. Well, not exactly rooftop; it was indoors. Sitting on the highest floor of the building, it benefited from a glass ceiling that made you feel like you were swimming in the sky.

The first time Elvin had seen it, his jaw had landed on the pristine white—of course—stucco deck and had stayed there for the better part of an hour. With bright blue tiles lining the sides and the bottom, the pool was a piece of the Mediterranean Sea in the middle of downtown Toronto.

He found Ray there, swimming laps back and forth, back and forth. Elvin grabbed a seat on a deck chair and watched Ray's thick arms glide across the water, his broad shoulders turning left and right, his feet trailing behind him in a lazy flutter kick. At the wall, he executed a perfect flip turn, somersaulting in the water and kicking up a splash before shooting off again in the opposite direction. Ray had been on the swim team throughout his school years and was even friends with some Olympic athletes.

It was a good ten minutes before Ray sprinted his last lap into the wall. He came up for air, panting, and stripped his goggles off. "Oh hey, how long have you been sitting there?"

Elvin shook his head. "Not long." And he would have gladly sat there longer. Watching Ray swim was a meditation of sorts, with the steady strokes and the methodical splashing of water.

Ray sighed and turned onto his back, floating away from the wall. He wore nothing but Speedos that hugged him so tight there was no mistaking how large he was. The defined muscles of his chest, stomach and thighs skimmed the surface of the water, sometimes dipping underneath like they were purposefully teasing Elvin. With Ray staring up at the sky, Elvin let his gaze linger.

One section of his brain examined the scene before him and registered nothing more than body parts—an arm, a leg, a torso. But combined in a package that was Ray, they called to something in Elvin that didn't get stimulated very often. He wanted to study every inch of Ray, memorize every patch of skin, every follicle of hair. He wanted to know how Ray would feel under his fingertips, how he'd taste on his tongue, how he'd smell with Elvin's face pressed right up against him.

Elvin looked away, dropping his gaze to the floor. Of all the people in the whole wide world, he had to develop these feelings for his boss. Figured. As a demisexual, sexual desire wasn't a thing for him unless he'd already established an emotional connection with the person. And since he didn't have much time for a social life, it wasn't that far-fetched that he would latch onto someone who filled so much of his day-to-day routine.

Elvin couldn't count the number of times he'd tried to convince himself that this crush was merely a side effect of proximity. His job was to take care of Ray and his hard-wiring had assumed it was entitled to be presumptuous. But the more Elvin tried to deny his attraction, the more he felt drawn to Ray. He'd long ago lost sight of the line that separated professional compatibility and personal chemistry.

He stood, emotions swirling, threatening to break free of his tightly held self-control. Coming over tonight had probably been a bad idea. He already spent his whole day catering to Ray, and now he was giving Ray his evening too. This was no way to maintain emotional distance.

"Hungry?" he called out as he headed back to the stairs. If he couldn't get emotional distance, then physical distance from Ray's naked body would have to do.

"Sure."

"I'll see what's in the fridge."

"I'll be there in a minute."

Elvin stood in front of the fridge, letting the cool air blow away the heat from the pool. The truth was he didn't want distance from Ray. Hell, he willingly showed up at Ray's condo first thing in the mornings, picked up his dry cleaning, chased away his one-night stands, then came over again to hang out over dinner. None of which were requirements of his job and he was certain that none of the other executive assistants at Jade Harbour did even a fraction of it.

Except he liked doing it. He liked spending time with Ray, how they bantered, the easy way they communicated. So whatever emotional entanglement he felt was entirely his own fault.

"Anything good?"

Elvin jumped at Ray's voice on the other side of the fridge door. He peeked around it to find Ray standing merely a foot away, dressed in low-slung pajama pants and a T-shirt that clung to his still-damp skin. He was drying his hair with a towel, sending the stinging smell of chlorine in Elvin's direction.

"Um…"

Ray raised an eyebrow.

"Yeah." Elvin pushed wide the fridge door to let Ray look inside. "What do you feel like?"

Ray leaned in to peer at the clearly labeled containers. He was so close that his body heat competed with the cool air of the fridge.

He should step back and give Ray more room, create that distance between them. But Elvin's feet stayed firmly stuck in place. He swallowed and tried extra hard not to sway toward Ray.

"The pad thai is always good." Ray looked over his shoulder at Elvin. "You know what you want?"

"Um, not really."

"How about the pineapple fried rice?" Ray suggested, holding up the box.

"Sure." Not because that was what he wanted, but because he could tell from the look in Ray's eyes that that was what *he* wanted.

Elvin took the two boxes from Ray and set about heating up the food on the stove. If he'd been home by himself, Elvin would have stuck them in the microwave and been done with it. He suspected that's what Ray would have done if he hadn't been there too. But he was there, and Ray didn't love the taste of food that had been radiated by invisible waves, so he went to the trouble. Because that's what he did. He went above and beyond for Ray. He sighed.

"Everything okay?"

Oops. He hadn't meant to do that out loud. Ray was

sitting on the other side of the kitchen island, wet towel tossed on the counter, watching him.

"Uh, yeah. I'm good. *You* okay?"

"Yeah, I am. The swim helped." Ray shook his head. "Damn, Ming really got to me today."

"Was it Ming? Or was it PFT?" Ming could be a persistent pain in the ass, but he was mostly harmless. Ray's family, on the other hand? From the stories he'd heard, they were the poster children for eccentric rich people. Elvin grabbed plates and utensils.

"In this case, both."

Elvin threw Ray a sympathetic smile. There wasn't much else he could say or do. Joanna had been clear in her desire to recruit more high-profile investors and they didn't get more high-profile than Phoenix Family Trust.

"Anyway, I gave Ginny a call. Left a message. I've done my part."

Ginny was one of Ray's cousins, if Elvin remembered correctly. A few years older than Ray and the most understanding of his life choices. She'd even married a "commoner," even though she still worked for the trust.

"That wasn't so hard, was it?" Elvin plated up their food.

Ray made an annoyed sound and picked up his fork. "Did I miss anything this afternoon?"

Elvin took up position on the opposite side of the kitchen island. "I downloaded everything we have on Caron Papers." He scooped up a spoonful of fluffy rice and shoveled it into his mouth. Hot and spicy. He sucked in some air to help cool down the food, and only then did he notice that Ray was frowning at him. "What?"

"First, sit down." He nodded to the seat next to him. "And second, wait till the food isn't going to burn your tongue before trying to eat it."

Elvin swallowed and checked his tongue. It felt a little singed, but still perfectly functional. He shrugged and ate another spoonful. See? It was fine.

"I said, sit down." Ray nodded again, more forcefully this time.

Elvin rolled his eyes and slid his plate across the counter. Then he made the long trek all the way around the ginormous island. By the time he got to Ray's side, Ray was already scooping a healthy portion of Elvin's fried rice onto his place.

"Hey! That's not fair!" He should have known Ray had ulterior motives.

"I want some rice too."

"There's another box of it in the fridge."

"That's too much. I can't finish it all. I only want a taste." Ray gathered up a pile of his noodles and arranged them carefully on Elvin's plate. "Here. A trade."

Elvin pulled his plate back. "You're worse than my siblings."

"Am I?" Ray curated a spoonful of noodles, broccoli and chicken. "At least I gave you some noodles. Would your siblings do that?"

Elvin shoved another bite of rice into his mouth. He resisted the urge to speak with his mouth full and chose to ignore Ray's question instead. That only served to inflate Ray's ego even more and he smiled smugly as he ate.

Elvin tried some of his consolation prize noodles, savory and sweet with the perfect amount of fishy tang. He snuck a look at Ray's plate and spotted some baby corn that Ray hadn't given him. He reached over, grabbed one of the tapered yellow strands and popped it into his mouth.

"Hey!"

Now it was Elvin's turn to be smug. "Have some more rice." He pushed his plate toward Ray. "It's a trade."

Ray didn't look so impressed when Elvin turned the tables on him, but he still took an equivalent amount of rice. "No more trades. We're even."

"You started it."

Ray rolled his eyes.

It was childish. Juvenile, really. But as they finished their meal in silence, a comforting warmth filled Elvin to overflowing. *This* was why he gave so much to Ray. Because he gave so much back. They were even.

The dishwasher ran silently behind them as they sat side by side on one of the giant leather couches. Ray hadn't wanted to wait until the next day to dive into the Caron files and despite the late hour, Elvin felt weird going home when his boss was working. So he'd pulled out his own laptop and together they'd started sorting through them.

"We didn't install a new management team after we acquired Caron," Ray said absently, thinking out loud.

"That's unusual, right?" One of the first tasks after acquiring a portfolio company was typically to replace the existing management team with people that Jade Harbour had worked with in the past. People who had long histories with the portfolio company tended to be more loyal to that history than to the vision and goals of Jade Harbour. It was easier to get rid of them than try to win them over.

"Yeah, I wonder why we didn't." Ray frowned at his laptop. "Caron was family-run before we bought it. It doesn't make sense that we'd leave the management team as is."

Elvin made a note of it.

"Headquarters in Montreal?" Ray's frown deepened. "But isn't the mill up north?"

"Yep, in northern Quebec. I guess it's kind of hard to conduct international business from the middle of nowhere." That arrangement had been flagged in the original proposal to acquire Caron, but then dismissed as an immaterial concern.

"That's not a good idea." Apparently Ray disagreed. "How are they supposed to keep an eye on things if they're not at the mill?"

"They make regular visits?" Elvin guessed.

Ray shook his head. "I don't like it."

Elvin could see the gears in Ray's mind spinning a mile a minute, making connections and identifying potential risks. This was why he was the best. He could outthink anyone at Jade Harbour, moving faster and arriving at conclusions ages before others even understood what was going on. He was like a master chess player, playing the game several moves ahead.

He shook his head again. "I really don't like it."

"You think there's something sketchy going on?" Elvin wouldn't be surprised if there was. Very few people in the business and finance world were entirely innocent. Sometimes, one had to bend the rules to get stuff done.

"I don't know yet. But they've certainly left themselves exposed." Ray sighed, closed his laptop and stretched his arms up. When he relaxed, he draped his arms across the back of the couch, conveniently behind Elvin's shoulders. It was such a teenage movie theater move that Elvin had to bite his lip from laughing out loud. But it wasn't a move, because Ray wouldn't make a move on him. Ray was stretching.

"I'll have to pay them a visit. Before the end of the week would be best."

Elvin nodded, careful not to bump Ray's arm behind him. "I'll make arrangements." He typed a note into his laptop before closing it too. "I should go."

Ray let out a small sigh. Or maybe just a loud breath. "Yeah." He paused. "Okay."

Elvin stood and busied himself gathering his things. "I'll see you tomorrow."

"Sleep well," Ray called to him from the couch. Other than turning his head to watch Elvin leave, he hadn't moved a muscle.

Every cell in Elvin's body wanted to crawl back there and snuggle up under Ray's arm again. But no. That was not going to happen. He swallowed and turned back to Ray's front door. "You too," he called before letting himself out.

Chapter Four

Montreal's Quartier International had many beautiful historic buildings going for it, but unfortunately Caron's office wasn't in one of them. Taking up the third floor of a squat concrete building dating from the Cold War, the inside looked as depressing as the outside.

There was no one at the reception desk when Ray arrived and he had to go wandering through empty hallways until he found someone who could announce his arrival. Some intern showed him into a conference room that smelled a little musty, like it hadn't been used in a long time.

He'd visited countless Jade Harbour portfolio companies over the years, many of which had their own unique brand of weird. They ranged across every industry imaginable:

technology, oil and gas, health care, real estate, entertain-
ment. Some were better managed than others, but none
were as starkly bleak as Caron. If he didn't know better, he
would have guessed that this was *not* a Jade Harbour company; they wouldn't finance an operation this embarrassing.

Ray pulled out his phone and shot off a quick message to
Elvin. You're not going to believe what this office looks like.

He didn't have to wait long for a reply. Why? Is it nice?

No, it's the most despondent thing I've ever seen. He
snapped a quick photo of the conference room and sent it
off to Elvin.

It doesn't look that bad.

Ray rolled his eyes. Of course Elvin would give them
the benefit of the doubt. Trust me. It's bad.

A middle-aged white man poked his head into the room.
He wore a sweater vest over a short-sleeved white button-
down, and the top of his head shone like it'd been recently
polished. "Hello. I'm Gilles Champagne," he said with a
heavy French accent. He pushed thick glasses up his nose
as he took a seat opposite Ray.

Ray wasn't sure what he'd been expecting when he'd
read Gilles Champagne's biography, but it certainly wasn't
the dowdy figure in front of him. In an industry where
image mattered as much as skill, it was hard to believe that
this guy was in charge of a Jade Harbour company. "I'm
Raymond Chao, operating partner at Jade Harbour."

"Yes, yes. I have been expecting you." Gilles started

laying out folders and papers and binders all over the conference table like he was preparing for an exam. "You are here to ask questions about Caron."

"It's really more of a conversation." Ray eyed all the materials in front of him. Sometimes CEOs were visibly nervous when he showed up to audit them, so he couldn't blame Gilles for wanting to be overprepared.

"An IPO, wow." Gilles folded his hands in front of him, which Ray took as a signal that he was ready for whatever Ray threw at him. "Very exciting, no?"

"Ah, well, we manage IPOs pretty often."

"Yes, of course, excuse me." Gilles chuckled and adjusted his glasses. "You must have done this many many times at Jade Harbour."

"Yeah." Ray cocked his head. "Have *you* led a company through a public offering before?"

"Me?" Gilles looked a little shocked. "Oh, no, no, never. This is my first time and there is so much to learn."

"Right." That raised more questions than it answered. "And how did you get involved with Caron?"

"Oh!" Gilles eyes lit up. "I have been an employee of Caron for many years. Many years."

"Uh-huh." Ray waited for him to continue and Gilles stared back at him unblinkingly.

It took several awkward moments before Gilles got the message. "I was a junior accountant," he explained. "And was promoted."

"All the way to CEO?" It wasn't an unheard of path to the top, but certainly unusual.

"It took many years," Gilles was quick to add.

"What did you do before coming to Caron?" Ray remembered Gilles' biography listing more than one company.

Gilles hesitated, his gaze darting around the room like he was looking for answers that might be written on the walls. "Uh, I thought we were talking about Caron today."

Ray narrowed his eyes at the clumsy attempt at redirecting the question. "Are you not a part of Caron?"

"Yes, yes, of course. But you want to know about before Caron."

"That's right." Ray stared at the guy and silently dared him not to answer the question. Didn't he realize that the more he tried to avoid the question, the harder Ray was going to press? People only hid stuff that was sketchy, exactly the types of things Ray was most interested in.

"I was an, uh, accountant. For many companies here in Montreal."

Again, answers that led to more questions. Ray pulled Gilles' bio from the folder Elvin had prepared for him. "It says here that you were the CFO of a logistics company, a health foods company and a nursery that grew houseplants." He put the paper down to find Gilles practically squirming in his seat. "Now you're telling me you were just an accountant?"

"Uh, no, I was, uh, in charge of the finance department." Was that sweat beading on the guy's head? Sure enough, he pulled a handkerchief out of his pocket and wiped it over his brow.

"Is it too warm in here for you?"

"No, no. I am fine." Gilles stuffed the handkerchief back into his pocket.

Ray sat back in his chair. He couldn't count how many times he'd done one of these top-to-bottom audits on a portfolio company. Obviously the outcome everyone hoped for was a clean bill of health, but there were always issues that needed addressing—employee complaints, shoddy bookkeeping, facilities that weren't quite up to regulation. Then sometimes there were bigger concerns, like personnel conduct or inappropriate use of funds.

Here, though? With Gilles looking like he wanted to be anywhere else in the world? It left an uneasy feeling in Ray's gut, one that he got whenever he was about to stumble onto something serious. He didn't know what it was yet, but one thing was for sure: if Jade Harbour wasn't careful, they were going to be in for a shit storm.

"Okay." Ray sat up straight and braced himself for a long afternoon. The only way to uncover the issues—big or small—was to go through the company with a fine-toothed comb. He'd need to read every line of every account, examine every purchase order and contract on file. By the time he was finished, the only thing left to do would be colonoscopies of the staff. "Let's get started."

Elvin had booked him into his favorite boutique hotel in the heart of Montreal's Old Port. It had uneven stairs, creaky floorboards and a hint of that old building smell that was impossible to imitate in new builds. His suite was the largest the hotel had to offer, with original stone walls and a Juliette balcony overlooking the Saint Lawrence River. Ray toed his shoes off the second he got inside and tossed his jacket onto the enormous four-poster bed.

He dropped into a plush wing-back armchair and propped his feet up on the matching ottoman. God, what a long day. He'd made Gilles walk him through each and every piece of paper the guy had brought into the conference room, looking for inconsistencies, discrepancies, anything that didn't add up.

To his credit, Gilles appeared to be an excellent accountant—leadership qualities to be determined. Every single row of numbers added up. He knew every company policy by heart. He could recite the financial health of every one of Caron's clients. And he could name all the employees on payroll, including how long they'd been with the company and the name of their dog.

There had been nothing out of the ordinary, and yet that sinking feeling persisted.

Ray pulled out his phone to find a message from Elvin waiting for him.

Let me know when you've checked in.

He tapped out a quick response. Just got in. Going to go find food soon.

I made a reservation for you at the restaurant downstairs. You liked the rack of lamb you got the last time you were there.

The lamb? When did he have that? It must not have been that good if he couldn't remember it. But then, it had to be decent if he'd mentioned it to Elvin. Ray shrugged. He could go for lamb. God knew he needed something hearty after the day he'd just had.

Great. Thanks. At least that took care of figuring out where to eat.

How did the meeting at Caron go?

Long. Painful.

Did you find anything interesting?

Nope.

That's good?

Maybe...

Gilles might know Caron inside and out, but his odd reaction to being asked about his history was strange. Executives were often asked about their past experiences and most had polished spiels at hand. Was Gilles flustered because he wasn't practiced in the art of business small talk? Or did he have something to hide?

Ray set his phone on the ottoman and went to the bathroom. He relieved his bladder, washed his hands and splashed some water on his face. His reflection in the mirror looked tired, and slapping his cheeks to bring up some color didn't help. He yawned for good measure. Ugh. Food. Then bed.

The last few times he'd been in Montreal, he'd had pretty good luck finding someone to warm his bed. Not that he often had trouble with that. But he wasn't sure he'd be able to stay awake long enough to make it worth someone's while. It was a shame, though, since he always slept better with another body beside him. And if he ever needed a good night's sleep, it was tonight.

He wiped his face with a towel and went to grab his phone before putting on his shoes and heading downstairs. The restaurant host seated him in a private booth with a view out onto the cobblestone streets of Old Montreal.

A waiter appeared with a carafe of water and the menus. Ray didn't bother taking them. "You have a rack of lamb on the menu?"

"Oui, monsieur. It is poached in olive juice, with a side of roasted artichokes and potatoes."

"Sounds good. And any Château Climens Barsac?"

"Oui, the 2014. A very good vintage."

Ray nodded. "Perfect."

"Bien sur." The waiter bowed his head before backing away.

Ray sipped his water while gazing out the window at tourists wandering the streets. His phone buzzed. Did you make it to your reservation? said the text from Elvin.

Yes. And got the lamb.

Good. Need me for anything else?

Ray cringed and checked the time. It was already late for dinner and definitely past the hour when Elvin should have signed off work. Yet here he was, checking in on Ray.

No. I'm good. Good night.

You too.

Ray turned his phone screen side down and tapped on the back of it. He asked a lot of Elvin, way more than any of his colleagues asked of their assistants. But Elvin never complained and if Ray was honest with himself, he kind of liked having Elvin waiting on him hand and foot.

No, that sounded bad, even in his head. Elvin waited on him because that's who Elvin was. Ray doubted he could stop him even if he tried. But he'd be lying if he said he didn't like it. Elvin made cappuccino better than anyone Ray had ever met. Elvin was organized and on top of things. Elvin could anticipate his needs before he even knew what they were.

Like tonight. How had Elvin known he'd want lamb for dinner? How had he known that Ray would be too tired to venture far from the hotel? It was like Elvin could read his mind—better than he could himself.

Still. That was no excuse for working Elvin as hard as he did. He should pull back, make sure Elvin's personal time was strictly personal time. No sending messages making sure that Ray—a full-grown adult—managed to check into a hotel he'd stayed at a dozen times before.

The waiter returned with his plate of food and the bottle of wine he'd ordered. With a practiced hand, the waiter poured the wine and handed the glass for Ray to taste. It was good, fruity and rich at the same time. It would go well with the lamb, which was tender and falling off the bone. The olive juice had penetrated the meat, giving it a nice tang. Every bite was heaven, a foodgasm.

Ray reached for his phone to tell Elvin how good dinner was. No, wait. Elvin was off for the night. He'd *just* told himself to respect Elvin's personal time. But it was a shame not to share delicious food with someone else.

Ray had eaten plenty of meals alone over the years. Hell, he'd been eating alone since he was a kid. Even during the rare times when he was visiting his parents or his grand mother, they never bothered to include him in their dinner plans, leaving him to fend for himself with whatever was in the fridge. He was used to it, but that didn't mean he liked it. Food was meant to be shared. And while he *could* polish off a whole bottle of wine himself, he was well past the age when he could bounce back the next day.

He sighed and stuck another piece of artichoke in his mouth. Suddenly the delicate folds of the vegetable didn't taste as good as they had a minute ago. He put his fork and knife down, picked up his glass of wine and scanned the restaurant. He was the only solo diner. Everyone else looked like they were work colleagues or older couples on dates. Everyone had someone.

He finished the wine in his glass and poured himself another. He would *not* finish the bottle on his own, but he could have a second glass.

His waiter was cute. Maybe Ray could chat him up and give him his room number. He took another sip of the wine. No—waiters got off work too late and Ray didn't want to wait that long. And going elsewhere to find a warm body was too much hassle, which meant he was stuck. Here. Alone. Eating a delicious meal. Sleeping in a gorgeous bed. Alone.

God, he was tired.

Chapter Five

Ray took a sip of champagne and surveyed the room. The lighting was dim and the air hummed with the whispers of guests huddled in groups of three or four. Others stood pensive in front of paintings while silent waiters glided past with trays of drinks and bite-sized finger foods.

He'd arrived about thirty minutes ago—late to the party—hoping it would already be in full swing. Or at least, as lively as a fine art fundraiser could get. But other than the occasionally loud guffaw from a group in one corner, the other attendees seemed content with their quiet milling around. He glanced at his watch. How much longer did he have to stay before politely bowing out? Too long.

The clear, crisp clink of silver on glass rang through the air as the host called for everyone's attention. Finally.

"Hello, everyone, thank you for coming to tonight's fundraiser—"

"You look like you're about to bolt." A hushed voice came from over Ray's shoulder.

It belonged to a petite woman with dark skin and wide eyes, long black hair styled in elegant curls framing her heart-shaped face. Her pink lip gloss gave her an air of innocence that contrasted with the bold purple off-the-shoulder dress and killer stilettos she wore.

"I was thinking about it." Ray turned his body just enough to create intimacy without invading her personal space. A move that was more subconscious than practiced. "Were you?"

She gave him a quick once-over before refocusing on the host at the other end of the room. "Maybe. If I had a good reason to."

Ray smiled, turning on the charm. She had approached him, had struck up a conversation without prompting. Who was he to step away from such an enticing opportunity when it presented itself.

"I don't suppose drinks would cut it."

She held up her own glass of champagne. "Nope."

"Perhaps great company?"

"For engaging conversation?" She lifted one eyebrow, her lips curling into a half smile.

"Sure. We could debate the merits of privacy versus security in the modern era of the internet." He took another sip of champagne, careful not to let his gaze linger too long on the beautiful woman next to him.

"Oh, I'm all for privacy. You know, being an attorney and all."

Ray shifted a little closer. "Privacy's good. It's great. I know a few private places we can escape to."

She turned, bringing her within an inch of him. Chin raised, she looked up at him, lips parted slightly. The scent of her perfume surrounded them, something fruity and musky all at the same time, and Ray wondered where the fragrance would be the strongest. He'd have to investigate to find out.

"As appealing as that sounds…" She ran a perfectly manicured finger down Ray's chest, hooking it in an opening in his shirt. "I have a policy of not sleeping with clients." She straightened the finger and used it to push him away.

There was very little force in her single finger, but Ray moved back all the same. Client? He was certain he'd never met her before. He wouldn't easily forget someone like her.

Her smile grew at the confusion on his face, her eyes twinkling in mischief. "Oh yes, Mr. Raymond Chao. I know who you are."

Ray crossed his arms in mock irritation. He had to hand it to her, she had him fooled. "I'm afraid you have me at a disadvantage."

"Denise Washington," she said, but the name didn't ring any bells. "My firm has taken on Jade Harbour as our latest client."

Ray nodded. It made sense now. But the gorgeous Ms. Washington had made a critical error. "In that case, Jade Harbour is your client. Not me."

She laughed. A delicate sound that rang high and light. "Client by proxy."

Ray narrowed his eyes and leaned in again. "I'm not convinced. Maybe you should use your lawyerly ways to change my mind."

"Hmm." She drew circles across his chest with that damned finger. "Tempting."

Ray caught her hand and brought it to his lips to plant a quick kiss. "And?"

"And I'm afraid I'll have to decline." She extracted her hand. "I have an early day tomorrow. An important client meeting." She winked at him.

He chuckled at her playfulness. "I suppose that means I'll be seeing you tomorrow morning."

She raised her shoulders as if to say, *you caught me*. But in fact, Ray was pretty sure she'd caught him.

He didn't usually sit in on meetings with the law firms that Jade Harbour had on retainer. It wasn't his department, and frankly, maintaining ignorance of the rules made his job a lot easier. But it wasn't every day that he got turned down by someone he propositioned. In fact, he couldn't remember the last time it'd happened. This Denise Washington had more charm and grace than anyone he'd considered taking to bed in a long time. So if sitting through a boring legal meeting meant he'd get to see her again, he may be willing to make an exception.

"Does this mean you stalked me to this fundraiser?" Ray turned away from her and began a slow stroll around the perimeter of the room. Denise fell easily into step next to him.

"I normally like to keep tabs on what my clients are up to," she admitted. "But in this instance, we'll have to chalk it up to pure coincidence."

A waiter stopped as he passed by them, offering a plate of tiny crepes. Denise picked one up and popped it whole into her mouth. She let out a small sound of approval as she chewed. Ray smiled at the casualness of the move, how she didn't care whether it was polished enough for this crowd. Elvin would appreciate that—her quickness and efficiency. Ray took a smaller bite, careful not to get crumbs on his shirt.

"Do you know anyone here?" he asked. The party was attended by the usual philanthropy crowd, people Ray had met dozens of times before, but he couldn't match names to faces. They took turns hosting these things, sometimes with art auctions, other times with large-scale gala dinners. Always with a black-tie dress code and an entrance fee that started in the thousands. They raised money for children's welfare, medical research and whatever else would make them look like compassionate citizens of society. But Ray had always thought it hilarious that they spent thousands to make thousands when every single person in the room could simply donate double the amount without the accompanying fanfare.

But then, that was the point, wasn't it? The fanfare. The need to let everyone know that they had more money than they knew what to do with and a reluctance to give it away without getting something in return.

"A few clients," Denise acknowledged. "But believe it or not, I'm actually here for the art."

"Really?" That was a first.

She laughed and shook her head. "I know. It's unheard of. Someone coming to an art fundraiser because they actually have an interest in what's on display."

If Denise hadn't been alluring before, she certainly was now.

"Which piece of art, exactly?" Ray glanced at the walls around them. The paintings were a modern, color block style that he didn't really understand.

"That one." Denise nodded at a large black square.

"The black one?" Ray didn't want to judge. People could like what they liked. But he didn't see the appeal of that particular piece.

"Yes. The more you stare at it, the more it speaks."

Ray would rather stare at Denise, who wore a dreamy expression on her face. "And what does it say?"

She took her time responding, tilting her head as if to hear the painting better. "Right now, it's telling me that loneliness wears many disguises. It lurks in the corners and pounces when you're least prepared." She turned, gazing up at him with a look that was so piercing it was almost painful. "And that the cure comes from where you'd least expect it."

In his office at Jade Harbour, Ray stared out the window at the sparkling towers in Toronto's Financial District. Denise's words had stayed with him all night and into the morning. He'd laughed it off initially and she'd followed suit. The intense moment brushed aside as if it hadn't happened at all. Then he'd escorted her out to a waiting taxicab before he grabbed another to go home by himself.

But he couldn't shake the words. Loneliness wearing different disguises, pouncing when least expected. If that wasn't the truth, he didn't know what was. How many times had he been living his life, perfectly content, then *wham*—the feeling of being utterly, devastatingly alone hit him so hard, he could barely breathe?

It had happened more when he was a kid, but as he got older, he'd found ways to keep the feeling at bay. Social events to fill every evening. Inviting people home so his bed was never empty. Learning how to charm, how to woo, how to make people love him. But all his tactics weren't working as well these days, were they? He'd wake up feeling alone even though there was a warm body next to him. He wandered through parties as if he was watching from the other side of bulletproof glass.

Even his work, which had been essential to filling his days with something productive, was getting repetitive. Companies with the same old problems. Executives with the same old vices. All the fixes were the same. He was bored. Worse than bored. He'd become apathetic.

A knock on his door roused him from his downward spiraling thoughts.

"I'd toss you a penny if we still had them." Elvin came to stand in front of his desk.

Ray shook his head and pushed himself to his feet to stretch. "My thoughts aren't even worth that much."

A look came over Elvin's face, a mix of worry and amusement. "In that case, perhaps you'd like to daydream through that meeting with legal you asked about this morning. They're about to start."

Ray came around the desk and gave Elvin's shoulder a squeeze. "Yes, I'll do that. Thanks for letting me know."

Introductions were being made when he let himself into the conference room. Mike, Joanna and a couple other folks from Jade Harbour on one side. Denise and her partners on the other. They all quickly shook hands and took their seats.

Denise looked as pristinely composed as she had yesterday. She wore a cream-colored pantsuit that brokered no argument as to who was in charge of her party. "Thank you for this meeting," she started. Her husky voice now sounded like steel being rolled across the wooden table. "We wanted to go over the pending cases at Jade Harbour and anything you feel might be on the horizon."

Ray tuned out the rest. He didn't actually need to hear any of it, didn't know enough to contribute, and frankly couldn't have cared less. But he watched Denise. The way she jotted notes on her pad of paper, the way her hair slid over her shoulder. The way she turned her gaze to the person who was speaking, giving them her undivided attention, daring them to try to fool her.

Then she glanced in his direction. A quick look that most people would have missed. But not Ray. She knew that he had no business here. That his presence was entirely due to her. And she liked it, liked that she had the power to bring him here and keep him here.

Ray leaned forward in his chair, bracing his elbows on the table. Was she the cure to his loneliness? She certainly was unexpected. But the longer he listened to her grilling his colleagues, the more he realized that no, she had better things to do than get mixed up in his baggage. His cure would have to come from somewhere else.

Chapter Six

"Hello?" The familiar herby smell of Chinese medicine hit Elvin in the face as he entered his parents' house. Some people wrinkled their nose at the bitterness, but it always reminded Elvin of home, family and belonging. Today, the aroma was particularly strong.

"You've returned?" his dad called out from the living room in Cantonese. Elvin followed the sound to find him sitting in his massage chair, semi-reclined, a historical Chinese drama playing on the TV.

"Hi, Dad. Mom bought you some Chinese medicine again?"

Dad grunted in acknowledgement.

"Is it helping?"

He grunted again, though exactly what the sound meant,

Elvin wasn't sure. Dad had had back pain for as long as he could remember, the result of some workplace injury when Elvin was still a kid. Seeing him pop over-the-counter medication was a familiar sight, occasionally supplemented by whatever concoction Mom's Chinese medicine doctor conjured up.

"Where are the kids?" Elvin asked.

"Backyard."

"By themselves?" The question slipped out before Elvin could stop it. "You know what, never mind." Because providing adult supervision was a concept his parents had never quite grasped. *He'd* grown up without them hovering over him, so why couldn't the younger kids? Yet another topic Elvin had given up arguing with them about.

He gave Dad a squeeze on the shoulder and wound through the house into the backyard. "The kids" were his three youngest siblings—Jessie, Joyce and Eason, who were six, eight and ten. Janice and Edwin were in high school and college, and were out at school or a friend's house more often than they were at home.

Elvin was the family's de facto third parent. He could change a diaper blindfolded and with one hand tied behind his back. He'd pretended to be his dad during phone calls with teachers countless times and had perfected his mom's signature.

The three youngsters were playing monkey in the middle, with poor little Jessie desperately trying to steal the ball from the older two. Elvin stopped inside the glass door, watching their little feet pound across the dry yellowing lawn, their high voices shouting and yelling for the ball. Only when Jessie tripped over herself and started crying did he open the door and step out.

"Don't play so hard!"

"DaaiGo!" Jessie used the Cantonese name for *oldest brother* as she picked herself up and hurtled toward him as fast as her short legs could carry her.

He bent down to scoop her up, swallowing a grunt as she landed in his arms at full force. "Hey, little girl."

"They won't give me the ball!" she cried, in English, into the crook of his neck.

Elvin sighed. Oh, the drama of small children. As hefty as the weight of the world. "You guys need to let her play."

"We are!" Eason called out as he ran over with Joyce. "She's the monkey!"

"Hi, DaaiGo!" Joyce launched herself on top of Elvin and Jessie in an attempted hug. But the weight of both girls had him tumbling to the ground.

Apparently, Eason thought that looked like fun because he jumped on too.

"Oof." They knocked the air out of him and it took a couple moments before he managed to push them off enough to breathe. "Jesus," he muttered.

"What?" Jessie asked.

"Uh, nothing." It felt weird saying anything remotely curse-like around his family. Not that his parents had ever instituted a no-swearing rule—hell, he wasn't sure his parents understood most English-language curses. But the last thing he wanted was one of the younger kids showing up at school and repeating some of the stuff he said when he was at Jade Harbour.

"Um, anyone hungry?"

All three tiny bodies jumped up and down, hands raised in the air. "I am!" they shouted in chorus. They raced to see who could get to the kitchen faster. Elvin followed more slowly. Pacing himself was key to making it through an entire day with his family.

He stopped in the living room on his way. "Dad, you want lunch? I'm going to make something."

Dad grunted and eased himself off the recliner. "There's leftover fried rice in the fridge. Just *ding* it in the microwave."

"Okay." He stood in front of Dad, offering his shoulder as support. Dad grabbed it and held on as he stretched, his face contorting into a look of pain before he settled back into something more tolerable.

They made their way slowly into the kitchen, Dad's steps slow and measured as he bent over at an awkward angle to relieve the pressure on his back.

Elvin resisted the urge to rehash their old argument. He'd said everything there was to say, but Dad was adamant about not going to see a doctor. Even physiotherapists or chiropractors were out of the question. Apparently it was more acceptable to suffer in silence than it was to admit to strangers that he needed help. It was ridiculous and Elvin got angry whenever he dwelled on it too long. Then Dad would get angry and Mom would try to step in with some new Chinese medicine potion. It never worked.

Elvin pulled out Dad's chair at the kitchen table and deposited him into it. The sigh of relief Dad let out when he was finally seated only served to annoy Elvin even more. He turned away and yanked the fridge door open.

On the top shelf was a giant box of fried rice and separate boxes of braised Chinese broccoli and char siu pork. It was food served at the restaurant where Mom had worked for years. She often brought home whatever couldn't be sold by the end of the night.

"Eason, grab bowls and chopsticks for everyone," Elvin called over his shoulder.

His younger brother scrambled to obey, noisily opening and closing drawers and cupboards and plonking things down on the table. Meanwhile, Elvin transferred the food onto plates and rotated them through the microwave, letting himself get lost in the droning hum.

Life could be seriously exhausting. Life with family could be especially exhausting. Imagine all the spare time he'd have if he wasn't constantly coming back to his parents' house to help cook and clean and take care of Dad and the kids. He could...see more musicals? He almost let out a bitter chuckle. His life was so consumed by family and work he wouldn't know what to do with himself if they were to suddenly disappear. How sad was that?

He set the heated plates on the table with a little more force than he'd intended, which garnered a disapproving look from Dad.

Oops. "Sorry," he muttered under his breath before going back for another plate.

If the kids noticed, they didn't let on. Instead, they dove into the food and all the noise that usually accompanied their presence was replaced with the quiet sounds of wooden chopsticks against ceramic bowls. Jessie stood on her chair, laying the top half of her body on the table to reach the communal plates in the middle.

"Here." Elvin took her bowl to fill it up before she dropped the whole thing and spilled food all over the place.

"Thanks, DaaiGo," she said with her mouth full. It was adorable and messy and heartwarming all at the same time. There was a matter-of-factness in her expression, like she knew he would always be there for her, watching out for her, catching her before she fell. There was so much implicit trust in the way she casually leaned her small body against him. Elvin picked up another piece of char siu and put it in her bowl.

His family was exhausting and then there were moments like these. Fleeting, almost accidental moments that made up for all the work and fatigue. Reminders that the bond holding them together was so strong that it was easy to take it for granted. They were a burden, yes. But Elvin wouldn't be the person he was today without them.

The kids finished eating with astonishing speed and after they put their bowls into the sink, Elvin let them go off and play again. How the hell they had so much energy was absolutely beyond him.

"Your mom should be home soon. She's working a half day today." Dad pushed his empty bowl away from him.

"I know." Elvin scooped it up and brought it to the

sink to wash. Mom had maintained the same schedule for years—waitressing at a restaurant in Chinatown for every lunch and dinner all week except for Sunday evenings.

She was nearing retirement age, but even though they hadn't talked about it, Elvin had a feeling she'd keep working past sixty-five. With Dad forced into early retirement because of his back, there were still too many household expenses and no way their government pensions would be able to cover it all. Never mind college tuition for five more kids.

As if on cue, a car pulled into the driveway. Elvin turned the water off and went to meet Mom at the door.

"Ah, you're here. There are groceries in the car." She stepped past him and took off her shoes, leaving him to bring the bags inside.

He managed it in one trip, dropping everything on the kitchen floor with a loud thud. She'd already pulled on the rubber gloves and had her hands wet washing the dishes.

"Mom, I was going to finish that."

She waved a wet hand in his direction. "Put the vegetables away."

He exchanged a knowing look with Dad, who was still sitting at the table. Mom had a habit of finishing tasks before others got around to it, as if she couldn't wait for things to be done a second slower than she wanted. It was partially the reason why Dad rarely did anything around the house. Why bother when Mom always got it done ahead of time?

Elvin sighed and opened the bag closest to him. It was

full of leafy greens, most of which he recognized but didn't know the names of.

"How is work?" Mom asked over the clanging of dishes and sloshing of water.

"Fine."

"Fine? What does fine mean? Is fine good or bad?"

Elvin shot Dad another look, but he was no help, staring at the table and absent-mindedly drawing invisible circles with his finger.

"It's good. It's busy."

"Your boss is good?" Mom turned the water off as she carefully balanced the last bowl on the mountain of dishes in the drying rack.

"Yeah, Ray's fine." They'd met him a few times at the family picnic Jade Harbour held every few years. Handsome and charming, Ray had easily won his parents over with his fluent Cantonese. Now they thought he was a superhero, could do no wrong, a savior who was doing Elvin a favor by giving him a job. To be fair, Elvin's own opinion of Ray wasn't that far off, but he wasn't about to admit that to his parents.

"You be good to Ray." Mom waved a finger in his face as she helped him finish putting away the groceries.

"I'm good to him!" If only they knew the extent of it. Actually, knowing them, they'd probably applaud it.

With all the groceries shelved in their appropriate spots and all the dishes clean, Mom finally sank into an empty chair with a sigh. Guilt washed over him. If he felt tired, he could only imagine how Mom felt. Working on her feet all the time. Taking care of this family with no end in sight. Exhausting was an understatement.

Elvin sat with his parents and reached into his pocket for the small folded piece of paper. "Here." He slid it across the table.

"What's this?" Mom snatched it up and unfolded it. She took a second to read the number he'd written out on the check, nodded, then refolded it.

Dad kept staring at the table like he hadn't noticed the exchange.

"Is that enough for this month? I can write another ch—"

Mom shook her head and cut him off. "It's enough. Thank you."

Her words landed like comforting soup that was still a little too hot. They hurt and soothed at the same time, a bittersweet sensation that Elvin wasn't sure he'd ever understand. He nodded his acknowledgement and the moment passed, never to be mentioned again.

Chapter Seven

"Hello?"

"I almost fainted in shock! Could it actually be cousin Ray leaving a message on my phone?"

Ray rolled his eyes. Ginny had always had a flair for the dramatic. But then, he couldn't really blame her. It'd been ages since he'd voluntarily reached out to a family member and even longer since he'd spoken with Ginny specifically.

"Yes, Ginny, it is actually me." Ray swiveled around in his chair, using his foot to push it left and right.

"To what do I owe the pleasure?" There was a lot of background noise coming from Ginny's end of the line. Almost like she was in the middle of a restaurant. "I can't imagine you called just to catch up."

Ray smirked. "How's the husband? The kids?" he asked, if only to prove her wrong.

"They're fine. The youngest is starting college in September. In design." Ginny sounded exasperated. "Whatever that is. Why don't they study something practical? What is she going to do with a degree in design?"

Ray stifled a laugh. The fact that Ginny was allowing her youngest to study something as frivolous as design at all was a huge step forward from their parents' generation. If he'd tried that with his parents, they would have refused to pay his tuition. "Kids these days," he offered in commiseration. "I can't believe you have kids in college."

"Ha! The oldest graduated two years ago! Hold on." Ginny shouted instructions to someone in Cantonese. Something about making sure the place settings were right. "You haven't been around for too long. They don't even know what Uncle Ray looks like."

That was the one drawback to being so cut off from his extended family. He didn't get to see his niblings grow up. If he was honest with himself, Ginny wasn't so bad. She gave him a hard time about being the family black sheep, but it was mostly in jest. Back when the scandal broke that he didn't want to work for PFT, it'd been difficult to figure out who was actually pissed at him and who was simply keeping their distance. It'd been easier to write off everyone than risk rejection after rejection.

"Yeah, sorry about that." After a while, Ray had gotten used to the status quo. But hearing about Ginny's kids made him want to know more about what was going on in their lives.

"You'll have to make it up to us." Ginny shouted at someone again, loud enough that Ray held his phone away from his ear. "Anyway, like I said, you didn't call to see how we're doing. What do you need?"

Ray cringed at Ginny's stark comment. She was right and there was no point in denying it. "Do you know if any Phoenix Family Trust people will be in Toronto soon?"

"Hold on." There was some shuffling, like Ginny had put the phone in her pocket. When she came back on the line, it was quiet in the background. "What's this about?"

He had her full attention now. "I've been asked to set up a meeting between PFT and Jade Harbour."

"We met with you a couple years ago." There was a slight but distinctive change in Ginny's tone. No longer was she cousin Ginny, happily giving updates about her kids. Now she was executive Ginny, shrewd about business and money making.

"Yes, I know. And I also know that an investment commitment wasn't right for Phoenix at the time. But we'd like to maintain the relationship in case things change."

Silence from the other end of the line. He'd always known this was going to be a tough sell. It was one thing to decline an investment opportunity because it wasn't the right fit. But Ray had always suspected that PFT's reluctance to do business with Jade Harbour had more to do with him than anything else. It wouldn't do to be seen supporting a Chao who had turned his back on the family, would it?

"Ginny?"

"You know the likelihood of securing a commitment from us is practically nil. We already have investment partners in your asset class."

Ray ran a hand over his face. "I know. But—"

"So why waste everyone's time?"

Ray grimaced. Ginny wasn't trying to be mean, he knew. It was the reality of their situation, no matter how much Ming and Joanna wanted to believe otherwise. Grudges in his family were real and they would sooner cut off their own leg than capitulate to Ray. He sighed audibly.

"I'm sorry, Ray, but I don't see what good it would do." Ginny wasn't the type to soften her blows, so a word of apology, no matter how superficial, meant a lot coming from her.

"Yeah. I know." If only he could convince Ming and Joanna to get it too. Then maybe they'd stop pestering him about it all the time. "Listen, can you just let me know if anyone from Phoenix is coming through? Even if it's junior staff. They just want to meet people with PFT business cards."

Ginny let out a sound perfected by all annoyed Chinese mothers. One that made clear that she was being forced against her will and that someone would pay for it. "Fine. I will check with a few people. But Ray, I have to warn you. If word of this gets back to your father or any of the uncles—"

"Yes, I know, I know. They'll have the head of anyone who agrees to meet with us."

"They have ears everywhere," Ginny warned.

Ray had no doubt that they did. Deeply rooted in a culture built on relationships and connections, the Chaos prided themselves on the extensive network of people they knew. Being able to gather information from sources all over the world was key to how they'd built their wealth.

"We'll be discreet, don't worry."

"It's my job to worry."

Ray chuckled. He could only imagine the amount of anxiety raising kids involved. Managing personnel issues for the family company could only add to the stress. Not for the first time was he grateful that he'd managed to extricate himself from PFT and his family.

"Okay, unless there's anything else, I have to go." Ginny must have been on the move. The earlier background noise was growing in volume.

"That's all. Please keep me informed if anyone comes through Toronto," he reiterated. Ginny hadn't actually agreed to help him and he needed at least that.

She huffed. "Yes, yes, I will keep you informed."

"Thank you." Ray breathed a sigh of relief. "I owe you one."

"You owe me more than one," she shot back. "Okay, bye."

The dial tone droned before Ray could sign off himself. He dropped the phone on the desk and covered his face with his hands. It was over, thank fucking god. He'd made the call, passed along Joanna and Ming's request. What PFT did with that wasn't his concern.

A knock sounded at his door. "Um…you okay?"

Ray looked up to find Elvin standing sheepishly in the middle of his office. "Yeah, I'm fine. What's up?"

"I ran into Ming in the kitchen just now—"

Ray groaned out loud. "Not him again." Why was the guy always popping up everywhere?

"Yeah, well, we were chatting and—"

"What were you chatting about?" The question popped out before Ray consciously thought of it.

"Huh? Oh!" Elvin's face lit up. "There's a new musical called *Abroad* that's a huge hit on Broadway. It's coming to town soon, but tickets haven't gone on sale yet. Anyway, it's probably going to sell out quickly because Clarissa Davis is playing the lead role. She's Broadway royal—are you listening to me?"

Ray had kind of tuned out after the word *musical* and was admiring the gleam in Elvin's eyes instead. There was an intensity to them whenever he spoke about musical theater, kind of like he was gazing into a parallel universe that Ray couldn't see. But no, he hadn't been listening to the actual words coming out of Elvin's mouth.

"You know what? Never mind." Elvin shook his head.

This must be why Elvin went to Ming to talk musical theater, and Ray didn't like it. If Elvin was passionate about this stuff, it should be the least Ray could do to feign interest, right? But Elvin had moved on.

"Apparently, Ming's going with you to the Caron mill."

It took a moment for Ray to catch up. When he did, he shot up from his chair. "What?"

Elvin shrugged like they were discussing whether it was going to rain in the spring. "That's what he told me."

"Why? There aren't any investors up there." And the last thing Ray needed was Ming looking over his shoulder while he was working.

"Something about getting a feel for the investment so he can sell the IPO better."

It sounded like a steaming bowl of shit and Ray tried to convey as much in the look he pinned Elvin with. "I need to talk to Joanna about this." He headed for the door. If she wanted a thorough audit, then Ming couldn't tag along.

Elvin raised a hand, stopping Ray in his tracks. "I believe this was her idea."

"What?"

Elvin winced at his volume.

"Sorry."

"It's okay."

Ray flopped onto the couch, stretching out so his feet were propped on the armrest. Ming was already ruining his day and now he'd be ruining the entire week.

"Don't hate me, but I don't see what the big deal is." Elvin had taken the armchair and was looking at Ray like he was a misbehaving child. "Sure, Ming's a little annoying sometimes, but he's really not that bad."

"Because you can geek out about musicals together. I don't have anything to talk to him about." And frankly, Ray had no interest in finding out whether they had other interests in common. "Can you imagine having to spend forty-eight hours straight with someone who you have nothing to say to? It's torture. Pure torture."

Elvin didn't look convinced. But that was because he didn't go on business trips very often. The first criteria when evaluating a business traveling partner was whether you could get stuck in an airport together for a whole day without wanting to kill each other. Ming definitely didn't pass the test.

"I think you're blowing it out of proportion."

"That's easy for you to say. You're not the one who has to travel with Ming." Wait. Ray swung his legs off the couch and sat up. Why hadn't he thought of this before? "You're coming with us."

Elvin's eyebrows shot up. "What?"

It was the perfect solution. Ray jumped to his feet. "You'll be the buffer. You can keep Ming occupied so he's not breathing down my neck. I'll be free to do what I want and if there are any logistical hiccups, you're right there to handle them."

Elvin didn't look nearly as excited as Ray felt. In fact, he kind of looked concerned. Like maybe Ray had lost his mind.

"What? This is a great idea!"

"I don't know." Elvin rose and headed toward the door.

"What's there to know? Wait, where are you going?"

Elvin paused and sighed, his shoulders slumping like the weight on them had gotten too heavy to hold up.

"Hey." Ray went to him and turned him around so they

faced each other. "What's wrong?" Elvin's shoulders were tense under his fingers and Ray kneaded the muscles to soften them.

Elvin's brow furrowed as he studied Ray. Then he looked away and shrugged Ray's hands off. "You want me to tag along to handle Ming for you."

"Yeah."

Elvin stiffened.

Shit. What had he said wrong? "And to help me with, you know, work," Ray added. It didn't have the effect he'd hoped for.

"I don't know. It's really last-minute." Elvin took a step back.

It was only a few inches, but it felt like a chasm had opened between them. Ray tried to close the gap, reaching for Elvin to bring them back together. "The flight isn't until tonight."

Elvin was shaking his head, looking anywhere else but at Ray. "My parents might need my help."

Ray knew an excuse when he heard one. "With what?"

"I don't know. Stuff. What if the toilet floods? Or one of my siblings needs a ride somewhere? I can't just take off and leave them hanging."

None of those sounded like actual reasons, but more importantly, Ray had solutions for each one. "If the toilet floods, we can send a plumber to their house. If anyone needs a ride, we can send a car. Do they need food? We'll order food for them. Is the house dirty? We'll hire a cleaner." Ray bent down a little and leaned to the left to get into Elvin's line of sight. "Whatever they need, I'm sure we can find someone else to help out. They'll survive two days without you."

Some of the stiffness eased from Elvin's posture, but not nearly enough for Ray's liking. He took Elvin by the arms, just above his elbows, and gave him a gentle shake. "Come on. Say you'll come with me. I need you."

That must have been the magic phrase. Elvin sighed and rolled his eyes. The corner of his mouth lifted a fraction.

"Please?" Ray put on his best puppy dog eyes. "I can't do this without you."

The last of Elvin's tension melted away. "Okay, fine."

"Yes!" Ray threw his arms into the air.

Elvin reached up and pulled them down again. "Easy. I might have agreed to your ridiculous plan, but it doesn't mean I have to like it."

Ray slung an arm around Elvin's shoulders and gave him a tight side hug. "You say that now, but I guarantee you'll have a great time. I mean, you're traveling with me! What's not to enjoy?"

"Enjoy? I thought this was a work trip and I'm supposed to be distracting Ming for you, right?"

He had a point, but Ray wasn't about to let that dampen his mood. "Details." He waved away Elvin's comment. With Elvin along, there wasn't a scenario that the two of them couldn't deal with together—Ming included. How had it taken him so many years to come up with the idea?

Ray patted Elvin on the chest. "Seriously. It's going to be great."

Elvin gazed at him, one eyebrow cocked in skepticism. Ray put on a winning smile that grew wider as Elvin's skepticism faded. They were pressed side to side, Ray's arm still around Elvin's shoulder. Their faces were mere inches away from one another.

They'd been this close plenty of times in the past. Hell, Elvin had seen him wearing nothing but a swimming suit in the pool. But there was something about that moment, about the way Elvin was looking at him like he could do no wrong.

Ray swallowed around the lump that had suddenly formed in his throat. He let go of Elvin and took a step back, but that feeling persisted. Elvin's scent clung to him, fresh and minty, and Ray unconsciously took a deep breath. It was so familiar, so comforting. Before he knew what he was doing, his body had taken him closer to it.

"Ray?" Elvin whispered.

Elvin's voice was quiet, so quiet. But it echoed through the hollow space in Ray's chest, a space he'd gotten so used to that he hadn't realized it existed.

He stumbled backward and turned away. "Yeah, uh… I'll pick you up on the way to the airport." He marched toward his desk and busied himself with the random items scattered on it.

He didn't hear Elvin move. Didn't hear the door close. But he knew the second he was alone. He always knew the moment Elvin exited the room, he realized.

Why was that? And how come he'd never noticed it before?

Ray cleared his throat and shifted on his feet. What was wrong with him? God, had he become so dependent on Elvin that he couldn't function without Elvin in the room with him? Jesus, he was a fucking mess.

He glanced at the clock. If he left now, he could squeeze in a quick swim before heading to the airport—and picking Elvin up along the way. Ray grabbed his suit jacket and slung it over his shoulder. He turned toward his door and breathed a sigh of relief to find Elvin's desk unoccupied.

Good. He wasn't sure he'd trust himself to string together a sentence at this point. He hurried out while he still had the chance.

A swim would clear his head and then everything could go back to normal.

Elvin was already on the sidewalk with a full-sized suitcase when Ray's car pulled up. The driver popped the trunk, got out to help Elvin with his bag, then opened the backseat door for Elvin to slip into the seat next to Ray.

"Did you bring your entire apartment with you?" Ray asked.

Elvin furrowed his brow. "What do you mean?"

"Your suitcase." Ray chuckled. "I've never seen anyone bring something so big for a two-night stay."

Elvin pointed a finger in his face. "You might be accustomed to throwing a few things in a carry-on for a business trip, but I'm not. How am I supposed to know what I need? I have to be prepared."

Ray nodded, trying to hold back his laugh. "Except I'm

sure they have stores, even in northern Quebec, where we can, you know, buy things."

"But what if they're far away and we don't have a car? What if they're closed by the time we get there? You never know."

"Most hotels have all the essentials."

Elvin tensed. "Yeah, about that." He shot Ray a sidelong glance before staring resolutely at his hands clasped in his lap.

"What about it?"

"Um, well, there aren't exactly many hotels in that area. The nicest place I could find was a bed-and-breakfast."

Ray had stayed in plenty of bed-and-breakfasts before. Elvin should know that he wasn't too picky about that, as long as the place was nice. "Cool. I'm okay with that. What's the problem?"

Elvin cleared his throat and shifted in his seat. "Well… the reservation was originally only for one room. Because, you know, you were traveling alone."

Oh, he knew where this was going. "Uh-huh."

"So I called them to change the reservation."

"Uh-huh."

"And they only have one extra room available."

Two rooms. Three people. The math didn't quite work and Ray's heart skipped a beat at the prospect. "Okay."

"I mean, I can sleep on a couch if they have a living room or something. Or I guess I could stay in Ming's room if he's okay with that. You can still have your own room."

The idea of Elvin sharing anything with Ming was not

something that sat well with Ray, never mind a bedroom or, god forbid, a bed. "No, no. You're not sharing a room with Ming."

Elvin looked a little lost, but he nodded anyway. "I'm sure they have a couch somewhere. I'll figure it out."

"You're staying with me." It was the most obvious solution, even if it rattled around uncomfortably in that hollow spot inside Ray.

But Elvin didn't seem to think it was such a wonderful idea. "Are you sure?"

"Of course I'm sure. Why wouldn't you stay with me?" His words came out a lot more confident than he felt. On the surface, it made complete sense. They already spent so much time together. Elvin knew all the ins and outs of his life. What was the big deal about sharing a bedroom? It would be fine. Yeah, it would be totally fine.

Elvin shrugged, but he still looked uncertain. "I don't know. I thought you'd like some privacy."

Ray sighed and reached over to grab Elvin's hands before he sprained a knuckle with how hard he was twisting his fingers. Sure, he might have his own reservations, but he wasn't about to add any more stress to the situation than there already was. Elvin stilled under his touch.

"Do you really think I need privacy from you?" The idea itself was kind of absurd. "You know more about me and my *private* life than anyone else on the planet. Hell, you probably know more than I do."

Elvin gave him a shy smile. "I probably do."

Seeing Elvin smile soothed the lingering uneasiness Ray

had. "There you go. It's settled, then. We'll share a room and Ming can do whatever the hell he wants on his own."

Elvin nodded and took a steadying breath. He untangled his fingers and flipped one hand over to clasp Ray's.

Ray should have pulled his hand back then, but he didn't want to. Their palms fit together like two pieces of a puzzle and the feeling of Elvin's fingers wrapped around his sent warmth through Ray like he'd never experienced before. It wasn't a burning touch, nothing sizzled or zinged. Just a steady smoldering of embers threatening to build and build and build.

Elvin glanced at him, eyes wide, lips parted. He must have felt the warmth too. How could he not when it was so visceral for Ray? A small sound escaped Elvin's throat. He might have been trying to clear it, but it drew Ray's gaze to Elvin's neck. Long and strong, with the collar of his shirt wrapped snugly around it. Elvin's Adam's apple bobbed and Ray had the sudden urge to learn what it tasted like. He leaned in, drawn to that patch of skin right underneath Elvin's jaw where his pulse would be the strongest. Ray wanted to feel it beat against his tongue.

Suddenly, Elvin turned away, pulling his hand from Ray's. "Um, thanks." He fiddled with his collar and fingered the spot where Ray had wanted to leave his mark.

Ray sat back, dazed and numb. He fumbled at the door and rolled the window all the way down. Cool evening air blasted into the car and he sucked it in like he'd been underwater for minutes.

What the hell had just happened? Had he been holding Elvin's hand? Leaning in?

If Elvin hadn't put a stop to it, Ray would be sucking on his neck right now and leaving a hickey for all the world to see. God, what was going on?

Elvin was his employee, his subordinate, and Ray had always prided himself in knowing when to use his own power and position of privilege. Strong-arming executives into cooperating with Jade Harbour? Sure. Intimidating his juniors in compromising situations? Absolutely not.

It had never been a problem before. He'd never even gotten within miles of the line. Now he practically had one foot on the other side.

Their car pulled into the airport and took the narrow lane down to the hangar where they were meeting Jade Harbour's corporate jet. And not a moment too soon. The car had barely stopped before Ray grabbed the door handle and pulled it open. He couldn't get out fast enough.

What must Elvin think of him? He had to apologize. Elvin would forgive him, right?

He turned, looking for Elvin. Only to find him talking to Ming.

Chapter Eight

Elvin had never been on the company jet before. He'd seen pictures of it, sure, and had arranged for Ray to use it plenty of times. Actually on the private jet with its dedicated crew? Never.

But any excitement he might have felt paled next to what happened in the car with Ray. What the hell *had* happened? His heart was still beating too hard and his brain operating on too little oxygen to fully comprehend it.

He'd been worried about the rooming situation because he honestly did not want to share a room with Ming. The guy was okay most of the time, but Elvin had his limits. Sleeping on a couch somewhere didn't sound like fun, but he'd done it enough times that a couple nights wouldn't be a huge deal. Not in a million years had he ever contemplated spending the night with Ray. That was way too intimate, the stuff of daydreams and fodder for his already unhealthy crush.

But Ray had been okay with it. No, he'd pretty much insisted they room together. Then they'd held hands. Then Ray had almost kissed him.

Well, it had felt like Ray was leaning in to kiss him. Which would have been fine and not fine at the same time? Who the hell knew? Certainly not Elvin, because he'd basically short-circuited by then.

It didn't help that Ming ambushed him the second they'd arrived. The dude must have had a coffee right before because he was bouncing off the walls a little. He carried on a one-sided conversation that Elvin was happy to ignore as they boarded the plane. Elvin took the first seat he found. He kept his head down as Ray slid into the seat across the aisle.

Ray hadn't really been about to kiss him. No way. They'd worked together for years and Ray hadn't shown the slightest interest in him that way. What a completely ludicrous idea.

But what if it was true?

Elvin had never imagined a scenario where his feelings for Ray might be reciprocated. Elvin stared resolutely out the window as the plane taxied down the runway and lifted off into the air, pressing him back against the seat. It was impossible. It had to be. What would Ray ever see in a guy like him? He was the assistant, for god's sake. And not one of those sexy secretaries in short skirts and high heels. He went on way too much about his family and geeked out on musical theater. Ray was classy, sophisticated, worldly. Elvin was the opposite.

It was merely a figment of his imagination. It had to be. He'd been visibly stressed and Ray, being the good guy that he is, was being supportive and reassuring. That was all there was to it.

The plane leveled off and the flight attendant, Alice, came down the aisle to take their drink orders. "Welcome aboard, gentlemen. Dinner tonight will be lobster tail with an arugula salad. The vegan option is portobello steaks with oyster mushrooms and asparagus for Mr. Rao." She nodded toward Ming. "Can I get anyone started on drinks?"

Ming launched into an involved conversation about which wines would pair best with his vegan dinner. By the time he'd settled on a choice, Elvin figured he'd give Alice a break.

"I'll have a glass of whatever white wine is easiest for you, please."

Alice nodded. "I can do that. And for you, Mr. Chao?"

"Lagavulin, sixteen-year, single malt. On the rocks."

"Coming right up."

Elvin snuck a glance in Ray's direction, but he was staring as resolutely out of his window as Elvin had been earlier. Conversation was out of the question with Ming sitting right in front of them. Then Ming fiddled with a latch on his chair and it swung around, locking into place facing Elvin.

"So, Elvin." Ming stretched his legs out. He wasn't that

tall, but his legs were long enough that Elvin had to shift his to avoid contact. "First time on the jet?" Ming clasped his hands behind his head, elbows sticking out to the sides.

"Yes, first time."

"What do you think?"

Elvin looked around, taking in the plush leather seats and low-pile carpeted floor. Solid wood paneling lined the curved walls, dampening the rumble and hum of the engine. "It's nice."

"Isn't it!" Ming leaned forward to slap Elvin across the knee. "You're a lucky bastard, you know?" Ming continued. "Not everyone at Jade Harbour gets to ride on the jet. Certainly no assistants. Ray must have called one in to get you on board this trip. Eh, Ray?"

Ray glared at Ming like he'd just stolen Ray's favorite toy.

"Aw, come on, Ray. What's with the bad mood? We're going to have a great time! You, me, Elvin. A boys' getaway!"

Elvin suppressed a groan by running a hand over his face. A boys' getaway with Ming was not as appealing a sell as Ming was making it out to be.

"Your drinks, gentlemen." Alice came back with a tray and handed out their respective glasses.

"Thanks, Alice. You're a doll," Ming said as he took his wineglass. He winked at her before taking a sip.

Elvin cringed but Alice laughed and shook her head. "You're too funny, Mr. Rao."

"I'm your favorite passenger!"

"That you are." Her smile seemed genuine, Elvin had to admit.

As much as Ming could be a little difficult to get along with, there was no doubt that the guy was good at his job. Anytime Elvin had seen him interact with a non–Jade Harbour person, they actually seemed to like him. Weird.

"Alice, I'll have another." Ray held up his empty glass.

"Whoa." Ming chuckled. "That was fast."

It was. There may not have been much scotch in the glass to begin with, but Ray had tossed the whole thing back in one gulp.

"Sure, Mr. Chao. I'll be right back."

Elvin dropped his gaze to his lap. The sullenness, the staring out the window, chugging expensive scotch like he was a college student with cheap beer. Ray wasn't merely in a bad mood, he was verging on angry.

A wisp of worry snaked its way through Elvin. It settled into his joints and wound around his gut, squeezing tight. Was it their almost kiss? Having to share a room? Or something else altogether? For someone who claimed he could read Ray like a map, Elvin was at a complete loss.

Was it possible that Ray had detected Elvin's affections for him? He'd always been so careful to not let on what he felt. But that moment in the car had felt so real that maybe his mask had slipped. Ray was an observant person. Elvin wouldn't put it past him to pick up on something so fleeting and subtle.

Was that what Ray was angry about? Perhaps he felt betrayed, or violated. It was true that Elvin had much more access to Ray's life than the average assistant. Theirs was a relationship built on trust and mutual understanding. It wouldn't be fair for Elvin to take the knowledge Ray entrusted him with and spin it into something more. That line between professional and personal had been blurry for a long time, but it was still there. No matter how strong Elvin's feelings, he had to respect that line.

He took a sip from the wineglass he held, but it tasted as bland as water. Ming chattered away, mere white noise in the background. Alice came back with their dinner trays, but Elvin found himself without an appetite.

"Hey, buddy, you're not eating?" Ming eyed his plate.

"I'm not very hungry." Elvin poked at his food.

"No? You don't want the arugula salad?" Ming pointed at it with his fork.

Elvin picked up his plate and held it out to Ming. "Help yourself."

"What's wrong?" The question came from Ray, across the aisle. His voice was stern, commanding, impossible to ignore even if Elvin had wanted to.

Elvin looked over to find Ray's eyes steely under a furrowed brow.

"Nothing."

Ray's eyes narrowed a fraction.

Elvin gulped. "Really. I'm fine. I'm not hungry, that's all." He forced himself to take a sip of the wine.

"You're never not hungry."

Ray had a point. If there was food available, Elvin ate. It was something drilled into him from childhood. Not having an appetite wasn't an option; they never let food go to waste.

Without warning, Ray reached across the aisle and put the back of his hand on Elvin's forehead. Ray trying to take his temperature was a joke, and Elvin would have laughed out loud if there wasn't such a strong undercurrent of tension on the plane. He pushed Ray's hand away. "I'm fine."

"I don't believe you."

"Well, I am," Elvin snapped a little harder than he had intended. He sucked in a breath. "Sorry."

Ray set his jaw and turned back to his plate. He arranged his fork and knife carefully and then pushed the plate away.

"You're not finishing that either?" Ming pointed to Ray's plate with a gleam in his eye.

Wordlessly, Ray handed it over and crossed his arms over his chest.

Ming glanced from Elvin to Ray and back again before shrugging and helping himself to their salads. "You guys are missing out. This salad is great. I love arugula."

"Good for you," Ray muttered.

If Ming had heard the comment, he didn't react. He munched away happily while Elvin joined Ray in his sulking.

This was ridiculous. If Ray was upset about something, he should come out and say it. How was Elvin supposed to know what he'd done wrong if Ray didn't tell him? He could only read Ray's mind so far.

"So Ray, about Phoenix Family Trust."

Elvin groaned out loud. Not this. Not now. How the hell did Ming not know how to read the room?

Ray's mood went from bad to worse. "What about it?" he nearly growled.

"Have you had a chance to talk to your father?"

"No."

Ming's expression fell. As if he'd actually expected Ray to have set everything up already. Just how clueless was he?

"When do you think you'll be able to? You know this is a priority for Joanna."

Oh, no. Elvin put a hand over his eyes. Everyone was loyal to Joanna. Everyone wanted to please her. But invoking her name now only implied that Ray wasn't as committed to Jade Harbour as everyone else was—nothing could be further from the truth.

"You think I don't know that?" Ray shifted forward in his seat.

Ming froze, finally realizing his mistake. "I'm sure you do! Of course you do! So, you know, what's the update?"

Ray's jaw worked back and forth and for a split second it looked like he might unleash a verbal lashing on Ming. Elvin reached for Ray's arm and gave him a tug backward. "You talked to your cousin, right?"

It took another second before Ray huffed. "Yes, I spoke with my cousin. She's the head of HR. I asked her to let me know if any PFT staff were coming through Toronto."

"We don't have to wait for them to come to Toronto. I'm happy to go to them!"

"Ming." Elvin shook his head. So much for his attempt at de-escalation.

But Ming didn't get the message. "What? I've been working on a presentation for them, catered to their interests and priorities. I think your father—"

"Ming." Elvin cut in. "Maybe now isn't the best time."

Ming looked at him, genuinely confused, then turned to Ray, who sat slumped low, arms folded across his chest. He looked like someone had stepped on his puppy.

Ming opened his mouth, but Elvin caught him before he spoke. "Not now."

Ming pressed his lips together and a crease formed between his brows. Now he looked like a toddler who wasn't getting a second helping for dessert.

Maybe it was a good thing Elvin had come along. Who knew what kind of trouble these two would get into if he wasn't there to defuse the situation. For a second, Elvin considered sending each man to opposite sides of the plane just to keep them out of each other's hair.

"Gentlemen!" Alice to save the evening. "We're getting ready to land. I'll have to ask you to spin your seat around, Mr. Rao."

"Of course, Alice. I'd be happy to." He sent Elvin one last disgruntled frown before reaching for the latch that would unlock his seat.

Elvin sighed and glanced at his watch. The flight had been short—barely an hour and a half. And yet it'd felt like a daylong ordeal.

He glanced over to Ray, who still looked upset, but not

as worked up as he had been a minute ago. "Hey," Elvin whispered. "You okay?"

Ray met his gaze, held it for a moment and then nodded.

Elvin nodded back, gave Ray's arm one last squeeze and sat back for the plane's descent. They'd work through this and figure it out. The almost kiss, the shared bedroom, Ming. Everything would be okay. It had to be.

Chapter Nine

Ming must have a death wish. He couldn't be more irritating if he tried to be. If Alice hadn't announced their descent when she did, Ray would have strangled him to just get him to stop talking.

It wasn't even that Ming wouldn't stop pestering him about Phoenix Family Trust. It was the way he did it. He was so eager, like Ray hadn't repeatedly told him to back the fuck off.

Ray jogged down the stairs and paced away from the plane. The black tarmac was lit by the bright airport floodlights, but beyond the lights, night had already descended. Ray lifted his face toward the inky sky and let the biting wind whip at his cheeks. After that flight with Ming, he could have used a swim. Short of that, this would have to do.

"Ray!" Elvin's voice brought him back to where the ground crew was coordinating with the flight crew to get the jet parked for the night.

Their bags had been offloaded and a taxi driver was stashing them in the trunk of an unmarked car. Elvin stood next to the open backseat door and Ming was nowhere in sight. Good. Maybe the earth had opened up and swallowed him whole.

No such luck. As Ray approached, he spotted the back of Ming's head already in the front passenger seat.

"You okay?" Elvin asked quietly when Ray was within earshot.

"Yeah. You?"

"Yeah."

"How far to the hotel?"

"Bed-and-breakfast." Elvin corrected him with a slight grimace, reminding Ray of their rooming situation for the trip.

"Right. Bed-and-breakfast."

"About an hour, I think."

"Wonderful." Another hour stuck in an enclosed space with Ming. Ray ran a hand over his face and sighed. "Might as well get on our way." He gestured for Elvin to climb in first and slid in after him.

Ming turned around in the front seat. "Was this the best you could do?" he asked, looking skeptically at the car's interior.

Elvin glanced quickly out the back window where the driver was stowing the last of their bags. "We're in a pretty rural part of the province, Ming. There isn't really a limousine service up here."

Ming didn't look impressed, but at least he let it go as the driver shut the trunk then climbed in behind the steering wheel.

Elvin leaned forward to confirm the address with the driver, and they finally pulled away from the plane and into the dark forests that surrounded the airport.

"How many people live up here?" Ming asked as he peered out the window. They passed a few buildings with the lights still on. But soon there was nothing but the shadows of trees dancing in the light of the moon.

"Eh...thousand, I think." The driver had a thick Quebecois accent and it was questionable how much English he understood, but that didn't seem to deter Ming, who tried valiantly to carry on small talk as they drove.

Better the driver than Ray. He happily tuned out the droning sound of Ming's voice and settled in for the long trip. In the reflection of his window, he could catch glimpses of Elvin when the moon shone at just the right angle. There was a tiredness to the way he held his head, in the slope of his shoulders. It'd been a long day, especially since Elvin had shown up at his condo first thing in the morning. Then Ray had to drag him out to the middle of nowhere because the thought of being alone with Ming was unbearable.

Ray turned to Elvin, who was twisting his fingers together in his lap. Without thinking, Ray reached out and untangled his fingers, taking Elvin's hand in his.

"Hey, sorry about all this," he whispered as quietly as he could. Ming and the driver were still going at their broken, halting conversation.

"About what?"

"Making you come on this trip. Ming."

"There's nothing to be sorry for." It was hard to see Elvin's expression in the dim interior of the car, but Ray could tell from the sound of his voice that Elvin meant every word.

Of course he did. Elvin gave all of himself without ever stopping to ask why. No wonder Ray had been tempted earlier that evening. Some part of him knew that if he asked for it, Elvin wouldn't say no. Elvin never said no. It was a problem.

They had to talk about it, but not with Ming sitting close enough to eavesdrop. Not at the end of a long day when they were both tired. Tomorrow would be a long day too. But perhaps tomorrow night. They could give Ming the slip somehow and hash out what had happened. They were long overdue for boundaries. Elvin needed to learn how to say no and Ray needed to learn how to take care of himself for once.

"Later," Ray whispered.

"Okay."

They slid into silence and eventually Ming and the driver did too. Ray must have dozed off, because the next thing he knew, they were pulling up in front of a large brick house.

"Is this it?" Ming asked, peering skeptically out his window.

"Yes," replied the driver.

"Looks like the photos on the booking site," Elvin added.

Ray raised a hand to rub his eyes, only to find that he still held Elvin's in his. They'd held hands during the entire drive, and the realization made Ray feel all warm and fuzzy.

Holding hands was most definitely on the list of things they shouldn't be doing as boss and employee, but in that moment, Ray couldn't find the will to be sorry about it. Hell, he didn't even want to let go of Elvin to get out of the car.

An older couple with matching heads of snow-white hair stepped out of the house onto the wraparound porch. Elvin managed to wrest his hand from Ray's and went to greet them. Ray hung back, only to regret it when Ming came to stand next to him.

"He's good, eh?"

Ray cast Ming some side-eye. "What?"

"Elvin." Ming nodded toward him. "He's good at what he does."

Pride swelled in Ray's chest. "Yes, he is." Elvin wasn't merely good, he was fucking fantastic.

Ming's lips curled into a smile that set Ray's nerves on edge.

"Why do you care?"

Ming turned his smile toward Ray and Ray could have sworn it grew wider at his question. Ming shrugged, a little too nonchalantly, purposely nonchalantly. "No reason."

Ray didn't believe that for a second.

"I've got keys!" Elvin came back, holding his hands up.

Ray swallowed his irritation and grabbed the key Elvin held out to him. He was done with Ming, done with confrontation, just done.

He climbed the few steps to the porch and let himself in. The elderly couple was nowhere in sight, but people were moving around near the back of the house. Next to a small reception table was the staircase and Ray took it two steps at a time to the second floor. There were four doors leading off from the landing, two of which were closed with light seeping out underneath. Ray checked the key in his hand and found door number three.

It was a cozy room with frilly curtains, solid wooden furniture and ruffles on the bed linen. Under the window sat a small writing desk and chair. A second door led into an en suite shower room with a slanted ceiling so low that he'd have to duck. But all in all, it was cute. Country rustic or something like that.

The window overlooked the front of the house and Ray caught the last of the taxi's taillights as it pulled away. Downstairs, the door creaked, then the floorboards creaked and finally the stairs creaked before Elvin appeared in the doorway.

He was huffing, with Ray's carry-on tucked under one arm and his own giant suitcase behind him. Ray could have slapped himself. He'd completely forgotten about their bags.

"You should have called me to come get my own shit." He took the luggage from Elvin and set it in one corner of the room. "Most places have people to carry bags for us."

"Yeah, I know. But the couple here are kind of older and

I didn't want to bother you." Elvin stood with his hands on his hips, surveying the room.

"Oh hey, yours is bigger." Ming poked his head in and peered around Elvin's shoulder.

Not him again. Ray stepped forward. "Well, there's two of us and only one of you, so—"

Ming raised both hands in defense. "I was making an observation. I didn't say I wanted to trade or anything. You need to chill out, man. Jesus."

Elvin wedged his way between them and gently pushed Ray back. "We're all tired. It's been a long trip. Why don't we call it a night, huh? We'll see you in the morning, Ming." He grabbed the door and moved to close it.

"Yeah, sure. Sweet dreams." Ming winked at Elvin right before the door clicked shut.

"What is that supposed to mean?" Ray took another step only to find himself crowding Elvin against the door.

Elvin took him by the arms. "Nothing. He doesn't mean anything by it. You know, half of what he says is only to get a rise out of you."

He did know, but he couldn't stop himself from reacting. "Yeah."

Elvin slumped against the door, head tilted to one side. Ray was standing so close, close enough to feel Elvin's breath on his skin, to smell the slight mustiness of a long day in Elvin's hair. The impulse to lean into Elvin was so strong, to rest his head on Elvin's shoulder. Ray forced himself to move back and ran a hand over his face.

God, he must need to get laid. That was the only explanation Ray could come up with. He was projecting his cravings onto Elvin and it was utterly unfair. They had to set things straight between them and figure out how to get back to the way they were before. Tomorrow night. They would find time to talk tomorrow. "I'm going to jump into the shower."

"Okay." Elvin looked relaxed and soft, like he needed the support of the door in order to remain upright. His eyes were half-lidded and his lips were parted and it was all Ray could do not to press into him and kiss the hell out of him.

Fuck. He needed to get a hold of himself. Ray scrambled into the bathroom and fumbled with the lock. As if a locked door between them provided some semblance of safety. He turned the shower on, stripped and stepped into the ice-cold spray, biting his lip to keep from crying out.

When Elvin had first brought up the need to share a room, Ray hadn't given it a second thought. Of course they'd share. He wasn't about to relegate Elvin to some couch when there was a perfectly good bed available. But now Ray wasn't so sure. Not when every glance at Elvin seemed to trigger that part of him that he didn't know how to control.

Ray had never had to fight these types of sexual urges before. If he was attracted to someone, he let them know. If they didn't feel the same way, he moved on. But here was Elvin and neither of Ray's options were any good.

He stood under the cold water until his fingernails turned an alarming shade of blue. He turned the water off and reached for a towel. Oh shit. The towels must still be neatly rolled into twin logs on the bed.

Ray cracked the door open. "Um, Elvin?"

"Yeah?"

"I forgot the towels."

"Oh."

Ray waited, but there was no movement on the other side of the door. "Can you grab one for me?"

"Oh. Yeah, sure." After some shuffling, Elvin shoved a towel through the narrow opening.

Ray took it, waited for Elvin to extract his hand and shut the door firmly. His heart was pounding, his dick was hard. So much for the cold shower. He dried himself quickly before realizing his other problem—he didn't have clothes to change into.

Ray breathed deep, willed his dick to go down and wrapped the towel loosely around his waist. He opened the door.

Elvin was hunched over his suitcase, which was sitting open on the floor. He looked up and froze when he caught sight of Ray. Crouched down as he was, Elvin's head was at the perfect height and when his jaw dropped opened, Ray's imagination took over.

Elvin on his knees. Elvin with his lips around Ray's cock. Elvin moaning as Ray threaded his fingers into Elvin's hair. It took every ounce of willpower Ray possessed to look away from the enticing image Elvin presented.

"Bathroom's all yours," he croaked, turning quickly, hoping Elvin didn't notice the tented towel.

"Thanks," Elvin responded. His voice sounded as hoarse as Ray's.

Ray kept his back to the room as he fidgeted with his own suitcase, daring to breathe only when he heard the bathroom door click shut. Oh, this was bad. This was very, very bad.

He tossed the towel on the floor and pulled on his pajamas. Screw brushing his teeth. There was no way he was risking going anywhere near the bathroom now. No, it was probably best if he was in bed with the lights off by the time Elvin came out.

Ray eyed the bed—was it him or did it look a whole lot smaller than the beds he normally slept in? He went over and pulled the covers back. Honestly, had he really been expecting a king in a small bed-and-breakfast in the middle-of-nowhere northern Quebec? Maybe *he* should try to find a couch to sleep on for the night.

Before he could decide what to do, the bathroom door opened.

Elvin's hair was wet and a drop of water hung off the tip of his nose. Ray swallowed, eyeing that drop and feeling the strangest jealousy that it got to slide down Elvin's skin.

He tore his gaze away from the damp man of a temptation standing a mere arm's length away. "The bed's small."

"Uh, yeah, it's a double." Elvin moved. Ray managed not to watch. "I can sleep on the floor."

Even if they zipped up Elvin's suitcase and leaned it against the wall, there wouldn't be enough room for a full-grown man to stretch out on the carpet. Plus, it didn't look like there was a second set of linens available.

"No, don't be ridiculous. We'll make it work," Ray said, even if he didn't quite believe it himself.

Elvin stood on the other side of the bed. "Yeah?" He looked as unconvinced as Ray felt.

Ray shrugged. He climbed in, careful to stay on his side of the bed. Elvin followed suit. Even though he was about to fall off the edge, Ray could sense Elvin's arm mere inches away from his own. This was going to end in disaster, for sure.

"Um, good night?" Elvin said softly.

"Mmm-hmm, good night." Ray flicked off the lamp on his side of the bed and Elvin did the same.

Light from the moon filtered into the room as Ray stared up at the ceiling. It wasn't going to be a good night. Nope, it was going to be a long, long one.

Chapter Ten

Elvin must have fallen asleep at some point during the night because he didn't remember when or how he ended up in this particular position. He was still on his back, but now Ray was wrapped around him like a twisting vine, one leg thrown over Elvin's thighs, an arm slung possessively across his waist. Ray's head was right next to his, chin on his shoulder, every breath sending a warm stream of air against his neck.

He'd never felt more comfortable in his whole life.

He closed his eyes and tried to commit the moment to memory. The weight of Ray against him. The warmth of another body in the bed. The mustiness of their combined scents. It was heaven and he never wanted to return to earth.

Ray made an adorable little sound, like a mini groan deep in his throat, then snuggled in closer, tucking his face right in the crook of Elvin's neck. The hairs on the top of his head tickled Elvin's cheek. Elvin leaned into it and soaked in the feeling.

This had always been a possibility when he first realized he might be sharing a bed with Ray. Who was he kidding? A part of him had hoped it would happen.

Ray let out a sigh and his breathing pattern changed, but he didn't move an inch. "Good morning," he muttered, lips moving against Elvin's skin.

"Morning."

"What time is it?"

The pale light sneaking in past the curtain suggested it was still early. Not too early for Elvin's internal alarm clock, but definitely too early for Ray. "I'm not sure."

Ray groaned, but still didn't move.

Did Ray not know the compromising position they were in? Shouldn't he be pushing Elvin away and jumping out of bed? Should *Elvin* jump out of bed? How was this okay?

"Want me to check?" Elvin held his breath, not sure which answer he wanted.

Ray tightened his hold. "No, it's fine."

Elvin exhaled with relief.

But that didn't mean he'd be able to go back to sleep. He was wide awake now, his mind racing. Ray couldn't possibly think Elvin was someone else. Did that mean this was okay? Or maybe was Elvin simply a warm body he was using as a human pillow? Elvin rolled the idea around in his mind, testing the weight of it.

He'd never really craved physical intimacy with anyone before. Even with the casual boyfriends he'd had in university, he'd never wanted to explore past the most innocent of touches. But Ray wasn't a boyfriend, and there was nothing casual about whatever the hell they were to each other.

Elvin stared up at the ceiling. Outside the window, the faint glow of the early sun grew brighter and brighter.

Beep! Beep! Beep! His phone blared from the nightstand. Ray groaned and brought a hand up to rub his eyes while Elvin reached out to turn off the alarm. He'd forgotten he'd set it last night, but obviously past Elvin was way more responsible than morning Elvin.

No longer bound to the bed by Ray's limbs, Elvin sat up, swinging his legs over the side. The air was cold and it sent a shiver through him. Every fiber of his being wanted to crawl back under the covers where it was warm and cozy and filled with Ray. Screw Caron and Jade Harbour and work. If he could spend the rest of his life lounging in bed with Ray, he'd die a happy man.

But life was never that simple, was it? There were bills to pay and rent to meet. There were family responsibilities and people who counted on him to be there. He hadn't been born into a life of leisure; he wasn't built for it.

It was nice while it lasted. A little moment of happiness that he could hold close to his heart and revisit whenever he wanted. It was enough. More than enough. Elvin went to brush his teeth and wash his face, keeping one ear attuned to any sounds that might come from the bedroom, but there were none. When he stepped out of the bathroom, Ray was again half-dressed, this time wearing his suit trousers and nothing else.

"Oh, sorry."

Ray stopped in mid-motion, about to put on his shirt. When had nudity suddenly become a thing for him? When had Ray's nudity become more than a slight distraction? His pants were snug around his hips, perfectly encasing his muscled buttocks and elongating his already long legs. With his arms raised, it left his sides exposed—tender skin that rarely saw the sun, a strangely intimate part of the body that Elvin wanted to trace with his fingers. Ray's nipples were little nubs surrounded by dark circles of skin. Would those patches taste any different from the rest of him?

Elvin swallowed. No tasting Ray. No touching. No looking at Ray, even, at least not like that. He turned away to fumble through his suitcase for clothes.

"I should be the one saying sorry."

Elvin turned at the comment. "What do you mean?"

Ray was buttoning up his shirt. It was safer that way, even if Elvin's hungry eyes ate up the last inches of skin on display.

"For this morning." Ray nodded toward the bed.

"Oh." It was thoughtful of Ray to apologize, and Elvin wasn't surprised he did. But it still cut deep, like what they'd done was something to be ashamed of. Those minutes they'd had in bed together were precious and Elvin would never be sorry for soaking in every last second. "It's fine. I didn't mind."

Ray nodded, tucking his shirt into his pants. "We should talk about it."

"About what?" Elvin clutched the clothes he'd chosen to wear, wrinkles be damned.

"About us."

Elvin swallowed, trying to wrest control over the ball of emotion spinning in his chest. They'd somehow drifted into a new dynamic over the past couple days and Elvin wasn't sure how they'd gotten there. Had he done something to encourage it? Had he wanted it so much it triggered something between them? Whatever it was, Ray was right about needing to talk it over. They had to put a stop to this before they went too far down the road.

"Yeah, okay."

"Tonight? We'll have to find a way to ditch Ming."

Elvin nodded. "I'll think of something."

"Great. Thanks." Ray went into the bathroom.

Elvin stared at the closed door. Twelve hours. He could delude himself for another twelve hours before reality would set in.

For once, Ming's chattering was a welcome distraction. It carried them through breakfast and the car ride to Caron's mill about twenty minutes away. If Ming detected anything strange going on between Elvin and Ray, he didn't bring it up. And since Ming wasn't the sort to *not* bring up something like that, Elvin felt a little proud of how well he was keeping it together.

When they finally got to Caron, there was no time to think of anything else. They launched into full work mode.

The mill staff had not been given a heads-up that Jade Harbour was coming for an on-site visit. Catching them off guard was a deliberate tactic—they couldn't prepare ahead of time and cover up all the dirty little corners they didn't want anyone to see.

"Who are you?" the guard at the gate asked in French. The driver turned to Ming, but his repeated yells of "Jade Harbour" meant nothing to the guard.

Ray took over and in semi-decent French explained their surprise inspection. Unconvinced, the guard made them wait for the manager to come sort things out.

"We were not informed that you would be coming today." Pierre, the general manager, spoke in heavily accented English while frowning in disapproval.

Behind him stood another man, tall with broad shoulders. His orange-red hair and full beard matched the plaid-checkered lumberjack fleece he wore. He had his thick arms folded across his chest and he eyed each of them with a probing stare. Whoever the dude was, he was not friendly.

"I know. That was the point." Ray stood his ground against Pierre and the lumberjack. "Jade Harbour is entitled to unannounced visits."

The lumberjack muttered something low and in French that Elvin couldn't understand, but Ray apparently did.

"Go ahead. Call Gilles. I guarantee he'll be okay with this."

Pierre seemed to consider it for a moment before shaking his head. "No." He nodded toward the truck he had driven out. "Follow us in."

"Nice welcoming party," Ming muttered under his breath.

They drove to the middle of a large dirt square. On one side was a massive building with loading docks spaced out along the wall. Opposite were enormous piles of logs of various diameters. Elvin eyed the mountain of trees. If any one of those came loose, they'd be flattened into pancakes. The hum of drills and saws and other heavy machinery reverberated through the air.

The second the taxi doors were shut, the driver hightailed it out of there, leaving them standing completely out of place in the dusty industrial landscape. That didn't seem to faze Ray, or Ming either. Ming strolled up to the lumberjack and stuck out his hand. "What's your name?"

Mr. Orange Beard looked dubiously at Ming's hand before answering his question. "Olivier."

"Great. Nice to meet you, Olivier. What do you do around here?" Ming didn't seem the least offended by Olivier's slight.

"Warehouse manager."

Ming nodded to the big building on their left. "Is that the warehouse?"

"No."

Ming shot Elvin a glance and Elvin gave him a slight

shrug in response. Elvin found that Francophones some-times came across a little too curt. He'd always written it off as a lost-in-translation thing. But Olivier's attitude to-ward them felt too hostile for that.

"Why don't you give us a tour?" Ray suggested, mostly to Pierre, but Olivier jumped in.

"I will do it."

Pierre looked from Olivier to Ray and back before nod-ding. "Olivier knows the mill as well as I do. He can an-swer your questions." He didn't wait for a response before stalking off and disappearing through a door at the far end of the building.

"Come." Olivier started in the opposite direction.

Ming shook his head, unimpressed, as he followed. Elvin and Ray brought up the rear.

"I don't like the look of this," Ray said quietly.

"No kidding. Do unannounced visits always get such a warm reception?"

"That's just it. Operations on the up-and-up don't mind people dropping in. They have nothing to hide."

"So you think these guys are hiding something?" Elvin asked.

Ray held the door open for Elvin. "It's too early to tell. Keep your eyes peeled. I have a feeling things are about to get exciting."

Chapter Eleven

Inside, the mill was a maze of shadow and light. Industrial lights hung from high above, flooding the cavernous space with an eerie yellow glow. Oversized machinery was lined up in rows, churning away while sending vibrations through the concrete floor and through Ray's leather soles. Here and there were factory workers in hard hats and reflective safety vests poking at control panels and peering at gauges.

"Should we be wearing those?" Elvin asked in a stage whisper, nodding at the safety gear.

Ray shrugged. Olivier wasn't wearing any and he didn't seem concerned. In fact, he was marching up one aisle and down another so fast Ray barely had time to take in what the hell they were seeing.

The only thing slowing them down was Ming. He asked questions nonstop, forcing Olivier to explain how this process or that process worked. Ray stayed in the background, watching how Olivier reacted, his body language, the tone of his voice. They were in front of a machine that looked no different than the dozens of others they'd passed. Olivier was pointing at a lever that was supposed to cut giant sheets of paper into the right size for storage and shipping. His explanation was simple and straightforward, almost a little too simple—this thing cuts that thing and the other things move stuff over somewhere. He probably didn't think they could understand anything more complex. Yet, the more Ming asked for details, the more curt Olivier became, like he was in a hurry to brush them off.

As Olivier spoke, something else became clear. Ray knew just enough French to know that Olivier's accent sounded different from everyone else they'd met so far. His English only carried a hint that it wasn't his first language. He must have grown up in a larger city, learned English early and used it on a regular basis. With language skills like that, it seemed odd that he would end up in the middle of northern Quebec working at a paper mill.

Their last stop was the warehouse where finished products were stored before they were shipped to the customer. One side of the warehouse was made up of pallets stacked up to the ceiling. On the other side sat giant rolls of paper, placed end upon end.

"Watch out." Olivier motioned for them to step aside as

a forklift drove by. Once it had passed, he stuck his hands on his hips. "That's the end of the tour."

"Wow, this is amazing. It really is." Ming gazed up at the rows of paper products with wonder.

Elvin looked pretty impressed too. Ray? Not so much. "How long have you worked here?" he asked.

It was a simple question, but Olivier's closed expression shut down even more.

"Why is that important?" Olivier crossed his thick arms over his thick chest and grew several inches in height.

"Because I asked you." Ray squared off with him, raising his chin. He wasn't about to be pushed around by an ill-advised display of machoism. "If you don't want to answer the question, I can just as easily check the employee records."

Olivier tried to stare him down. Ray stared right back. Eventually, Olivier gave in. "Almost one year."

Ray did a bit of mental math. "After Jade Harbour acquired Caron."

"Correct."

"Where did you work before this?"

Olivier's expression grew even darker, if that was possible, and for a second Ray really thought Olivier wouldn't respond. "Berry Pulp & Paper, not far from here. Before that at Laurent Wholesale & Distribution in Sherbrooke."

Sherbrooke wasn't far from Montreal. That could explain Olivier's English. But Ray didn't like how hesitant Olivier had been. Was there something in his past that he didn't want Ray digging into?

He made a mental note to check Olivier's employment history. If he'd been brought on board after the acquisition, Jade Harbour should have access to his HR records.

Another forklift drove past them, carrying several rolls of paper. Ray watched it inch away before turning back to Olivier. "Take us to the office. I want to look at your files."

There was another silent stare down before Olivier finally relented. He turned on his heel and walked away without waiting to see if they'd follow.

Elvin leaned in as they made their way back through the warehouse. "Does he seem unusually pissed off to you? I feel like we're trampling over his mother's grave or something."

"Or he's got a surly disposition," Ray offered.

Elvin looked dubious. "I'm only asking because I don't want to end up getting fed into a wood chipper."

Ray gave him a shoulder bump. "Don't worry. I'll make sure you get home in one piece." He nodded toward Ming. "No guarantees for Ming."

The management offices were on the second floor, small and dingy compared with the vastness they'd come from. There was a lingering scent of cigarette smoke, most likely due to the yellow residue on the walls. Pierre was in one office, talking on the phone. The other office held a messy desk, but no people. In the open area were several more desks in various states of tidiness, with a row of metal cabinets at the far end.

"What do you want to see?" Olivier asked.

"Everything."

Olivier cast him a sidelong look. "What do you mean?"

"I mean everything. Supplies, inventory, orders, client lists, vendor lists, employee records. Everything." People always thought Ray was joking when he said this. They stopped laughing when they found themselves pulling apart their entire computer system and all their files to get Ray what he wanted.

"How are you going to read all of that?" Olivier hadn't moved from his spot leaning against an unoccupied desk.

"Don't worry about it. That's my problem."

Pierre hung up the phone and joined them. "Is everything okay?"

Olivier glanced at him, then back at Ray. "Yes, everything's fine." He stood and walked around the desk to sit in front of the computer. "Everything is digital. If you had asked in advance, we could have prepared a copy for you to take home."

"Still don't understand the concept of a surprise audit, do you?" Ray responded, standing behind Olivier.

Pierre blanched at the comment and Elvin looked uncomfortable. Ming was trying to hold in a burst of laughter. Ray could only imagine the size of Olivier's scowl.

Olivier pushed his chair back suddenly and Ray had to jump to get out of the way. "Here. The files you want." He waved at the computer screen, which showed a series of folders, all labeled in French. Then he stalked away, not waiting for Ray's response.

They watched Olivier barrel through the door leading back into the factory and it slammed shut with a force that made Pierre wince. For a second, no one moved or said anything, until Ming broke the silence.

"Well, he's not in a very good mood, is he?" Ming picked the nearest chair and made himself comfortable in it. "I'm assuming we're going to be here awhile?"

Ray took the chair Olivier had vacated. "It'll be faster if we all pitch in."

From the corner of his eye, Ray saw Ming rubbing his hands together, grinning like this was what he'd been waiting for all trip. "Put me to work. It's not like there's anything else to do around here."

Ray glanced up from the computer screen to make sure he'd heard Ming correctly. He hadn't expected Ming to volunteer himself. But hey, if he was willing, Ray wasn't about to object. Because there was at least one thing Olivier was right about—reading through all this material was going to take a really long time.

He turned to Pierre. "Is there somewhere we can print stuff out?"

Pierre printed to a large printer-copier that sat outside his door.

"Good. We'll call you if we need you."

Even with three pairs of eyes, it would have been impossible to go through all of Caron's files in one day. But Ray had to admit they were making better progress than he'd anticipated.

Elvin's efficiency was never in question. But Ming was surprisingly methodical and had great attention to detail.

More than once he'd flagged something that seemed odd so they could investigate further when they made it back to Toronto.

They copied files as they went, printing some out to make cross-referencing easier. Soon, they'd taken over the entire office, with stacks of paper scattered across every horizontal surface. Olivier and some other guys had come through a few times, stopping in to talk to Pierre or work at a computer. But for the most part, everyone left them alone.

Elvin closed a folder he'd been organizing and leaned back in his chair, stretching his arms out overhead. "Finished the vendor list. Nothing abnormal that I could see."

"Good." Ray checked what was left for them to go through. "I want to do a rundown of inventory, matching their records with what's on the floor. It'll be easier with two of us covering the warehouse."

"I can help." Elvin stood and stretched some more. He'd taken off his suit jacket at some point and rolled up his sleeves, exposing his forearms and their light dusting of hair. Now, as he held his arms in a circle in front of him and twisted side to side, the image triggered memories of last night and this morning, memories that Ray had managed to ignore for most of the day.

Not now, he scolded his wayward penis before daring to stand. "Ming, you okay here?"

"Yep," he answered without looking up. "I'm in the middle of this general ledger and it'll be a while still."

"Let's go." Ray grabbed the inventory list he'd printed and led the way to the warehouse with Elvin by his side.

He hadn't been surprised when he woke up wrapped around Elvin. It was how he normally slept with whoever happened to be in his bed. What had been surprising was how much he hadn't wanted to get out of bed. With every other lover, the intimacy that came with sex faded as soon as the sun broke over the horizon, but with Elvin the intimacy had only felt stronger without the sex.

He was in dangerous territory and he had no idea which way was out. Before last night, there'd been a line, however faint, but at least it'd been clear what he'd had to do. Now? Fuck, they'd gone so far past the line, he didn't know where it was anymore.

The problem was, he liked this next-level intimacy with Elvin. It was tantalizing. Like he'd gotten a sample bite and now his mouth watered for more. Tonight. They were going to talk and sort out a plan for the future. It might be too late to go back to the way things were only a week ago, but it wasn't too late to make sure they didn't end up somewhere neither of them wanted to be.

Ray pushed open the door to the warehouse and promptly walked into Olivier.

"What are you doing?" Olivier asked, like Ray was trespassing.

"Inventory." He held up the papers in his hands.

Olivier didn't budge.

"Are you going to let us pass?"

Olivier didn't look like he wanted to, but Ray took a step forward anyway and Olivier shifted enough for them to squeeze through.

"He really doesn't like us," Elvin whispered.

"Too bad for him."

Elvin snuck a glance backward and his eyes widened in alarm. "He's following us."

"Probably making sure we don't burn the place down or something." Ray handed Elvin the inventory. "Ignore him."

He checked which aisle they were in front of and then pointed to the first page in Elvin's hand. "I'm going to read out the serial numbers on each of these pallets and you can cross them off on the list."

"Got it."

They worked like a well-oiled machine, easily falling into step like they'd done inventory checks together since they were children. Olivier was never more than a few meters away, watching them, talking into his walkie-talkie, then watching them some more.

At one point, Elvin tried to assure him that they didn't need supervision, but he merely nodded and continued to stand guard. Whether he was guarding Ray and Elvin or the warehouse was anyone's guess.

They were nearing the halfway point when things got interesting.

Olivier spoke rapidly into his walkie-talkie, too quietly for Ray to hear what he said. But not a minute later, a forklift came around the corner and sped down the aisle toward them.

"Whoa." Elvin jumped back as the huge metal prongs barely missed him.

"What's going on?" Ray asked.

Olivier was busy directing the forklift driver. They stood back as the driver maneuvered around them, picked up a pallet sitting at the far end of the aisle and zoomed away. When Ray glanced questioningly at Olivier, he found himself at the receiving end of a death stare.

He pointed to where the forklift had disappeared. "What was that about?"

"Nothing." Olivier's eyes were hard, like he was daring Ray to press the point.

Ray wasn't one to back down from dares. "Stay here," he said to Elvin. "Keep checking serial numbers."

"Where are you going?" Elvin asked.

"To find that pallet." Ray started down the aisle, first walking, then running when he realized Olivier was following him. Good, better he deal with Olivier than Elvin. "Where did you take the pallet?"

"Nowhere."

Ray stopped when he reached the middle of the warehouse. He scanned the area, but all the pallets looked alike. Damn it, he hadn't managed to grab the serial number before the forklift had taken it.

Forklift. The driver was strolling across the warehouse floor, stripping off his gloves as he went.

"Hey!" Ray jogged up to him.

The driver stopped short, eyes wide with surprise and a touch of fear. He backed away a few steps before he bumped a giant roll of paper.

"Don't say anything!" Olivier shouted at the driver in French.

Ray pointed at the guy. "Where did you put that pallet?"

"He doesn't speak English," Olivier said to Ray, trying to step in between them.

"I think he does. Where did you put that pallet?" Ray sidestepped Olivier once, then again, before physically pushing him away. "Where?"

The driver shook his head, lips pressed together like he was afraid the answer might fall out of his mouth. Ray got up close. "Where is it?"

His gaze darted to the right, then to Olivier, then finally back to Ray. The movement was small and quick, but it was enough. Ray followed it and found two single pallets sitting on their own. It had to be one of the two.

"Which one is it?" he asked the guy, who kept shaking his head.

No matter. He could deal with two pallets.

"Did you find it?" Elvin came jogging up. Trust Elvin to be there when Ray needed him.

"It's one of these. Find the serial numbers."

Olivier stood watch, hands on hips, as Ray and Elvin scoured the pallets for the label that identified the product inside and customer. The driver sulked behind Olivier, muttering apologies that everyone ignored.

"I don't see one," Elvin said, circling his pallet.

"Mine's here." Ray read out the serial number and Elvin checked it off the list.

Ray turned to Olivier. "Why doesn't that pallet have a label on it?"

Olivier stood stone-faced, silent.

"I asked you a question."

"I don't answer to you."

That took Ray aback. If Olivier didn't answer to him, then who the fuck did he answer to? "Excuse me?" Ray got up close and personal, chin lifted to look Olivier in the eye. "What did you say?"

"I don't answer to you," Olivier repeated, more slowly this time.

He could mean Pierre, or even Gilles. But something in Olivier's eyes told Ray that he meant neither. There was something else going on here and Olivier didn't want them to find out what it was.

Ray couldn't help the grin that tugged on the corner of his mouth. Joanna wanted skeletons. Well, they'd just stumbled on a whole warehouse of them.

Ray turned to the driver, who was still hovering nearby. "Give me that." He pointed to the box cutter sticking out of the driver's pocket.

The driver looked nervously at Olivier. *Wrong move, buddy.* Ray walked over and grabbed it off the guy. If people didn't give him what he wanted, he was prepared to take it.

He extended the blade and started cutting away the plastic shrink-wrap holding the pallet together.

"What are you doing?" Elvin asked.

"Seeing what's inside here." Under the shrink-wrap were boxes of what looked like computer paper.

"Uh, do you think that's a good idea?" Elvin stared wide-eyed behind him. "He's coming."

Ray glanced over his shoulder in time to catch Olivier's advance. He ducked, raising an arm to shield himself, but Olivier did nothing more than loom over him.

"Stop!" His voice was so loud and forceful, the sound blasted over Ray like a physical wave.

"Oh my god, Ray. Do what he says," Elvin begged from the other side of the pallet.

Ray peered at the orange-red giant. He looked bigger than he ever had before, and he probably weighed twice what Ray did. His hands were curled into fists at his sides, but something about him gave Ray the sense that he wouldn't get physical. If he was going to use force, wouldn't he have done it already?

Slowly, Ray lowered his arm and stood up straight. "No."

Olivier's face turned as red as his hair. "I said, stop!"

"And I said no."

"Ray!"

"It's okay." Ray slipped out from Olivier's shadow, making his way around the pallet to Elvin. "He's not going to hurt us, are you, Olivier?"

When Olivier didn't move, Ray reached for the closest box and cut open the plastic ties that held the lid on. "No, I don't think you are."

He lifted the lid and threw it on the floor, never taking his eyes off Olivier.

"It's paper," Elvin said.

Ray glanced down and, sure enough, the box was full of white computer paper.

No, that couldn't be right. Olivier would never be so protective over computer paper. Ray wiggled a couple fingers between the top package and the edge of the cardboard box, then lifted the package out of the way.

Elvin gasped.

Olivier looked like he was about to explode.

Ray reached in and pulled out a rounded bundle covered in plastic. "I don't know what this is, but it definitely isn't paper."

Chapter Twelve

Holy shit. Holy shit.

That was a brick of drugs. A brick. Of. Drugs. That Ray was holding.

Ray was holding a brick of drugs.

"Put that back." Olivier pointed at Ray, and he didn't look like he was going to take no for an answer this time.

"Ray, put it back," Elvin whispered. They'd barely escaped a beating from Olivier and he had no interest in finding out what Olivier would do if Ray tried to take The Brick Of Drugs.

Ray tossed the plastic-wrapped package into the box and it landed with a heavy thump. Then he brushed his hands together like there was some residual powder on his palms.

Jesus fucking Christ. Drugs. In a box of paper. At a

company that Jade Harbour owned. Jade Harbour owned drugs. What were they going to do? They were going to die. Jesus Christ, they were going to die.

Ray pointed right back at Olivier. "I want to talk to your superiors." As if he was in a position to negotiate anything.

"Ray." Elvin grabbed Ray's arm. "What are you doing?"

Ray shook him off and started around the pallet toward Olivier. "Who do you work for?" He went right up to Olivier, who stood at least half a head taller and was twice as wide. Ray looked tiny next to the orange-red giant and yet he didn't look the least bit intimidated. How the hell did he do that?

"I said, who do you work for?" Ray shouted.

But instead of getting bigger and more aggressive, Olivier seemed to deflate. "You need to leave."

Leave? What did he mean? He was going to let them walk out of here? Elvin came up behind Ray and took him by the shoulders. "Ray, come on. Let's go." They needed to get out before Olivier changed his mind.

Ray shook him off again. "I'm not leaving until you tell me who you work for. Who's your boss?" He was practically poking Olivier in the chest.

What was he thinking? "Ray!"

"Listen to me carefully." Olivier bent his head and hissed the words through clenched teeth. "Leave and forget what you've seen here. Don't speak of it to anyone and you won't get hurt."

"Is that a threat?" Ray bit out his words just as harshly.

"No. It's a warning."

Elvin grabbed Ray and pulled as hard as he could. "Ray!" They needed to get Ming and get the hell out of this place.

Ray dug in his heels. "This isn't over. I will find out who you work for. *That's* a warning." Then he let Elvin lead him away.

"What the fuck was that?" Elvin kept hold of Ray, hurrying him through the warehouse.

Ray went, all resistance gone. His eyes were unfocused, like he was replaying the confrontation with Olivier in his mind. "It doesn't make any sense."

"No fucking shit. I'm not sticking around to find out what he'll do if we don't leave." Elvin pulled out his phone and frantically tried to find the number of the taxi company as he ran toward the management office. He hit dial and held the phone up to his ear, only then realizing that Ray had slowed to a stop behind him. "What are you doing? Come on!"

Ray looked at him, confusion marring his brow. "I don't think he'll hurt us."

"We're not taking that chance." Elvin marched back to drag Ray away just as the taxi dispatcher answered his call. "Hi, we need a car at Caron as soon as possible. Like now, please."

"Sir, please wait while I find the next available driver."

"Damn it," Elvin muttered. He jogged up the steel staircase two steps at a time and burst through the door of the management offices. "Ming!"

Startled, Ming nearly jumped out of his seat. "Yeah?"

"We're leaving!" Elvin started stacking every piece of paper he could get his hands on.

"Already?"

"Yes, already!"

"Allô? Monsieur?" The dispatcher came back on the line. Elvin put the phone to his ear again. "Yes, I'm here. I'm here."

"The closest driver can be at the Caron mill in twenty minutes."

"Twenty minutes! That's not soon enough. We need to leave now!"

A warm hand settled on his shoulder and Ray gently pried the phone out of Elvin's tight grasp. "It's okay," Ray spoke into the phone. "Twenty minutes is fine. We'll be waiting outside." He hung up and handed the phone back.

"Why did you do that? We can't wait that long!"

Olivier could change his mind at any moment and it wasn't like they'd be difficult to find. Elvin could see the headlines now—three employees of renowned private equity firm disappear in the forests of northern Quebec.

"Breathe." Ray held him by both shoulders and gave him a shake. "Breathe. Everything's going to be okay."

"Can someone tell me what the hell is going on?" Ming asked, hands on hips.

Elvin started to answer, but Ray put a finger on his lips. "Listen to me. We're going to get to the bottom of this. Everything will be fine."

Elvin pulled Ray's hand away from his mouth. How was Ray so calm? Like this was something he saw every day? "How do you know that? You were holding a brick of drugs!"

"What?" Ming came around the desk to stand next to them. "Did you say drugs?"

Ray cringed a bit, like he'd been hoping to keep that little detail from Ming. "Yes, there were drugs hidden in a pallet of computer paper. Most likely cocaine. Montreal is a distribution hub for the Mexican cartels."

"What!"

Ray lifted one hand from Elvin's shoulder and planted it on Ming's. "Calm down. Both of you. Hysterics are not going to help the situation."

Ming's jaw hung open as he glanced back and forth between Elvin and Ray. "You're joking."

If fucking only. Elvin would take a bad joke over Olivier killing them over a shipment of drugs any day.

"Unfortunately, no. But again, there is no reason to panic." Ray slowly let go of their shoulders. "A car is on its way. We'll pack up in here and go outside to wait for it. You both with me?"

"Yeah, sure." Ming looked more confused than terrified. But then, he hadn't been in the warehouse when Olivier threatened them.

"Elvin?" There was concern in Ray's eyes, in the way he said Elvin's name. But there was also surety; Ray's natural confidence that he was in full control of the situation. If he couldn't trust in Ray, what could he trust in?

Elvin forced himself to take a steadying breath and nodded. "Yeah. Okay."

"Good." Ray took a step back and surveyed the space. He pointed to the empty office next to them. "Where's Pierre?"

Ming frowned. "Uh, he left a few minutes before you guys got back. Didn't say where he was going and I didn't ask."

"Olivier must have called him." Ray grabbed a nearby box.

"That's bad, right?" A fresh surge of adrenaline rushed through Elvin's veins. "Pierre's the boss. He won't be as lenient as Olivier."

Something hit him in the chest and only after he grasped at it did Elvin realize Ray had shoved the half-filled box at him. "Don't worry about Pierre. As long as he's not here, he won't get in our way."

Ray pointed Elvin toward a nearby desk. "Pack everything up. Ming, make sure we have digital copies of everything we can access. Let's get out of here before they get back."

Elvin jumped into action. He could pack; he knew how to pack. Gather papers, drop them in the box—the familiar motions helped make their fucking wild circumstances a little less bananas. By the time he put the lid on the box, Elvin almost felt normal.

Ming tucked the flash drive into his pocket and they each grabbed a box. Ray paused by the door. "Ready?"

"Yeah, let's get out of here." Ming shouldered his way past Ray.

Elvin was less eager to venture from the relative safety of the office. "What if someone tries to stop us?"

"Ignore them and keep walking. I'll handle them."

Elvin nodded. If Ray said he would handle them, then he would handle them. They hurried to catch up to Ming. Around them, the machines still rumbled and the industrial lights cast deep shadows, but they didn't come across a single soul.

"Where did everyone go?" Elvin asked. The factory floor was far from inviting, but with it abandoned, it was downright creepy.

"Who cares?" Ming responded. "There's no one to stop us. That's all that matters."

Ming was right. Still. There'd been dozens of people around before—where did they disappear to?

Ming crashed through a door with a red exit sign hanging above it, not bothering to hold it open for Elvin and Ray. The latch mechanism was loud enough to be heard above the hum of machinery and when the door slammed shut, Elvin cringed at the boom.

"Jesus Christ," Ray muttered before opening the door himself with careful, measured movements. "He has no concept of being subtle."

Elvin wasn't in the mood to argue about Ming, especially when he could understand the need to get out of there as fast as possible. Sometimes subtlety was overrated. Out in the courtyard, the midafternoon sun beat down on them as if there was not a care in the world. They were alone there too. The forklifts sat empty, engines off, drivers gone.

"Now what?" Ming dropped his box on the dusty ground.

There was nowhere to take shelter, nowhere to hide if someone came looking for them. "I say we start walking." Elvin took a couple steps toward the main gate. "We can intercept the taxi on the road."

Ming eyed his box. "But this thing is heavy."

"You'd rather stand around waiting for them to come back?" Elvin glanced at the door they'd come through, half expecting it to open to a mob on the other side.

"No, Elvin's right. Let's walk," Ray chimed in. "They've cleared out to let us leave, so let's go."

Ming rolled his eyes, hands on hips. "Of course you'd side with him."

"I'm not siding with anyone," Ray shot back. "You can stay here by yourself if you want." He turned toward the gate and Elvin followed.

There was a shuffle as Ming grabbed his box and hurried to catch up. "We're like fucking fugitives, running through the woods to escape the law."

"Hardly," Ray muttered.

"I can't believe this," Ming continued. "Do you know how much these shoes cost? This gravel is going to destroy them."

"Would you rather lose a pair of shoes or your head?" Elvin was beginning to understand why Ray disliked Ming so much.

"You owe me a new pair, Ray."

"Yeah, yeah. Whatever. Just keep walking."

Ten minutes later, they reached the main entrance. The gatehouse was deserted and the gate itself was wide open.

Elvin rested his box against the gatehouse wall. "This is weird."

"It's weird." Ming was bent over at the waist, hands on his knees, trying to catch his breath.

"Come on." Ray shifted his box from one hip to the other. "Let's keep going."

Ming groaned loudly. "You're killing me."

Elvin shot him a stern look. "Not funny, Ming."

"What? Too soon?"

"Too fucking soon." Elvin hoisted his box and left him behind.

They walked in a single file, Ray at the front, Ming bringing up the rear. Gravel and grass crunched under their feet. Wind blew through the trees to their left and right. Occasionally, a twig snapped, the only indication that they might not be alone in the wilderness. It was at least forty-five minutes before a plume of dust appeared on the horizon.

"It's the taxi!" Ming shouted with a sudden burst of energy. He ran forward, awkwardly hoisting his box in midair.

"Hey, wait!" Elvin shouted after him, but Ming had already taken off.

"Relax." Ray continued at their steady pace. "If Olivier or any of his goons wanted to hurt us, they'd have done it back there."

"You don't know that." The image of Olivier looming over Ray was crystal clear in Elvin's mind. He could still feel the spike of fear that had pierced through him at the sight.

"I'm pretty confident. Olivier said so himself. If we don't tell anyone, we don't get hurt."

"You'd trust the word of a drug lord?"

Ray had the audacity to chuckle. "He doesn't strike me as one. Besides, drug lords don't hang out at paper mills doing the menial labor. Olivier answers to someone else and he's not going to act until he's directed to."

If that was supposed to make Elvin feel better, it didn't. There was still plenty of time for them to change their minds and it wouldn't be difficult for Olivier or his bosses to track them down. They'd stumbled upon a drug smuggling operation, for fuck's sake. Drug smugglers were bad people, dangerous people. Didn't people in Mexico get murdered by cartels for looking at them the wrong way?

They had to go to the police and report what they'd found. At the very least, they'd have to tell Joanna and Jade Harbour's legal team. This wasn't something that Elvin or Ming, or even Ray, could resolve on their own.

"Come on, guys!" Ming had already stashed his box in the trunk of the taxi and was climbing into the passenger side seat. Ray was several feet in front of him and Elvin jogged to catch up. With their boxes safely stowed, they settled into the car and rode back to the bed-and-breakfast in silence.

Like nothing happened. Like it was any other day on the job.

★ ★ ★

Elvin dropped into a chair back at the bed-and-breakfast. He bent forward and held his head in his hands. They'd made it. Well, sort of made it. The bed-and-breakfast wasn't entirely in the clear, but at least they weren't walking down a single-lane road through the forest.

God, he was tired and wired at the same time. His body was operating on nothing but adrenaline. He wanted to run a marathon and he wanted to lie down and sleep forever. He kind of wanted to throw up.

"Hey." Ray crouched down in front of him. "You okay?"

"Yeah." Even though he wasn't.

"We should probably eat. We skipped lunch." Ray looked entirely serious.

"How can you eat now?" Talking about it made Elvin's stomach churn.

"Our bodies need sustenance."

Elvin sat back and slumped down in the chair. "I can't eat anything. Not if I want to keep it down."

"Okay." Ray stood up. "I'm going to see if I can scrounge something up."

He went to knock on Ming's door. As they chatted softly in the hallway, Elvin pulled out his phone. He hadn't had a chance to check it since the morning, though the thought of answering emails now felt so inconsequential compared to what they'd been through.

But it wasn't emails that greeted him. His phone was packed with notifications of missed calls, voicemails and text messages from practically everyone in his family.

Janice: "DaaiGo, Joyce isn't feeling well and Mom and Dad can't decide if we should take her to the hospital."

Janice: "DaaiGo, can you call me back? Joyce can't breathe."

Mom: "Elvin, we go to hospital now. Joyce is feeling no good."

Edwin: "DaaiGo, we're in the emergency room and the pediatrician wants to admit Joyce. They're still running tests to figure out what's going on, but they don't like that she's not breathing well. She's been coughing a lot and has a fever too. Call us back."

Dad: "Elvin, where are you?" In the background of the voicemail: "He's in Quebec, for work, remember?" Dad: "When you back? Joyce is in hospital."

With each passing message, his stomach twisted and twisted until he wasn't able to move. The timestamp on the last message was more than an hour ago. How had he not heard his phone's notifications all afternoon?

"Ray!"

"Yeah?" Ray popped his head back inside. Ming was right behind him. "What's up?"

"Joyce. She's in the hospital." He held out his phone as if his sister was inside it.

"What happened? Is she okay?" Ray took the phone from him and scrolled through the messages.

"Who's Joyce?" Ming stood in the doorway.

"My sister. She's only eight years old."

"Difficulty breathing. Coughing. Fever," Ray read out loud.

"Shit. Doesn't sound good." Ming didn't sound all that sympathetic, but Elvin couldn't have cared less about Ming.

"What do I do?" he asked Ray.

He was stuck hours away in another fucking province, running from a drug cartel while carrying boxes of evidence that they weren't even sure was going to be useful. Now his kid sister was in the hospital and his family had been trying to reach him for hours. He knew a last-minute business trip was a bad idea. "What do I do?"

It took a moment for Ray to answer. He scanned their suitcases, the boxes, Ming. "We're going home. Right now." Ray pushed Ming out the door. "Get your stuff packed. Then call the flight crew to get the jet prepped for departure. I want them ready to take off the minute we hit the tarmac." He came back and held out Elvin's phone. "Where's the number for the taxi company? We'll need another driver ASAP."

Elvin took it with shaky hands. Taxi company? How was he supposed to find their number?

Ray moved through the room, grabbing clothes and stuffing them into suitcases. "We're done here and your family needs you. There's no point waiting until the morning." He slipped into the bathroom and came out with his arms full of their toiletries. But instead of packing them away, he dropped them onto the bed.

"Hey." Ray bent down in front of Elvin again. "Stay with me." He wrapped his hands around Elvin's. "Can you find the number for the taxi company?"

"Taxi company."

"Yes, we need a car right away."

With hands that felt like they belonged to someone else, Elvin navigated through his phone, hitting the wrong icons several times before he managed to find the call history. "Phone number."

"Great. I'll take it from here." Ray took the phone from him, dialing it with one hand, while still holding Elvin with the other. "You believe me when I say everything's going to be okay, right?"

Elvin nodded. He did believe. Or at least, he wanted to believe. But everything was so fucked up that he had no idea what okay meant anymore.

"Hi, we need a car at—" Ray turned to Elvin. "What's the address?"

Elvin blinked. What was the address? Hell, he barely remembered where they were. "Um…" He squeezed his eyes shut and wracked his brain before it came to him. "Woodlands Bed and Breakfast."

Ray repeated the name and confirmed that a driver would be there within thirty minutes.

Ming popped back in. "Hey, I called Alice. They're on their way to the airport." Ming nodded at Elvin. "Is he okay?"

"He's fine." Ray squeezed Elvin's knee. "Right?"

Elvin nodded again, but he was far from fine. He wasn't cut out for this kind of drama and adrenaline. Running from drug lords, calling up private jets for last-minute escapes. This was Ray's world. He was supposed to watch from the sidelines.

The taxi driver made it in record time, and within twenty minutes of Ray's decision to go home, they were on their way. They'd been in Quebec for less than twenty-four hours and it was twenty-four hours too long for Elvin. If he never set foot in this part of the country again, he would not be disappointed.

"Hang on." Ray gave his knee a squeeze. "We're almost there."

He'd kept a hand on Elvin's arm, shoulder, back, knee since Elvin's mini-meltdown in their room. It was a grounding touch, keeping Elvin tethered to the here and now. Without it, he would have spun out of control ages ago. But that physical connection was a constant reminder that Ray was in charge and he would get them all home in one piece.

Elvin slipped his hand into Ray's and held on. Who knew something so simple as holding hands could do so much? Mean so much? It was the only thing allowing him to breathe, to take the next step forward, to survive until he was reunited with his family.

True to their word, the flight crew had the jet ready when they reached the airport. It took no time at all to load their suitcases and boxes of materials and strap themselves into their seats. The next thing Elvin knew, they were hurtling down the runway and catapulting into the air.

Chapter Thirteen

Even Ming had been silent during the flight back to Toronto, thank whatever deity above that took mercy on them. After an early service of drinks, Alice dimmed the cabin lights and everyone settled in for the short flight. Ray sat next to Elvin, holding his hand, as much for his sake as for Elvin's. He wanted Elvin to know he was there, that he could take care of him. But Ray also needed to know that Elvin was still with him.

He'd seen a lot of weird things over the years. Rich and powerful people thought they could get away with all sorts—secret affairs, drug habits, shady business dealings—and they didn't care about being discreet. But finding drugs at a portfolio company was a first, even for him. Not to mention dragging boxes of evidence down a winding forest road, then scrambling for a last-minute flight out of the province. It was more excitement and adventure than usual, to say the least.

But now that they were safely descending into Toronto, the question was what the fuck he was going to do. Going to the police would be the upstanding citizen's only real option, but Ray had never claimed to be an upstanding citizen. Police involvement was too risky. It would introduce unknown players that Ray couldn't trust or control. Everything would get documented for a public record, and if anything was leaked to the press—which was a real possibility—they'd have a public relations disaster on their hands.

Then there was Olivier. He fit the image of a rough-and-tumble enforcer, but something about him struck Ray as odd. He replayed all his encounters with the orange-red giant, but there was nothing specific Ray could point to. Except perhaps the threat Olivier uttered: *Don't tell anyone and you won't get hurt.* Like he was willing to pretend nothing happened if Ray did the same. Why would he let them get away so easily? None of it added up.

The plane touched down with barely a bump when the landing gears hit the tarmac. Then the lights in the cabin came back on.

"We called ahead. There should be cars waiting for you at the hangar," Alice said as the plane taxied.

"Thanks, Alice." Ray turned to Ming. "I'll take the boxes with me. You go home."

Ming looked directly into Ray's eyes. "Fine. But I'm seeing this audit through. No brushing me off. Deal?"

He might be annoyingly obnoxious, but Ray couldn't deny that Ming had proven his worth. Besides, he knew too much. They couldn't risk Ming taking matters into his own hands. "Deal. But don't say anything to anyone, not even Joanna. We need to know what the hell we're talking about before we let anyone else in."

"Yeah, sure. I can do that."

Ray hoped to god that Ming could keep his mouth shut. Too much was at stake.

Alice got the door open and Ming was the first one out.

Ray turned to Elvin. "You ready? Time to go."

Elvin nodded stiffly and together they made their way off the plane. There were multiple cars waiting on the tarmac and Ming was already talking to one driver, who was stashing his suitcase in the trunk.

Ray approached the other two. "We're going in the same car." He pulled Elvin to his side. "First drop-off at Toronto Medical Centre and then a second at my place."

"I'll take you." One of the drivers moved to gather their bags and Ray got Elvin stowed in the backseat.

"Hey." Elvin grabbed his hand before Ray could shut the car door. "Thanks."

It was rare to see Elvin so vulnerable. He was always on top of things, organized and efficient. Ray couldn't remember a time when Elvin was ever at a loss. He took Elvin's hand and raised it to his lips for a kiss. Lines be damned. Elvin needed reassurance and Ray wasn't about to let propriety stop him from giving it.

"You don't have to thank me."

Elvin gazed up at him, eyes glistening under the bright floodlights of the airport tarmac. "Still."

It was a single word of appreciation to anyone else, but for Ray it filled all the empty spaces inside him. Elvin trusted him, believed in him, and that made Ray feel more alive than he'd ever felt before.

They made it to the hospital in less than twenty minutes. But when they got there, visiting hours were over.

"You can come back tomorrow morning at eight." The nurse at the counter was a little older than them. Her hair was pulled back in a severe bun and her glasses sat halfway down her nose.

"Nurse Pineda, isn't it?" Ray leaned over the counter and smiled.

"Yes." She eyed him over the rim of her glasses.

"You can make an exception for us, can't you? This is Joyce's older brother, Elvin." Ray clapped Elvin on the shoulder. "We were told she'd been asking for him and took a last-minute flight back from Quebec to see her."

He glanced at Elvin, who still looked a little shell-shocked. "He's been distraught, inconsolable. It would mean the world if we could go see Joyce. Just to make sure she's okay with our own eyes."

Ray gave her a flirty head tilt. "I'll make it up to you. What's your favorite coffee? Or tea? I'll get it delivered."

Nurse Pineda's expression didn't change an inch during Ray's speech. Her eyes said she'd heard the same thing a million times before and she wasn't a fool to fall for them. But then she glanced at Elvin and there must have been something in the way Elvin was barely holding himself together that struck a nerve with her.

"Fine. You can go. But be quiet about it. If I hear even a squeak, you're getting kicked out." She pointed them in the direction of Joyce's room. "And I'll have a pumpkin spice latte."

When Ray quirked an eyebrow, she gave him a stern look. "I know it's not the right season, but I want one anyway. You can get it?"

The woman asked for it, who was he to deny her. "Of course. Coming right up." He led Elvin away before Nurse Pineda could make more demands.

Joyce's room was at the end of the hallway and the bed closest to the door was empty. She was nothing more than a small lump under the thin hospital linens, with tubes and wires connecting her to beeping machinery.

"Oh my god," Elvin whispered as he rushed to her side.

Ray followed more slowly, closing the door behind them. Next to the bed, in an uncomfortable-looking armchair, sat an older man with a significant paunch. Mr. Goh had been asleep and woke up as Elvin leaned over Joyce.

"Elvin?"

"Dad, what happened to her?" Elvin spoke in Cantonese.

"The doctor said pneumonia." Mr. Goh shifted in his seat, but didn't get up.

"Pneumonia? How did she get pneumonia?" Elvin brushed stray locks off Joyce's forehead and tucked the blankets more securely around her.

"Who knows?" Mr. Goh shifted again. He looked like he wanted to stand up, but couldn't quite manage it himself.

Ray came around the bed and offered a hand in silence. When Mr. Goh noticed, his eyes lit up. "Mr. Chao? What are you doing here?"

"Please, call me Ray," he responded in Cantonese. "Do you need help? Here, I'll steady you."

After only a second of hesitation, Mr. Goh held onto his arms and together they leveraged him to his feet. Mr. Goh sighed and groaned and stretched. "That chair is too low."

It also had a huge dip in it, evidence of zero support left in its structure. No wonder the older man couldn't stand up by himself.

"Are you okay, Dad? Why are you sleeping in that chair? Edwin or Janice should have stayed." Elvin frowned in disapproval.

"Aiya, they both have school tomorrow. I'm an old man with nothing to do."

"Well, now you're going home." Elvin looked to Ray. "Can you?"

"Of course." Ray had instructed the driver to wait for them downstairs. They could leave at any time.

"Thanks." Elvin came around the bed and gently pushed Mr. Goh toward. "Ray'll take you home, Dad. I'll stay with Joyce."

"No, no, I can stay."

"Don't argue with me, Dad. Go home. You can come back tomorrow."

Mr. Goh looked from Elvin to his daughter, who was

asleep, taking short, shallow breaths. His shoulders slumped and he closed his eyes, nodding. "Okay. I'll be back tomorrow with your mother."

"I'll get him home, then swing by your place for some fresh clothes." Ray held out his hand. "Key?"

"No." Elvin pushed his hand away. "You should go home too. I'll be okay."

As if Ray was about to let Elvin stay at the hospital all night on his own.

"You've already done so much. I wouldn't have made it without you."

All words of argument died on Ray's tongue. He would have gladly done all of it again and more if that's what Elvin needed. Hell, there wasn't a single thing Ray wouldn't do for Elvin.

He pulled Elvin into a hug, chest to chest, ear to ear, his arms around Elvin's shoulders while Elvin threaded his arms around Ray's waist. They both breathed deep and sank into the embrace. He got Elvin home today. But Ray couldn't count the number of times Elvin had swooped in to rescue him when he was in trouble.

"Don't thank me. Seriously. We're a team. This is what we do."

Elvin pulled back so they could see each other. "We take care of each other?" His tone was uncertain, like the idea was novel, though appealing.

Ray liked the sound of it too. "Yeah, we take care of each other." He pulled Elvin in for one more hug then let him go.

Ray joined Mr. Goh in the hallway and matched the older man's slower stride as they made their way to the elevator.

"Thank you, Ray. Really, really. Thank you." Mr. Goh looked him in the eye. "For watching out for Elvin all the time. Mrs. Goh and I feel a lot more at peace knowing he has an understanding boss like you."

What kind of stories had Elvin been telling his parents? "Please, Mr. Goh. It's Elvin who watches out for me. I would be lost if he didn't keep me on track."

"I'm glad he is doing well at his job." Mr. Goh shuffled into the elevator when the doors opened.

"He's better than good." Ray pressed the button for the ground floor. "He's the best there is."

Chapter Fourteen

Ray blinked and cringed. Damn, his body hurt. The hospital room was still dark, lit only by medical equipment beeping in the background. He slowly unfolded himself from the decrepit chair where he'd somehow managed to fall asleep. Ray checked his watch; he'd only gotten twenty minutes of shut-eye.

Elvin was a few feet away, sitting in the other chair with his head resting on the bed, pillowed by his arms. His breathing was shallow and steady—still asleep. Joyce was still asleep too, curled up on her side, clutching a stuffed elephant to her chest.

Ray could see the resemblance between the siblings. They had the same nose, the same chin, inherited from Mr. Goh. Their eyes were from Mrs. Goh. In fact, all the

Goh siblings looked similar, which Ray had to admit was a little creepy. The first time he'd met Elvin's family at one of Jade Harbour's family picnic days, it'd been like seeing a dozen mini Elvins running around. It'd been hilarious.

He reached into his pocket for his phone and quickly scanned through the messages waiting for him. Most of them he ignored, but the one from Joanna had a high-priority flag next to it. She wanted an update on the Caron audit.

Ray sighed. That was a clusterfuck. He needed more information. Who did Olivier report to? Who else at Caron was involved? How the hell did all of it get past Jade Harbour's due diligence process? Ray went to his contact list and scrolled down to a number that had been saved without a name. He tapped out a quick message and hit send.

When he looked up from his phone, he found Joyce staring at him.

"Hey, good morning," Ray whispered.

She blinked groggily but didn't say anything.

"I'm Ray, Elvin's friend."

Nothing.

"How do you feel?" Ray tried again.

Joyce shrugged, a tiny movement, but enough to cause Elvin to stir. Joyce froze and Ray held his breath too, but Elvin settled back down. He needed the sleep, however uncomfortable it might be.

Ray eased himself out of the chair, bending backward to work the stiffness out of his back. "Do you want Timbits?"

Joyce considered his request with the solemnity of a child

before nodding her head once. Of course Joyce wanted Timbits. Who wouldn't want perfectly round bite-sized doughnuts?

"I'm going to go downstairs and get some for all of us, okay? I'll be back soon."

Joyce nodded again and Ray let himself out.

The Tim Hortons in the hospital lobby was already bustling, though the sky outside was still dark. He stood in line, feeling a weird solidarity with the other customers. Hospitals could be scary with the unpronounceable medical language, giant machines that did who knew what and the sterile aroma that made the place smell gross. But everyone knew what to do in a Timmy's line, they knew the menu by heart and could trust the drinks to taste exactly right. It was a bubble of normalcy, so simple and modest that it was kind of novel.

It was Ray's turn to order. He went up to the cashier and his mind blanked. Fuck. He couldn't remember the last time he'd actually had a Tim Hortons drink. And for the life of him, he couldn't remember what Elvin drank. Had he ever known? How embarrassing.

"Two large coffees. Black with cream and sugar on the side." Plain old coffee would have to do.

"Anything else?"

"And a box of Timbits."

He was right outside Joyce's room when his phone rang. Juggling his haul, he managed to pull it out of his pocket without dropping anything. It was cousin Ginny.

"Hey." Ray sandwiched his phone awkwardly between his ear and his shoulder.

"Hi, Ray, I'm sure you know this already, but I figured I'd call because I said I would."

He had no idea what Ginny was talking about. "What do I know?"

"Your parents. They're coming to Toron—" Sirens on her end of the line drowned out the rest of her sentence, but Ray had caught enough.

"They are?" That was news to him. But then, his parents never informed him of their travel itineraries.

"I don't know the exact dates, but it sounded like they'll be there for a week." Ginny shouted away from her phone, instructions to her driver in Cantonese.

"What are they doing here?" His parents almost never came to Toronto; there wasn't anything to do. Shopping was in New York or London or Paris. Vacations were in the south of France or Italy or Greece. They had property and businesses in Singapore, Bangkok and Tokyo.

The only reason they came to Toronto was to see Ray's grandmother—oh, fuck. When was her birthday? That must be it. Even though she lived less than an hour north of the city, it'd been at least several months since Ray had last spoken to her. He was a bad grandson, he knew, but it wasn't like she ever reached out to him either.

"I mentioned Jade Harbour to your father, to see if he'd be willing to take a meeting with them," Ginny continued.

"And?" Ray didn't bother holding his breath.

"He didn't reject the idea completely."

That was more than Ray had expected. *Maybe Ming will get his meeting after all.*

"If you want to set something up with him, you can arrange it with his assistant." Ginny shouted at her driver again and then came sounds of her climbing out of the car. "Do you have her number?"

No, Ray didn't even know who his father's assistant was. The last thing he wanted to do was speak to her to schedule a meeting. Elvin could probably take care of that for him, right?

"I'll send you her contact. I've got to go. Bye!" Ginny hung up before the last syllable of her sign-off died.

Ray maneuvered his phone back into his pocket before pushing open the door. Elvin was awake already, standing over Joyce and frowning down at her.

"Good morning." Ray set the cooling coffee and Timbits on the C-shaped hospital bed table.

"Morning," Elvin mumbled. "You're still here."

"I bought coffee."

"Thanks."

"DaaiGo?" Joyce's voice was small, but there was no second-guessing the way she was staring at the Timbit box.

Elvin shook his head. "Joyce, it's first thing in the morning. And you're sick."

Ray popped the box open and brought it around for Joyce. "People have doughnuts for breakfast." He ignored the glare Elvin sent his way. The poor kid was miserable. A little ball of fried dough and sugar wasn't going to hurt.

Elvin rolled his eyes, but didn't object again. "Did the doctor come around while I was asleep?"

"Not while I was here." Ray picked out one of the sugar-powdered Timbits and took a bite.

Joyce giggled at him.

"What?" He ran the back of his hand across his mouth, knowing he was smearing the powdered sugar all over his face. "Did I get it? How about now?"

"No!" Joyce squealed.

"Well, it sounds like you're feeling better." Elvin turned toward the door. "I'm going to go find a doctor."

He let himself out before Ray could remind him to take one of the coffees.

There was a tug on his shirt. When he glanced down, Joyce was looking up at him with the biggest puppy dog eyes.

"Can I have another one?"

As if Ray would ever say no. He held out the box. "Take as many as you want. Just don't tell your DaaiGo."

Ray walked into his big empty condo and collapsed on the giant white leather sectional. Coming home was surreal after the last couple days. It was hard to believe any of it was real.

From the moment he'd woken up, Elvin had been in full problem-solver mode. Between the nurses and the doctor, then the full Goh family squeezed into the hospital room, Ray had barely managed to speak one word to Elvin. Not that he'd minded. He'd stepped back and watched Elvin work his magic.

Somehow, Elvin kept his parents calm and his siblings occupied while dealing with Joyce's discharge papers. By midmorning, the box of Timbits had been demolished and Joyce was sent home with a two-week prescription for antibiotics.

Only as the family was wheeling Joyce out of the hospital did Elvin slow down enough for Ray to catch a moment with him.

You didn't have to stay. To which Ray had rolled his eyes.

I'll be in the office later this afternoon. Ray had told him not to bother. It wasn't like he was going into the office himself either.

Elvin had given him a sad, tired smile before following his family into the elevator.

Ray had come home. Alone.

He let his eyes drift shut as he lingered on the edge of consciousness. His body wanted to sleep, but his brain whirred at a hundred and twenty kilometers an hour. Everything had happened so fast, he hadn't had the chance to think things through, understand what was going on, decide on next steps. Ray picked himself up from the couch. There was only one thing to do.

Sliding into the pool was both a wake-up call and a warm blanket wrapping around him. He pushed off the wall, glided under the surface and emerged into practiced strokes and kicks. Stroke, stroke, breathe. Stroke, stroke, breathe. Get to the end of the pool, flip turn, glide.

His brain slowed to a respectable sixty as his body went through the familiar motions. Water rushed past his ears, drowning out any sound from the outside world, drowning out thoughts that threatened to take on a life of their own. There was nothing else but the steady swim through the pool until Ray was truly blissed out.

He lost count of how many laps he did or how much time had passed. He only stopped when his muscles told him they'd had enough. Ray flipped onto his back and gazed up at the skylight, bright with the midday sun. If he closed his eyes, he could almost imagine he was in the middle of the ocean, the sun beating down hot and heavy on him.

He floated until his stomach rumbled, reminding him that he hadn't eaten since…he couldn't remember. He lifted his head and blinked.

"Hey."

"Hi." Elvin sat on a nearby lounge chair. Changed into fresh clothes. Hair wet from a recent shower. Dark bags under his eyes. Shoulders slumped like the weight of the world was pressing down on him.

"What are you doing here?" Ray swam toward the wall closest to Elvin.

He shrugged. "Seemed like a better idea than going back to my place."

"How's Joyce?" He folded his arms on the edge of the pool and hung off the wall.

"She's okay. Breathing better than she was yesterday,

apparently. But there were too many people in that house and I told my parents I needed to get to work."

Ray shook his head. "You know you don't need to do that."

Elvin met his gaze and managed a small smile. "I know."

Ray returned it. The swim had worked the adrenaline out of his body and now Elvin was here to fill him up again with…what was this feeling he got whenever they were together? It felt like strength, like potential, like they could handle anything life threw at them. They were a team—the dream team. And if they stuck together, they could never fail.

He planted his palms on the deck, kicked his legs and hoisted himself out of the pool. He didn't miss the way Elvin's gaze trailed down his body, following the sluice of water flowing over his skin. Standing up, he waited until Elvin slowly surveyed him from toes to head before extending a hand in invitation.

Elvin took it and stood from the lounge chair.

"I'm glad you're here," Ray whispered.

"I'm glad I'm here too." He took a small step toward Ray, and they were inches apart. Elvin fully clothed. Ray wet and in nothing but his Speedo. Elvin's gaze dropped to Ray's lips, so intense it competed with the sun shining from above.

"Elvin." Ray's voice was hoarse. His breathing was ragged. His heart kicked up a notch. None of it had anything to do with the workout he'd just completed.

Elvin lifted his gaze to Ray's and there was such longing

and hunger there that Ray couldn't bear to deny him. He raised his hands to cup both of Elvin's cheeks and leaned forward to bring their foreheads together.

"Elvin," he said again, the two syllables conveying all that he wanted and all that he didn't dare to have.

A small, desperate sound escaped Elvin's throat. A little meow that tugged at Ray's heart.

"Are you sure?" Ray asked, because he didn't know if he'd be able to stop once they started.

In response, Elvin closed the space between them, pressing their lips together in a kiss that seared Ray down to the bone.

Chapter Fifteen

He was melting and floating and bursting all at the same time, his brain and body nothing more than a mass of firing neurons. Elvin clung to Ray like his life depended on it, pressing himself against him and getting soaked in the process. It didn't matter. Nothing mattered except getting closer. Deeper.

A sob broke out, followed by a hiccup, and only when Ray pulled away and brushed his hair back did Elvin realize those sounds had come from him.

"Hey." Ray ran a thumb over his lips and on instinct Elvin snagged it between his teeth. Ray sucked in a breath. "Elvin," he warned.

Elvin gave the thumb a lick and released it. He'd never done anything like that before. Had never imagined it was something he'd want to do. But with Ray standing in front of him, naked, wet, with eyes so full of concern, Elvin couldn't help himself. Years of carefully maintaining his distance, of concealing his feelings behind his job description, evaporated, and all he could do was pull Ray toward him and bury his face into the crook of Ray's neck.

"Shh." Ray rubbed long strokes across his back. "It's okay. Everything's okay."

Was it? Elvin wasn't sure.

Joyce would recover. Kids were resilient. But that was the least of their problems.

They'd found a cache of drugs at Caron. They might have targets on their backs.

They were in some seriously dangerous relationship territory. Going back to what they were didn't feel like a viable option anymore and moving forward had been out of the question for so long that Elvin couldn't quite accept it either. He didn't see a way out.

He hiccupped again.

Ray's stomach growled.

Laughter bubbled up in Elvin, uncontrolled and a little hysterical. He laughed until he was shaking, until he could barely catch his breath. Ray chuckled along with him, holding him up when Elvin nearly collapsed from sheer exhaustion.

"Come on. Let's get out of here before you fall into the pool." Ray led him away. "Mind if I grab a quick shower?"

Elvin shook his head. "Mind if I borrow some dry clothes?"

"Be my guest. You know where to find stuff better than I do."

Elvin took his time picking out a new outfit in Ray's walk-in closet while Ray did his thing in the bathroom. Then, emboldened by the ups and downs of the past forty-eight hours, Elvin climbed onto Ray's bed and lay spread-eagle.

Satin sheets and a glorious pillow-top mattress had Elvin's eyes drifting shut in no time.

He woke as the mattress dipped.

"Good nap?" Ray asked. He lay on his side, propped up by an elbow, gazing down at Elvin with lashes still damp from his shower. He smelled clean, fresh, soapy. He smelled like comfort, familiarity and belonging.

Elvin rolled toward him and snuggled in close to Ray's chest.

"God, Elvin. You're killing me," Ray groaned, but he wrapped his arms around Elvin all the same.

"Mmm," Elvin hummed. He certainly wasn't doing either one of them any favors, but it felt so damn good to be close to Ray. He took a deep breath, imprinted the feeling of his face pressed against Ray's chest, and somehow found the strength to pull away. "I suppose we should eat."

Ray sat up next to him, his hand still on Elvin's hip. "Yeah, I suppose we should."

They made their way to the kitchen, arm in arm, then opened the fridge door. It was stocked with ready-made meals, as usual, but none of them appealed to Elvin. He wanted something bad for him. Something greasy or fried.

Something he needed to eat with his hands and then lick sauce off his fingers.

"Want to order wings?" Ray asked, as if he'd read Elvin's mind.

"Yes."

Ray kept—or rather, Elvin kept—a stash of take-out menus in one of the kitchen drawers. He pulled them out now and flipped through them. "Korean fried chicken?"

"Yes." Ray stood behind him, wrapping his arms around Elvin's waist and resting his chin on Elvin's shoulder. "I want the green onion and soy garlic ones. And the ones covered in gochujang."

"And the corn topped with melted cheese," Elvin added. "Because we need veggies."

"Sounds good."

Elvin reached for his phone and called in the order. "Delivery in about thirty minutes."

"Perfect." Ray took his hand and led him to the couches. "Come sit with me."

They arranged themselves on a couch, Elvin's legs thrown over Ray's, Ray's arm around Elvin's shoulder.

"We need to talk."

Elvin sighed and leaned his head on Ray's shoulder. He knew they did. But talking meant leaving behind this no-man's land that allowed them to be whatever they wanted. Elvin wasn't prepared to leave yet. "Okay."

Ray planted a kiss on the top of Elvin's head. "I'm your boss."

When he didn't continue, Elvin nodded. "I know."

"There's a power imbalance here and I don't want to abuse my position."

Elvin lifted his head to look at Ray. Is that what he thought he was doing? "You're not abusing anything."

"Are you sure?" The conflict was so evident in Ray's expression that Elvin pulled him in for a quick kiss on the cheek.

"Absolutely. I haven't done anything I don't want to do."

"Still. Sometimes people don't know what they want or don't want when faced with a person who has a lot of power over them."

Elvin took a second to examine himself even when his gut instinct railed against it. What Ray said was true, but Elvin's feelings had developed so gradually and such a long time ago that he was certain he wasn't being coerced.

"You're not forcing me. If anything, I'm probably forcing you."

Ray chuckled. "How's that?"

Elvin shrugged and settled his head back on Ray's shoulder. "I'm here all the time. I arrange your whole life." He paused to let the thoughts floating at the back of his mind make their way onto his tongue. "Maybe I'm convenient," he whispered.

Ray's arm tightened around him, and Ray pressed another kiss to his head. "Don't ever say that about yourself." He placed a finger on Elvin's chin and lifted it so Elvin had to look up at him. "You are amazing and I…"

He what? Elvin waited for Ray to gather his thoughts, even though the anticipation was making his heart race like he'd run a sprint. He what? Was it good? Bad? Embarrassing? Inappropriate?

Ray dropped the hand he held to Elvin's chin and turned away from him.

"Ray." If he had to wait a second longer, he was going to combust. "What is it?"

Ray chuckled. "You're amazing." He shook his head and smiled back at Elvin. "You're amazing and you don't even know it. You single-handedly hold your entire family together and you also run my life down to the smallest details. You have this superpower for anticipating everyone's needs before they even know what they need. But, who takes care of you?"

Elvin blinked at the tears that were suddenly stinging his eyes. He turned away, swinging his legs off of Ray's and tucking them under himself. Who took care of him? No one. He didn't need to be taken care of. He was fine.

He leaned back against Ray, seeking the solidity that he offered. Who took care of him was a question he'd never stopped to consider. He rarely had needs that he couldn't handle himself. He was young, healthy, capable. He had a good job and could pay for his own living expenses and for his family's. What else was there?

So why the hell was he crying?

Ray gently wiped away the tears trickling down his cheeks, replacing them with soft kisses, nose rubs, touching foreheads. Where they'd grown five-o'clock shadows, their cheeks were rough against one another's. But even that sensation pulled Elvin deeper into whatever it was that was building between them.

"If you'll let me, I can take care of you," Ray whispered in his ear.

It sent a fresh wave of tears down Elvin's cheeks.

"No one should go through life without another person to lean on."

A sob broke from Elvin's throat, followed by a hiccup.

"It's okay to need or want help."

A knock sounded at the front door. Neither of them moved for a moment before Ray gave Elvin a squeeze. "Let me go get that."

While Ray went to the door, Elvin found a tissue and cleaned himself up. No one had ever offered to be there for him, to be the person he could lean on. He wasn't even sure he knew how to lean on someone else. The idea sounded so unlike the person he'd tried to be his whole life, the person he hoped he was. Logically, he knew no one was superhuman; it was normal to need help every once in a while. But it sounded weak and vulnerable, like he couldn't hold his own shit together.

"Food's here." The fragrant aroma of spices and barbecue filled the room as Ray brought over the food delivery.

In silence, they unpacked the bags and spread the feast out on the coffee table. Ray went to get plates and cutlery and bleached-white fabric napkins.

"Those are going to get stained." Elvin pointed to them, his voice nasally from his crying.

Ray shrugged. "So I'll get new ones."

Of course he would. Elvin set his aside and pulled the stack of paper napkins toward him instead. He dug into the gochujang chicken wings. Sticky and spicy with a hint of sweetness, the skin was still crisp underneath the sauce, and the meat was absolutely succulent. He polished off the wing and dropped its boney remains on his plate.

Next to him, Ray had taken a fork and stabbed a mini drumstick. With his other hand, he picked up a knife and proceeded to cut the meat off the bone.

"Seriously?"

"What?" Ray maneuvered the knife and fork like he was carving a turkey. "This way my fingers don't get dirty."

"It's wings. Your fingers are supposed to get dirty. That's the whole point." Elvin held up his hand to show the bright red sauce staining his fingers.

Before he knew what was happening, Ray leaned forward and wrapped his lips around one of his fingers. He swirled his tongue around and around and when he pulled off, Elvin's finger was clean.

Ray sat back with a satisfied grin. "Mmm, that sauce is good."

Elvin swallowed, all thoughts of food banished from his mind. "Um…" He stared at his hand like it belonged to someone else. Except he'd definitely felt Ray's tongue on his finger. Wet and hot. Light suction and then cool air on damp skin.

"You okay?" Ray asked innocently as he picked up a perfectly sliced piece of chicken and put it in his mouth. "Need help?"

Elvin grabbed a napkin and wiped his hands. When Ray had made his offer earlier, Elvin was pretty sure he hadn't meant licking his fingers. Though Elvin wouldn't mind more of that type of assistance. There were other places on his body that could get messy during a meal.

He shook his head as his imagination kicked into overdrive suggesting all the different ways he could get dirty with Ray. He might have had fantasies before, but that was before the kiss upstairs, the full-body hugs and cheeks pressed against cheeks. Now that he knew what it felt like to have Ray's tongue on his finger, he could only imagine what it would feel like on his chest, his stomach and lower.

He cleared his throat, shifted position on the floor and reached for another chicken wing. Elvin never got random hard-ons. It wasn't a thing his body did. But as Ray chuckled quietly beside him, his dick was definitely chubbier than it had been moments before.

"I'm fine," he said, more to himself than to Ray.

"Mmm-hmm."

Elvin huffed and shot Ray a playful glare. "Eat your food."

Chapter Sixteen

Ray was sure that glare was meant to put him in his place.
But who could blame him if he found it more sultry than
stern?

Eat his food? He could think of any number of things
he'd like to put in his mouth that he bet would taste just
as good. But he had to behave. It was too easy to flirt
with Elvin. Too satisfying to see the hint of pink on Elvin's cheeks and the way desire so clearly worked its way
through Elvin's body.

"Okay, okay. I'll stop." He served himself some corn.
Any nutritional benefit the kernels still contained was can-
celled out by the layers of melted cheese. He'd put a fork-
ful in his mouth when his phone rang.

Unknown Caller.

"Hello?"

"Yeah." The man on the other end of the line didn't introduce himself. He didn't have to. It'd been Ray who had reached out.

He pushed himself up off the floor, sending Elvin a quick smile as he walked around the couch. "Thanks for calling me."

"What do you need?"

"Have you ever heard of a company called Caron Papers?" Ray paced as he spoke.

Elvin moved onto the couch and watched him walk back and forth with a look of concern.

"No."

"I found drugs in their warehouse and I want to know where they came from, why they're there and who's behind it all." Ray ran a hand through his hair at the memory of staring Olivier down and cutting through all that packaging.

The man wasn't fazed by Ray's revelation. "What kind of drugs?"

White powder could be any number of things. "I don't know for sure, but I'm guessing cocaine. Montreal's a hub for that, isn't it?"

"It is."

"Who moves cocaine through northern Quebec?" Ray snuck a glance in Elvin's direction. His face had gone paler than normal, making the bags under his eyes more pronounced.

"Mostly likely Greek mob out of Montreal."

Shit. They didn't play around. It was a public secret that a handful of Greek-Canadian families controlled the city's construction industry. Ray knew they dabbled in other areas, but he hadn't realized that street drugs was one of them.

"What is it?" Elvin whispered as he reached out a hand.

Ray took it and leaned against the back of the couch. "Greek mob, huh? That doesn't sound pretty."

"It's not. But I'll do a bit of digging and get back to you."

"Okay, thanks."

The man hung up.

"Who was that?" Elvin asked.

Ray brought his hand up for a kiss. "My guy. You know, the one who used to work in military intelligence."

"You mean the guy who does illegal shit for you without getting caught?" Elvin didn't look impressed.

"It's not illegal this time. We need to figure out who's behind the drugs, and better him than us. He can do it without raising suspicions, and we should stay as far away from those people as possible." Ray came around the couch and sat down next to Elvin.

"Why aren't we just going to the police?" Elvin asked.

Ray shook his head. "We can't. Not without backlash against Jade Harbour. Can you imagine what our investors would do if they found out one of our portfolio companies was a front for a drug ring?"

Elvin's eyebrows shot up to his hairline. "Investors? Who cares about them? What about all the people who might get hurt because of those drugs?"

Ray appreciated Elvin's sense of propriety, especially since he apparently didn't have any. "Those people will get their hands on drugs one way or another."

Elvin pinned him with a stern look that did its job making Ray feel bad. He raised his hands in defense. "Trust me, I don't like it, but it's true. The drug trade exists because people want it. If we report this to the police, they might arrest Olivier, or maybe they'll even shut down a part of the operation. But someone else will take over and the cocaine will flow again. If the government truly wanted to address the drug issue, they'd create more social programs to help people kick their addictions."

Elvin didn't look convinced, but he did reach over and grab another chicken wing.

"Babe, I wish it were as simple as picking up the phone and calling the police. It would make all our lives a whole lot easier. But you know as well as I do that cops are rarely the answer." Ray picked up his plate and carefully scooped some corn onto his fork. He took a bite, then noticed Elvin was holding his wing in midair. "What?"

Elvin blinked once and flashed a quick smile. "Nothing." He dropped the wing on his plate and reached for a napkin. "So, if we're not going to the police, what are we going to do?"

Ray set his plate on the coffee table and sat back so he could gaze up at the chandelier. "I haven't figured it out yet."

"What *have* you figured out?" Elvin leaned one elbow on the back of the couch and propped his head in his hand.

Ray sighed. "I need to know who we're dealing with first. If it's a small operation that started at Caron recently, then maybe we *should* go to the police. We could issue a press release about how we're cooperating with law enforcement and all that. But if it's bigger, if it really is the Greek mob, then I doubt even the police will be able to touch them."

"Isn't that something for them to worry about?"

"It's not that simple." Ray shifted so he faced Elvin. "Jade Harbour owns Caron, so we're ultimately responsible for everything that happens there. If word gets out, people are going to ask questions that I don't think we have the answers to. Who did the due diligence on Caron before we acquired the company? How did we not know this was happening under our noses?"

"Those are good questions." Elvin looked as skeptical as any rational person would be. "I want to know the answers myself."

"Exactly." Ray pushed the logic a little further. "Since we don't really have answers, the next question people will ask is whether Jade Harbour was involved. Maybe we knew about it all along. Hell, maybe we're the ones orchestrating the whole thing."

"That's ridiculous."

"It's what they'll think."

Elvin huffed and turned to sit cross-legged on the couch. The permanent crease he wore between his brows deepened as the full ramifications of their predicament sank in.

"So you see why we have to keep this under wraps."

Elvin nodded, though he didn't look happy about it.

"Hey." Ray reached over and smoothed out Elvin's frown with his thumb. "Let's not get carried away with this right now. I've got my guy on it and there's nothing else we can do tonight."

Elvin looked at him incredulously. "How can you turn it off like that?"

Ray shrugged. He just did. He would be the first to admit that they were in deep fucking shit, but why waste mental energy on something he couldn't control? Besides, he could think of a dozen more pleasant ways to stay occupied.

"You worry too much." Ray rested his chin on Elvin's shoulder and blew a light stream of air across his neck.

Elvin's breath hitched. "Worrying is like breathing for me. I'd die without it."

"Hmm," Ray hummed, with his lips against Elvin's skin. "That sounds like a challenge."

"Yeah?" Elvin's voice was breathy.

"Yeah." With a finger on Elvin's chin, he turned Elvin's head to give him a kiss. Ray could taste the gochujang, spicy and sweet, the earthy tang of green onions. He nipped Elvin's lower lip and slipped his tongue inside his mouth when he gasped. Elvin met him with his own tongue and Ray had never felt anything so erotic in his life.

It was a soft, tentative dance. Forward and retreat as they tested each other's boundaries and grew bolder with each pass. Ray had kissed dozens of people in the past, but right

now he was no more than the inexperienced yet eager teen-
ager learning how sensitive his lips were.

God, Elvin was delicious. More than delicious. The
most intoxicating thing ever. He made tender little me-
owing sounds that urged Ray to bring him closer, hold
him tighter. Ray shifted and they fell lengthwise onto the
couch, Ray on the bottom and Elvin on top. Elvin wasn't
a small guy and he pressed Ray into the cushions, a delightful, satiating weight.

Ray ran his hands up and down Elvin's back, then down
to his ass, where Ray filled his palms and squeezed. Elvin
squealed in response and lifted himself off Ray. His lips
were pink and swollen. His eyes half-lidded with desire.
He swallowed thickly and then climbed all the way off to
sit on the floor.

"What's wrong?" Ray put a hand on Elvin's shoulder.

Elvin tensed under his touch.

"Elvin?"

He dropped his chin to his chest before speaking. "I've
never… I've never done this before."

It took a second for the words to sink in, but when they
did, a sense of elation soared through Ray. It was silly. A
twisted sense of male pride to think that no one else had
ever touched Elvin that way—the way he would, if things
panned out how he wanted.

But after that initial strut through the schoolyard, Ray's
sense came back to him. He took a seat next to Elvin,
shoulder against shoulder. "You haven't?"

Elvin shook his head. "I mean, I've kissed guys before but..." He didn't need to say any more.

Ray's sexual history was no secret to anyone, least of all Elvin. But they'd never talked about Elvin's sexual past. Ray knew Elvin wasn't the dating type, but he'd figured Elvin had gone through some sort of experimental stage—hadn't everyone?

Hearing Elvin confirm he was a virgin didn't surprise Ray, though. It fit, somehow.

"Is that...bad?"

Ray chuckled. "No, babe. It's not bad. It's what it is."

That didn't have the reassuring effect Ray was expecting. Instead, Elvin's frown slipped back into place.

"I just never found the right guy. I'm not a blushing violet or whatever, I just never wanted to have sex with anyone before."

"That's cool."

"I don't want you to think I'm, like, I don't know, a prude or something."

The thought had never crossed Ray's mind. "I don't think you're a prude."

"I'm demisexual."

Of all the things Elvin could have said, Ray hadn't been expecting that one.

"You know what that is, right?"

Ray gave him a look of mock offense. "Of course I know. Sexual attraction comes after emotional attachment. I know my sexualities."

Elvin nodded, though he didn't look as impressed as Ray felt he should have. "Right. So, you know…"

Ray took a guess and completed the sentence for him. "If you're willing to engage in physical intimacy with me, it means you've formed an emotional attachment to me."

Elvin rolled his eyes. "When you put it that way, it sounds so clinical."

Ray couldn't have disagreed more. The chemistry between them was so potent it was combustible. He should have known that it was fueled by emotions that ran deep. So deep they bordered on love.

Ray sucked in a breath as the reality hit him like a freight train. It was possible that Elvin loved him. It was probable that he loved Elvin back. And here he was coming on to Elvin like he was another of Ray's one-night stands. What the fuck was wrong with him? Elvin wasn't someone he could screw and toss aside. The thought alone made Ray sick to his stomach.

This thing with Elvin was…love? How the fuck had that happened? Yet Ray knew it was true like he knew the sky was blue and that Jade Harbour held investment meetings on Monday mornings.

He wrapped an arm around Elvin and brought their heads together. "There's nothing clinical about this." If anything, what they had was the absolute opposite.

"Yeah?"

Ray pressed a kiss into Elvin's temple. "Yeah."

Elvin snuggled closer and Ray held him tighter. Neither of them spoke until the sun started setting and painted the sky a rainbow of pinks, purples and blues.

Chapter Seventeen

A tap on Elvin's desk announced Ming's arrival. He hiked one hip up onto the edge of the desk and bent forward to rest his elbow on his knee. Looking past Elvin into Ray's office, he asked, "How's your sister?"

Elvin hadn't spoken to Ming since parting ways at the airport two nights ago. He was surprised Ming even remembered what had happened with Joyce. "She's okay. Her fever broke last night."

Ming nodded. "And uh, what about, you know?"

Wasn't that the million-dollar question? Ray had told him to be patient as they gathered more information, but Elvin didn't like the idea of carrying on as if everything was normal. They had to do *something*.

"I still have this thing." Ming waved the flash drive between two fingers.

Elvin had forgotten about that. "Have you looked through it?"

"Some. I made a copy of it for safekeeping." Ming slipped the drive into his pocket.

Safekeeping was a good idea. The question was, from who?

"Where is he, anyway?" Ming nodded toward Ray's office. "Shouldn't he be scouring the boxes we hauled through the forest?"

"He's out."

Ming cocked an eyebrow at the tired excuse.

"Really. He is. Caron isn't the only portfolio company he's working on."

Ming let out an unimpressed chuckle. "It should be."

For once, he and Ming agreed on something.

"Doesn't matter. You're the one I really wanted to talk to."

Elvin wasn't sure he liked the sound of that. "Oh?"

Ming reached into his jacket's inner breast pocket and pulled out two long pieces of paper.

It took a split second for Elvin to figure out they were tickets. And another second for him to read the name printed on them. He gasped and snatched the tickets out of Ming's hand. "Are you serious?"

"As a heart attack." Ming looked pleased as punch with himself. "*Abroad.* Opening night. Orchestra seats."

Elvin hated to admit it, but he was impressed. *Abroad*

was the hottest musical on Broadway this year. It featured some of musical theater's biggest stars and had won nearly every Tony it'd been nominated for. The touring cast was coming to Toronto, but tickets had sold out in minutes and Elvin hadn't managed to get any.

"How did you get these?" He examined the tickets to make sure his eyes weren't fooling him.

"Please." Ming polished his nails on his shoulder. "Ray isn't the only one who knows people." He plucked the tickets from Elvin and carefully tucked them away.

Elvin watched them disappear into Ming's jacket pocket with a touch of melancholy. He wanted to see the show so badly and the tickets were so close and yet so far.

"Go on. Ask me. You know you want to." Ming had him and they both knew it. "Oh, and did I mention the tickets come with backstage passes to meet Clarissa Davis?"

Elvin gasped again. "No."

"Yes." Ming's grin couldn't get more smug.

Clarissa Davis was a legend on Broadway. Perhaps the best singer, dancer, actor there'd ever been. People lined up overnight for a chance to meet her. Hell, people betrayed their best friends for a chance to meet her.

It wouldn't be so terrible to spend an evening with Ming, would it? It's not like they'd be carrying on a conversation. They'd show up, sit next to each other, meet Clarissa Davis, and then go their separate ways. No big deal.

Elvin braced himself. "Are you bringing anyone to the show?"

"Funny you should ask, Elvin!" Ming stood and tugged

on his jacket so the fabric lay flat. "As a matter of fact, I do have a spare ticket. Would you happen to know a theater connoisseur who would appreciate such a show?"

He was having way too much fun with this. "Lay off it."

"Oh, well, I guess you don't." Ming made to leave, ruining the effect when he glanced expectantly over his shoulder.

"Wait. Wait, wait. Can I go to the show with you?" Elvin rephrased his question.

"What show?"

Elvin grimaced. Shit. Ray was back early.

"Oh, Elvin and I were chatting about this wonderful show coming to Toronto soon. It's called *Abroad*. I doubt you've heard of it." Ming sounded like he was bragging, and Ray's expression went from curious to dark. "We were making plans to see it together, actually."

Ray frowned and for a split second Elvin thought he saw a touch of hurt. But then Ray's mask fell into place. "Oh?"

Elvin wished he could deny it, but everything Ming said was technically true. If only he didn't sound like he was trying to one-up Ray all the time.

Ray turned on his heel and marched into his office.

"Why do you have to provoke him like that?" Elvin asked.

Ming looked like he was about to play dumb, but then he shrugged. "It's too easy. I can't resist."

Figured. No wonder Ray disliked him so much.

Elvin led the way into Ray's office, and Ming made

himself comfortable on Ray's couch. "So, where are we at with Caron?"

From behind his desk, Ray glowered in silence. These two were worse than his siblings sometimes. "Ray doesn't think we should go to the police."

Ming nodded. "I agree. Nothing good can come out of that."

Ming's approval did nothing to lighten Ray's mood.

"What about Joanna? We need to tell her what's going on, right? And Mike, too." They would know what to do, and if they didn't, maybe they could bring in external legal counsel.

Ming shook his head. "No, we leave the legal department out of this for now."

"What?"

"I have to agree." Ray looked like the admission was physically painful. "We'll read Joanna in eventually. But we should have a couple solutions to offer before we do."

"But what about legal?" Elvin couldn't quite believe they were going to keep something so huge to themselves.

"What about them?" Ming jumped back in. "It's not like we're going to sue our way out of this."

"Elvin." Ray's voice was measured, carrying a note of caution. "We're not going to find a legal solution to the problem."

Meaning the solution was going to be illegal.

He glanced at Ming, who wore the same expression as Ray. Guarded, somber. There were elements of this job that were best left unexamined, and it appeared that this was going to be one of them.

Elvin nodded his understanding. This wasn't the first time he and Ray had found themselves in this position. He'd be lying if he claimed to be completely comfortable with it. But necessary evils and all that.

"Now that we're on the same page, I'll pick up where I left off?" Ming looked to Ray for direction.

"Caron's finances?" Ray asked.

"Yep." They'd split up the files at the mill and Ming had taken the financials. Apparently, he was some numbers genius.

"I was digging into their accounts, which they have a lot of. I mean, a lot. Way more than I would expect for a company of that size." Ming shrugged. "It's not illegal or anything, just weird. But now that we know about the drugs, maybe they're funneling illicit cash through some of those accounts."

Ray nodded. "That's a good place to start."

Ming pushed himself off the couch. "I'll let you know what I find."

The second the door closed behind Ming, Ray spoke up. "You're not really going on a date with Ming, are you?"

"What?" Who said anything about a date?

"The musical." Ray sat with his arms folded over his chest, chin jutted out a tiny bit.

If Elvin didn't know better, he'd have guessed that Ray was pouting. Because he was jealous? That was ludicrous. Ray was not the jealous type. Hell, he made a habit of taking home a different person every night of the week. If anyone had the right to be jealous, it'd be Elvin.

Ray's sexual conquests were an unpleasant reminder. He'd always been sweet and thoughtful with Elvin, but he was probably sweet and thoughtful with all those one-night stands too. And Elvin wasn't nearly as gorgeous or wealthy or well-connected as the people Ray normally took to bed.

He made for the door. "No, it's not a date. I don't even know if I'm going to go." He slipped out of Ray's office and shut the door before Ray could respond.

God, everything was such a fucking mess. Drugs and mobs, Joyce still on the mend, and he had to go complicating things with Ray. He should have kept his hands and his feelings to himself. Why did he have to go screwing up something so perfect?

Elvin stared at his computer screen, randomly clicking from window to window. Once in a while someone would walk past his desk and call out a hello. They looked so normal, so carefree, untouched by the drama plaguing his life.

There was a tap on the glass door behind him. It was Ray, who gestured for Elvin to join him. Elvin glanced at the clock. He'd been sitting mindlessly at his desk for thirty minutes already. It felt like a blink of an eye and it felt like forever.

"You need me for something?"

"Come here." Ray waved him forward. He waited until Elvin stood in front of his desk before sliding two sheets of paper across.

"What are these?" Elvin picked them up, scanning the

printouts. No, they couldn't be. How the hell had Ray done this?

"You want to see *Abroad*? I'll take you to see *Abroad*." Ray sat back in his executive chair, hands folded across his middle. With one foot, he swiveled the chair left and right.

Elvin held up the tickets. "But these are for the show in New York."

"I know."

Elvin looked at them again. "For tonight?"

"Plus reservations for dinner at Barcelona beforehand and backstage passes to meet Clarissa Davis afterward." Ray looked mighty pleased with himself.

"You did all this in thirty minutes?" Ray was resourceful, but this was fast even for him.

Ray's grin grew wider and his eyes sparkled in delight. "I called in a few favors. It helps to know people who know people."

No shit. Elvin sat in one of the chairs in front of Ray's desk. He scanned the tickets again. He should be flattered. Excited, even. But the only thing he felt was annoyance. He pushed the tickets back toward Ray. "I can't go to this."

Ray sat up straight, confusion washing away his humor. "Why not?"

"Because." It was so ludicrous. Who the fuck jumped on a plane at the last minute to go catch dinner and a show in New York City? The likes of Ray, that's who. People with so much money they didn't know what to do with it all. Not people like Elvin, who'd had a job since he'd been legally allowed to work. He'd scrimped and saved to put himself through school and his mom still worked at a minimum-wage job.

But it wasn't only that. Ray presented him with this outlandish present only after a confrontation with Ming. What was he trying to prove? That he had more connections than Ming?

"You're trying to outdo Ming and I'm not about to be a pawn between the two of you." Annoyance bubbled into anger in the middle of Elvin's chest.

"What are you talking about?" Ray stood. "I don't give a crap about Ming."

"Oh, please. I don't know what you think is going on between me and Ming, but I can assure you it's nothing. Ming is harmless. He likes to flirt. He likes to egg you on. And you fall for it every time." The words flowed out of Elvin's mouth without a second thought. Every one of them was true, but if he hadn't been so pissed that Ray was trying to buy him with a trip to New York, he might have found a more tactful way of saying them. Shit. Way to fuck things up even more.

The hurt on Ray's face was painfully apparent. He sat back down, slowly and with barely restrained control. "I didn't realize you felt that way."

"No, wait. Ray, that's not what I meant." Elvin went around the desk and crouched down to Ray's level. His heart felt like it was beating in his throat, racing to an erratic rhythm. "Why did you really buy those tickets?"

Ray turned to him, eyes like dual lasers boring into

Elvin. What was he looking for? What did he see? "Because I wanted to and because I could."

That wasn't an answer and yet that was all the answer Elvin needed. Normal people didn't do shit like this. But then Ray never claimed to be normal. He got what he wanted, when he wanted it, and nothing—no person nor circumstances—would stop him. The question was, did he want Elvin because Ming posed a threat Ray didn't like? Or did Ray want Elvin for himself?

Elvin dropped his chin to his chest. God, what a total and complete clusterfuck. "What about Caron? Don't we have to deal with that?"

"We are dealing with that." Ray stated matter-of-factly. "My guy is looking into the Greek mob."

"What about all the files we hauled back?" Elvin pointed to the boxes sitting in the corner of the room.

"One night away isn't going to make a difference."

"What about my family? What if something happens to them while I'm gone again?"

"We'll come back right away. Like we did last time."

God damn Ray and his solutions to everything. He made it all sound so simple, so easy. Like he could snap his fingers and all the world's problems would resolve themselves. Elvin wanted to believe it was true. Life would be so much more pleasant if it were.

"Elvin, I want to do this. With you. For you." Ray's voice was soft and almost a little hesitant, like he wasn't sure how Elvin would react. "It isn't about the money for me, you know that. This is something you want and it's something I can provide. What's so wrong about that?"

Elvin sighed. When he put it that way, nothing.

"Please?" Ray was practically begging. Ray never begged. "Let's go see the show."

Elvin wasn't sure he agreed with Ray's philosophy toward money, but Ray was right about one thing. He really wanted to see the show. On Broadway, no less! It would be rude to turn it down, wouldn't it? "Okay." Elvin gave in. "Let's go."

Chapter Eighteen

This was the third time Elvin had been to the airport in one week—more often than Elvin had been to any airport in the last year.

Not long after Ray had surprised him with the last-minute trip, he'd announced that there was a car waiting for them downstairs and they had to leave. No time to go home and change—his suit was apparently more than adequate—and they'd be home later that night.

Ray had arranged a private jet to fly them down to New York. It wasn't as nice as Jade Harbour's corporate jet, but it still had all the bells and whistles. Comfortable leather seats, individual side tables, a personal flight attendant to take care of all their needs.

"Welcome aboard, gentlemen," the flight attendant

greeted them. "If you'll take your seats, we're all ready for taxi and takeoff."

"I can't believe we're doing this." He'd been repeating that over and over as if the more he said it, the more real this would get. It didn't. Normal people didn't do this. He was as painfully normal as they came.

"Well, believe it." Ray settled into the seat next to him. He'd been a little short with Elvin during the drive over.

To be fair, Elvin had been a little short with him too. He was trying to do something nice, and Elvin appreciated the sentiment. But Ray was so ensconced in his world that he couldn't always see things from Elvin's point of view.

The cabin lights dimmed as the plane got into position for takeoff. They sat there, side by side in the dark, at a standoff. This was ridiculous.

"Ray," Elvin said. "Thank you for all of this." Regardless of his motives, this was a huge and thoughtful gift. Elvin would be an asshole to ruin it by being surly. He reached for Ray's hand and their fingers intertwined like it was the most natural thing in the world.

"You're not upset?"

Elvin wasn't so much upset as he was frustrated and confused. What were they doing and why were they doing it? Was it going to end in disaster? Was Elvin risking too much? "No," he said. "I'm not upset."

He wasn't about to find the answers he was looking for tonight, so he might as well enjoy the outlandishness of the trip.

Ray lifted their clasped hands and kissed the back of Elvin's. It was a soft and lingering kiss, with Ray closing his eyes and bowing his head. God, he really was gorgeous and caring. Elvin had never met anyone like him, and he was pretty sure he never would. It was a miracle that Ray would be willing to shower him with any gift, let alone something so extravagant. Elvin owed it to him to enjoy it.

For one night, he could hit pause on his life and be the Cinderella to Ray's Prince Charming. He'd worry about the real world after the clock struck twelve.

A car was waiting for them when they landed, and they were whisked away into the city. Elvin had never heard of Barcelona before, but Ray assured him it was the hottest restaurant in town. They pulled up in front of the building and a valet rushed over to open the door. Another valet ushered them onto a dedicated elevator that shot up to the penthouse restaurant, overlooking the busy lights of Times Square.

Inside, the lighting was minimal, but the billboards and signs outside more than made up for it, making the interior feel like the middle of a summer's day. Decorated with warm stone, the occasional multicolored mosaics and faux windows with Juliette balconies on the walls, it felt like they were in an actual European public square.

They were shown to an intimate table for two, tucked into a nook sheltered by trailing vines. When they sat down, their knees bumped together, which made Elvin smile. He shifted so his knee pressed against Ray's and he kept it there. It felt like a little secret the two of them shared, safe from the rest of the world.

The waiter showed up with a fresh carafe of water and informed them that they would be getting the preshow chef's menu, consisting of five tapas dishes, all inspired by the Catalonia region of Spain. The second the waiter turned to leave, Ray's phone rang.

With a frown, Ray pulled it out. "I have to take this. Sorry. Hello?" Holding the phone to his ear with one hand, Ray reached out with the other and Elvin grasped onto it.

He couldn't hear what was being said on the other end of the line, but whatever it was, it didn't sound like good news. Ray's frown deepened and his grip on Elvin's hand tightened.

"But you don't know for sure?" Ray asked. "Can you find out?"

More chatter from the other end until Ray finally said, "Okay. Keep me posted." He hung up and put his phone facedown on the table.

"Was that your guy?" The ex-military intelligence guy turned private investigator always tended to call at the oddest times, like he knew when he was most likely to interrupt something.

"Yeah."

Elvin was almost afraid to ask. "What did he say?"

"He thinks one of the larger Greek mob families are the ones behind the drugs we found at Caron. The Rousopouloses have been importing cocaine into Quebec for nearly a decade. From Montreal, they distribute all across the East Coast." Ray fiddled with the cutlery on the table, then took a sip of his water.

So it was true. All their suspicions and conjectures had been confirmed. It was kind of a relief, finally knowing what the hell they were dealing with. "Okay, so, what does that mean for us?"

Ray tapped his finger against the side of his water glass, his mind processing this new information at top speed. "We don't know for certain it's the Rousopouloses yet. But if it *is* them, they're no joke. They have their fingers in every part of Montreal's infrastructure. Nothing happens in the city unless they approve it." Ray shook his head, pausing as the waiter returned with two of their dishes.

"We're starting with pa amb tomàquet, fresh bread that we bake in-house, with a tomato and garlic sauce. And a plate of meats and cheese imported from Catalonia." He set the plates down and bowed before leaving.

"Wait a minute." Elvin leaned forward. "So we're actually dealing with a mob family here? Like the mafia? Organized crime?" Elvin could imagine it now. Some godfather figure sitting in the dark backroom of a store, surrounded by henchmen, the air filled with cigar smoke.

Ray picked at the food while he continued speaking, carefully layering thin slices of meat and cheese on the bread. "Yep. Looks like it."

Elvin slumped back into his chair. They'd seen some wild shit over the years: self-interested and corrupt executives; business people who exploited legal and regulatory loopholes for their own gain. But this was a whole other level of bad.

Ray took a careful bite of the pseudo sandwich he'd created. He chewed and swallowed before continuing. "The police have never been able to touch the Rousopoulo-ses. But there's a rumor going around that that's about to change."

"Really? How?"

"They're trying to infiltrate the family. Apparently, an undercover cop has managed to get in."

"Is that good?" Ray and Ming had been adamant that going to the police was out of the question, but if they were already involved, they might as well cooperate, right?

Before Ray could respond, the waiter returned with three more plates. "This is the bomba Barceloneta, ground meat wrapped in mashed potatoes, then fried to a golden brown, topped with aioli and brava sauce. The second dish is esqueixada, which is shredded salt cod, with onion, to-mato, bell peppers and olives, tossed in a light vinaigrette and sprinkled with sea salt. And lastly is the escalivada, where we grill eggplants, bell peppers and onions, gar-nished with anchovies. Enjoy!"

Ray helped himself to portions of each before he set down his utensils and tented his fingers. "They won't be able to work fast enough for our needs."

Elvin frowned. "What do you mean?" It seemed straight-forward to him. The cops could arrest Olivier and anyone else at Caron who was involved with the drug ring, and Jade Harbour would be free of the mess.

"It can take years for law enforcement to build a case and there's no guarantee that they'll be successful." Ray set about cutting the grilled vegetables into bite-sized pieces.

"Jade Harbour can't hold on to Caron forever. We have to sell it sooner or later or we'll lose any hope of turning a profit."

Profit. It always came back to that. But they weren't talking about some entitled prick who wanted to game the system for his own benefit. This was the fucking mob, so dangerous and organized that even the police couldn't bring them down. Ray and Ming's insistence that they go it alone felt like they were underestimating the seriousness of the situation.

"I don't know." Elvin shook his head. "Is it worth it? At some point, shouldn't profit come second to, oh, I don't know, the law? Our safety?"

"Safety?" Ray cocked his head like the thought had never crossed his mind.

"Yeah, safety. These people are dangerous, aren't they? And they know that we know. What if they come after us?" Saying the words out loud made the possibility that much more real to Elvin. What if they tracked them down in Toronto? What if they targeted his family? "Ray, this isn't like the other projects we've worked on. Are you sure we shouldn't tell the police what we know?"

Ray lifted his wine glass. "That's exactly why we shouldn't work with the police."

"What?" Ray's logic was going completely over Elvin's head. "Why?"

Ray pinned him with a look that was both solemn and stern. "Because they're dangerous. If the cops haven't been able to bring them down after all these years, what makes

you think that the little we know will help? If the Rousopouloses or whoever they are get wind that we're cooperating, we'll have even bigger targets on our backs."

Ray shook his head. "No, the safest course of action is to
befriend the Rousopouloses and somehow convince them
to relocate their operations elsewhere. We'll need to offer
them something they can't get anywhere else, something
mutually beneficial. Then once they clear out of Caron,
we dispose of it as quickly as possible."

"You're kidding me." Elvin couldn't believe what he
was hearing. They were seriously getting into bed with a
criminal organization. Because profits were more important than people, than the greater good, than any sense of
right and wrong. He shouldn't be surprised. Jade Harbour
had never claimed to be a humanitarian agency. They were
a business and they needed to make money.

"You're not eating." Ray eyed Elvin's mostly empty
plate. "What's wrong?"

"Nothing." He reached for his fork and stabbed a bomba,
but pushed it around his plate. "Have you ever thought
about what we do?"

"What do you mean?"

Elvin put down his fork. He had no appetite despite how
delicious the food smelled. "We've done some sketchy stuff
in the past."

Ray cocked an eyebrow. "I suppose."

"Mostly to bad people, though." Or at least that's how
Elvin had justified it to himself. Blackmail, coercion,

bribery—none of that was really wrong if it was the bad guys who lost out.

Ray chuckled. "Sure."

"But it's different this time. You're talking about working with bad people."

Ray paused for a beat before answering. "Yes, that's true."

"We're supposed to be okay with that?"

"I don't see any other option."

Elvin stared at Ray and he stared right back. How the hell had they ended up here? They were supposed to give Caron a clean bill of health, sell it to people who add value to the company, make some money, and everyone would walk away happy. Now they were debating their obligation to upholding morals.

"Hey." Ray reached across the table for his hand. "Everything's going to be okay. I promise. I'm not going to let anything bad happen."

Ray had always been true to his word, but Elvin couldn't help wondering if he was in over his head this time. "Are you sure?"

A flash of uncertainty skittered across Ray's expression, gone before it fully materialized. Anyone else would have missed it, but Elvin knew Ray too well. His confident smile and the cocky tilt of his head didn't completely mask his own doubts. "I'm positive."

Elvin didn't call him out on it. Fake it until they made it, right? If Elvin had learned anything from Ray over the years, it was to approach matters with self-assurance. Negotiate from a position of power, exude control. The opposition would be less likely to question them and more likely to fall in line.

Even if Elvin had trouble believing any of it himself.

He lifted Ray's hand and planted a soft kiss on it. Ray's belief would be enough for both of them. It had to be.

Chapter Nineteen

It was late by the time they made it back to Toronto. Over-all, Ray would rate the trip a success, dinner discussion notwithstanding. Watching Elvin sing along to every song during the show and then fan-boy over Clarissa Davis was totally worth sitting through a musical. Elvin had been on cloud nine all the way home, and Ray almost forgot the concerns Elvin had raised during their meal.

Almost.

Good and bad. Right and wrong. So much of what he did occupied the space in between, and the murkiness had never bothered him. There was a whole class of people out there who did whatever the hell they wanted with no regard to rules or laws or propriety. And they happily got away with it too. The stuff Ray dabbled in was nothing in comparison.

But then, he came from a world where one's character was defined more by dollar figures than anything else. Actions were only wrong if a person couldn't buy their way out of trouble. Hell, he'd used that tactic himself whenever it suited him.

A car picked them up from the airport and its first stop was Elvin's apartment. But when they got there, Elvin stared out the window, unmoved.

"Don't want to go in?"

Elvin smiled. "How did you know?"

It wasn't hard to tell. Ray had experienced the post-excitement drop in dopamine many times before. Coming back to reality could be a rough reentry. "Want to come to my place?"

Elvin nodded and Ray passed the instructions to the driver. When he settled back into his seat, Elvin snuggled up against him. It was the best feeling in the world.

Elvin didn't grow up like Ray. He had parents who were around enough to raise him. He had a family who needed and depended on him. They lived in a world where the rules actually mattered and people were held accountable for their actions. They were normal. All the money in the world couldn't buy that.

The car pulled up in front of Ray's condo. After handing the driver a generous tip, Ray led Elvin inside.

"Hey, Mohammad," Ray called to the security guard.

"Good evening, Mr. Chao, Mr. Goh."

Hand in hand, they rode the elevator up to the penthouse and then walked wordlessly to Ray's bedroom.

Elvin ran a hand over Ray's bed before sitting on the edge. He looked at Ray, eyes half-lidded from a full day of activities.

"Good day?"

"Mmm-hmm." Elvin gazed up at him with a soft smile. "It was." He held out his hand, and Ray took it. "Thank you."

"Of course."

"Let's not make a habit of it, though, okay?" Elvin gave him a tug to bring him nearer. "Impromptu jaunts to foreign cities are a little too rich for my blood."

"You'll get used to it."

Elvin shot him a scolding look and Ray chuckled. Spoiling Elvin was fun, all the more so because Elvin never took it for granted.

Elvin bent his head and ran his fingers delicately over Ray's hand, examining each knuckle and wrinkle. There was nothing erotic about it and yet Ray's dick perked to attention. Elvin traced the lines across his palms, his touch so feather soft it sent tingles all the way up Ray's arm.

"Elvin," he warned as his gut tightened in anticipation.

"Hmm?" Elvin didn't stop his thorough examination.

Ray breathed through it, willing his dick to behave. Elvin was a virgin, and anyone's first time should be carefully considered. Hasty after a long day wasn't Ray's idea of romantic. Ray cleared his throat and tried again. "Elvin."

This time Elvin peered up through his lashes and it was

everything Ray could do not to push him back onto the mattress and take him. "Ray."

Oh god, even the way Elvin said his name. Breathy, like he was too overcome to say it at full volume. Elvin took his hand and held it against his cheek, caressing it like it was the most treasured thing. He turned and pressed a kiss in the center of Ray's palm. Then a quick wet lick of his tongue and Ray almost came in his pants.

"Fuck, Elvin." Ray drew his hand back and rubbed his thumb over the spot where Elvin had licked him. It was hot, burning like Elvin's tongue had left a brand. "You don't know what you're doing to me."

Elvin gazed up at him, wide-eyed and innocent. Precious and exquisite. He was a gift, and who was Ray to be allowed to open it?

Ray sat down next to Elvin, careful to leave a gap between them. "Listen." He paused. He wasn't ashamed of or embarrassed by his active sex life. Sex was fun and he liked the companionship of having someone in his bed. But not everyone felt the same way. The last thing he wanted was to push Elvin to do something he'd regret in the morning. "I've slept with a lot of people."

"I know."

Yes, of course Elvin knew. But that wasn't the point. "Sex is…well, it can be fun, but it's also more than that. You know what I mean?"

Elvin was watching him with a furrowed brow. "Um, maybe?"

Fuck. Ray didn't even know what he meant, how did

he expect Elvin to read his mind? "What I'm trying to say is, don't do anything you don't want to do."

"Okay."

Ray nodded decisively. There. But then Elvin put a hand on his thigh and sent all his good intentions scattering. His dick was hard. Elvin had to have noticed. It was only an inch away from Elvin's fingers. So close.

"I'm not doing anything I don't want to do."

Huh? What? Ray swallowed, eyes fixed to the tiny space between Elvin's hand and his cock. Do what?

"Ray?"

He tore his gaze away to meet Elvin's. Elvin might have been an innocent, but there was clarity in his eyes. Unlike Ray, he wasn't clouded by the haze of desire. "Are you sure?" Ray asked. If they started down that road, he wouldn't be able to stop.

"I'm sure."

Oh god, how the hell had he gotten so lucky? Ray leaned in and caught Elvin's lips in a kiss, a mere press of lips against lips, but Ray poured every ounce of himself into it. All his desire and all his longing.

"Ray, please," Elvin whispered, and in those two words Ray heard all that he needed. He reached for his tie, pulled it free of his neck and dropped it on the floor.

Elvin made a noise of protest and bent to try to pick it up, but Ray caught him. "Leave it."

"It'll get wrinkled. Your clothes are too nice to end up on the floor."

"I don't care." He shrugged out of his suit jacket and tossed it next to the tie.

"Ray!" Elvin wriggled free of Ray's attempts to stop him and picked up the discarded clothing. It seemed that there was no preventing Elvin from taking care of him, not even with sex. Elvin placed the clothes on the armchair in the corner and held out his hand for the next article.

Easier to cooperate than object. Ray stripped as fast as he could, handing Elvin each item until he was left in his black boxer briefs.

Elvin's gaze roamed over Ray's body, pausing here or there for a second only to move on to the next patch of skin. Ray let him examine as much as he wanted, glorying in the attention. It made his heart pump and his skin flush and in that moment, he felt like he could conquer anything.

When Elvin finished his examination, he looked at Ray with wonder and awe. Ray's rapidly beating heart skipped a beat, sending his mind whirling with want for Elvin. How had this man escaped all the vultures in the world only to land at Ray's feet?

"Your turn."

Elvin moved slower than Ray did, undoing buttons with a slightly shaky hand. Ray took each piece of clothing he discarded and laid them carefully on top of his own on the chair—shirt, pants, socks—until Elvin was also in his underwear.

Beautiful didn't quite do Elvin justice. Pale, almost translucent skin covered a lithe body. Not overly muscular, but toned all over.

Ray held out his hand and Elvin placed his inside. Together they walked to the bed and climbed on. Ray lay on his side and Elvin slipped into a mirrored position facing him. An inch of air separated them from nose to toes.

"What do you want to do?" There was an entire world of sex to introduce Elvin to. He didn't want to move too fast or push any boundaries. They had time for that. Tonight should be about exploring sensations and learning what felt good.

"It doesn't matter, as long as I'm with you."

The trust Elvin placed in him was overwhelming. He'd had more sexual partners than he could count. He'd experimented with almost every kink and fetish there was. But none of that mattered when faced with Elvin, with the purity in front of him.

Elvin placed a hand flat on his chest. "Your heart is beating so fast."

"That's because of you."

Elvin swallowed, his Adam's apple bobbing. "My heart's beating fast too."

Ray put his hand on Elvin's chest, mimicking him. They lay there for a bit, breathing in and out together until their hearts beat as one, steady and in sync. Ray would have been content to lie there all night and all day.

"Let's go slow," Ray said eventually. "Whenever something feels good, say yes. And if something doesn't feel good, say no."

Elvin nodded.

"Ready?"

"Yes."

Ray leaned forward until their noses settled in next to each other, their foreheads pressed together. He brushed his lips against Elvin's, soft and light, then again.

"Yes."

Ray pressed in a little more, sneaking his tongue out to tease.

"Yes."

Ray sucked on Elvin's lower lip, catching it between his teeth and giving it a little nibble.

"Nuh…" Elvin moaned.

"Is that a yes?" Ray couldn't help chuckling.

"Yes." Elvin's voice was filled with need and Ray growled in response.

He went in for another kiss, a little more forcefully this time, bringing his hand up to bury his fingers in Elvin's hair. He nipped at Elvin's chin, then up his jaw, then bit gently on his earlobe.

"Yeessss." Elvin shuddered as Ray tugged on his ear.

He moved down Elvin's neck, his shoulder, his collarbone. Down the middle of his chest, then to one nipple and the other. He tasted Elvin's daylong salty, musky skin, relishing every "yes" that Elvin uttered in response. Down past his navel to the trail of hair that disappeared under the waistband of his briefs. Elvin's hipbones and inner thighs. The backs of his knees and the boney bits on his ankles. Ray dug his thumbs into the bottom of Elvin's feet and earned himself a long, low "yes" that sounded more like a moan than any discernible word.

"Ray." Elvin's arm was extended, reaching for him, and Ray gladly went.

He laid himself on top of Elvin's body, gently pressing Elvin into the bed. He slipped his knees between Elvin's thighs and smiled at Elvin's gasped "yes." Under the plain white briefs was a cock hard and leaking, pulsing against Ray's thigh.

"Yes?" Ray asked to draw out the moment.

Elvin grabbed Ray's ass and pulled him down. "Yes," he demanded.

Ray moved slowly, rolling his hips and varying the pressure against Elvin's dick. His own cock was a steel pole, pushing out of the top of his underwear, its tip brushing against Elvin's hot skin.

He tried to hold himself up on his elbows, both to give himself room to maneuver and to not crush Elvin. But the strength in his arms was zapped by the cries replacing Elvin's yeses and ethereal look on Elvin's face.

Ray dropped his head next to Elvin's so they were cheek to cheek. The roughness of their five-o'clock shadows only added to the pleasure coursing through him. Together they moved. Ray pushing Elvin down while Elvin pressed up. Their cocks brushed together through the two thin layers of cotton, so hot it was a wonder the fabric didn't catch on fire.

His orgasm was building. A subtle tightening deep in his groin that pulled at every sinew in his body. He held it off, wanting to live in the moment for as long as possible. He sank his teeth into the spot where Elvin's neck and shoulder met and bucked his hips hard against Elvin's.

"Ray!" Nails scraped down his back as Elvin arched off the bed. Hot wetness oozed between their bodies, triggering Ray's own orgasm.

He cried into the crook of Elvin's shoulder, allowing himself to come in wave after wave of blinding pleasure.

At some point, he'd collapsed onto Elvin while his brain was still floating somewhere in the stratosphere. Eventually, there was a poke in his side.

"Ray."

"Hmm?"

"It's getting hard to breathe."

"Oh, sorry." He managed to roll off, but he didn't have the strength to move any farther. Not that he wanted to. He wanted Elvin pressed against him every day for the rest of his life. If that meant locking themselves in the bedroom, so be it. He never wanted to be anywhere else.

"Ray."

"Hmm?"

"Was I…"

"Hmm?" Ray opened one eye to find Elvin gazing at him shyly.

His hair was a mess, his cheeks were rosy, and his lips were swollen. He was gorgeous.

"Was I, um, good?"

Ray laughed out loud. He couldn't help it. "Elvin," he said in between chuckles. "You were mind-blowing. If you were any better, I would have died."

Elvin grinned like he was proud of himself. "Good. You weren't so bad yourself."

"Not bad?" Ray pushed himself up onto an elbow. "Only not bad, huh?"

Elvin shrugged with one shoulder. "I don't have anything to compare it to. I wouldn't want to give a maximum score until I get a better sense of what's out there."

"Oh yeah?" Ray poked him in the tummy. "You're planning on making the rounds?"

Elvin played the innocent. "Maybe. I mean, unless you have other tricks up your sleeve."

Ray threw a leg over Elvin and leaned in to whisper in his ear. "Oh, I've got plenty of tricks. You're not going anywhere."

Chapter Twenty

The sun was barely up when Elvin woke with a smile on his face. It was the perfect temperature under the duvet and the bedsheets smelled like Ray. He let his eyes drift shut as images of the night before replayed in his mind. The musical, selfies with Clarissa Davis, and most importantly, sex with Ray.

Dear god, sex with Ray. Elvin had had no idea physical intimacy could feel so fucking good. Ray had been sweet and gentle and considerate and everything Elvin had known he would be. He'd never get enough.

Ray was still fast asleep next to him. He had one hand on Elvin's hip, like he needed to maintain their connection even when unconscious. Did he do that with his other lovers?

Elvin blinked at the unbidden thought. Where the hell had that come from? He tried to push it from his mind, but now that he was aware of it, he couldn't shake it.

What if he didn't measure up to Ray's other lovers? What if Ray got tired of him and wanted more variety? What if he was merely convenient?

It was getting hot under the covers and Elvin slowly eased himself to the edge of the bed. The air was chilly, but he needed that wake-up call. Last night had been the grand ball, but they were well past midnight now.

The only clothes Elvin had were dirty and he cringed at the thought of putting them back on. He let himself into Ray's walk-in closet. Wearing Ray's clothes didn't feel appropriate either, but what other choice did he have? He picked out the oldest shirt and jeans Ray had, then quietly padded out of the bedroom.

As the door clicked shut behind him, Elvin let out a sigh. He'd been in love with Ray for as long as he could remember, but Ray didn't feel the same way. The only thing that had changed was the threat of a crime boss and the shock of Joyce in the hospital. Elvin had felt vulnerable, helpless, with none of his usual control. He'd leaned on Ray for support and…had Ray taken advantage of him?

Elvin shook his head as he went into one of the guest bathrooms to splash water on his face. No, Ray didn't take advantage of people. He had no need to. People gladly gave themselves over to him, which was exactly what Elvin had done.

He'd been a willing participant. But now that they'd had

sex, now that Joyce was feeling better and the mob situation was sort of being handled, would they go back to the way things were before? Elvin wasn't sure he'd be able to do that. How was he supposed to put his feelings back into the box? Would he be okay if Ray started bringing home other one-night stands again?

He headed to the kitchen and started on breakfast, moving mostly on autopilot as the unending questions swirled in his mind. Ray had made no commitments to him. It wouldn't be fair of him to expect anything of that sort. If their working relationship fell apart because of this, would Elvin have to find a new job? Would he be able to find one that paid as well? What would he tell his parents when they asked why he was switching jobs?

His parents. Shit. He hadn't been over since bringing Joyce home from the hospital. Hell, he hadn't even called to check in on them. Elvin patted his pockets. Where the fuck had he put his phone?

As quietly as he could, he snuck back into the bedroom. Ray was still dead to the world, one arm flung over his head and one leg sticking out from the duvet. Elvin went to the chair where they'd left their clothes and pulled his phone out of his discarded pants. It was dead.

Damn it. What if his parents had tried to call and they couldn't reach him? What if Joyce had taken a turn for the worse or something else had happened to one of his siblings? Elvin rushed back to the kitchen and plugged his phone in.

"Come on. Come on." It took forever for the screen to

flicker back to life and another eon for messages and notifications to come through.

There was a text message from Janice asking for a ride to a friend's house. Another text message from Edwin asking to borrow his car. And finally a voicemail from Mom asking when he would be coming by for dinner and to help with chores. No emergencies. No crises.

Thank god.

He sank onto a kitchen stool and dialed his parents' landline.

"Hello?" A young boy answered the phone.

"Eason, it's DaaiGo. Are Mom or Dad there?"

"Hi, DaaiGo! Hold on!"

Elvin smiled at the thundering sound of small running feet, accompanied by screams of "Mama! Baba! DaaiGo's on the phone!"

"Wei?" Both of his parents picked up at the same time.

"Hi Mom, Dad."

"What's going on? Is something wrong?" Mom responded.

Elvin shook his head. No wonder he always jumped to the worst-case scenario. Guess who he learned it from. "Nothing's wrong. I'm sorry I missed your call."

"My call?" Mom sounded genuinely confused.

"You called me yesterday and left a message on my phone."

"Oh!" Mom tsked. She was probably waving her hand like she was shooing away an insect. "It's nothing. The washing machine was leaking but Janice cleaned it up."

Elvin cringed. Their washer and dryer were these old decrepit appliances from the nineties. He had no idea how they still functioned. "We should get it replaced."

"Aiya, that's too expensive. Your father already called someone to come fix it."

"Oh, okay." But Elvin doubted she heard him. She was busy shouting at the kids to eat their breakfast.

"Anything else?" she asked him.

"No, nothing else. I just wanted to make sure everything was okay at home."

"Yeah, yeah, everything is good. Come home soon, okay? Okay, bye bye."

Elvin dropped his head into his hands. It sounded like they had things under control. Guess they didn't need him so much after all. That was good, wasn't it? Then why did he feel like he'd been tossed aside?

Ray lumbered in just then, rubbing the sleep out of his eyes.

"Morning," he mumbled. "God, that smells delicious. Who were you talking to?"

"My mom. Sorry, did I wake you up?"

"Nope." Ray came over and gave him a quick peck on the mouth.

It was so casual, so second nature. It made Elvin's heart soar and his stomach plummet at the same time.

"How are they doing?" Ray picked up a cappuccino and held it under his nose.

"They're fine." And again, there was that odd sting of disappointment.

"See? I told you they'd be able to take care of themselves." He sipped the cappuccino and moaned. "This way, you can spend more time with me, because I've got to tell you, I could get used to waking up to this every day."

What an absurd statement. Elvin pinned Ray with his disapproving big brother look. "You *do* wake up to this every day."

"Mmm, not the same thing." Ray scooted in closer and wrapped an arm around Elvin's waist. "You're not usually wearing my clothes and I don't usually get to do this." He leaned in for another kiss. This time it was slow and sensual, a mix of minty toothpaste and bitter coffee.

Elvin melted into it. He couldn't help it. All doubts aside, Ray was simply irresistible.

Ray's pants vibrated. "Hold that thought." He put down his cup and pulled out his phone. "Hello?" he answered the call with a frown. "Tell me."

He went around the kitchen island to pace the room. "How do you know this?"

Elvin watched as the fuzziness of the morning cleared to make way for cold hard reality.

"So it's the Rousopouloses. Any developments on the police investigation?" Ray shot off questions with authority and command. "No clue who the undercover cop is? Where in the organization he is?"

Ray shook his head and ran a hand over his face. "Listen, I'm going to need to talk to them. In person. Can you set up a meeting?"

Elvin frowned. Set up a meeting? With the Rousopouloses? Of course. Ray would need to talk to them if the goal was to form some sort of partnership. But the idea didn't sit well with him.

"Let me know when it's done." Ray tossed the phone onto a nearby chair and ran his fingers through his hair so it stood up on end. "Looks like I'm headed back to Montreal."

"Are you sure that's a good idea?" Elvin already knew the answer, but he couldn't stop himself from asking.

"We don't have much choice." Ray came over and snuck his arms around Elvin's waist again.

"Why can't your guy do it?"

"That guy?" Ray nodded toward his phone. "He would never agree to represent us. Besides, this is too sensitive to hand off to anyone else. I need to deal with it myself."

"But it's dangerous." Elvin slid his hands up Ray's shoulders, around the back of his neck and onto either side of his face. What if these people didn't want to work with Ray? What if they'd rather tie up loose ends instead? "You can't go by yourself."

"I'm not going to put anyone else in harm's way." Ray kissed one of Elvin's palms, then leaned in for a kiss on Elvin's lips. "I'll be fine. I promise." He extricated himself from Elvin and went to examine the stack of waffles Elvin had made earlier.

Elvin usually put a lot of stock in Ray's promises, but he wasn't so convinced this time. Who knew what these people were capable of? "I'm going with you."

"What?" Ray held a plate of waffles in one hand and a bottle of maple syrup in the other. "No, you're not."

"I am. You can't go alone. It's not safe."

"Which is exactly why you're not coming." Ray set down the plate and bottle and went back to Elvin. "I know you're worried, but there's nothing to worry about. I've got it all under control."

That's what Ray thought, but he couldn't stop Elvin from following him.

"Let's not get carried away, okay?" Ray flashed a smile, one Elvin knew was meant to disarm him. "How about we dig into the breakfast you made? We'll deal with everything else later."

That was hard to argue with. Elvin nodded and went to take out the pre-made frittata he'd been heating in the oven.

"Oh my god, there's more!" Ray took an exaggerated inhale, slapped his hands over his chest and moaned. "I don't deserve you."

Elvin laughed at Ray's display, but his words bounced around in Elvin's head. Ray didn't deserve him? He might feel that way now when this thing between them was novel and new. But it would grow old eventually and Ray would want to move on. Like his family had found ways to move on.

He cut generous portions of the frittata and made up plates for each of them. Once they were seated at the island, Ray leaned over for a lingering kiss.

"Thank you," he whispered against Elvin's lips. "You're amazing."

Elvin leaned his forehead against Ray's, letting himself

soak in Ray's admiration. It wouldn't last forever, so he might as well enjoy it while he had it.

And when Ray finally tired of him? Well, he'd figure that out when they got there.

Chapter Twenty-One

Ming was sitting on Elvin's desk when they arrived at the office.

"Good morning! What do we have here?" Ming glanced back and forth between them, a massive smile on his face.

"What do you want, Ming?" It'd been a perfect morning so far and the last thing Ray wanted was Ming showing up to ruin it.

"Oh, I was just stopping by to see how my two favorite people in the world are doing." He hopped off Elvin's desk and wiggled his eyebrows. "How was the big night?"

Ray frowned. What the hell did Ming know about their night?

Elvin's eyes widened as his cheeks flushed. "What do you mean?"

"A little birdie told me that my invitation got outbid." He nudged Elvin with his elbow and shot him a knowing smile.

His invitation? Ray stepped forward at the thought of Ming propositioning Elvin. Who the fuck did he think he was?

Elvin maneuvered himself between them. "He means *Abroad*. Yes, we went to see *Abroad* in New York last night."

Oh. Ray backed down. How was he supposed to know what Ming was talking about when he grinned like that?

"Anyway." Ming chuckled and tapped on Ray's office door. "I'm here on business."

"What business?" Ray unlocked the door and led the way inside.

"I found something." Ming helped himself to a seat on the couch and opened up his laptop. "Better I show you."

Ray grudgingly sat down next to him. Just his luck that Ming was actually good at his job.

"Here." Ming swung the laptop around so Ray and Elvin could see the screen. There was a spreadsheet pulled up with rows and columns of numbers. "This is their general ledger. I've highlighted the relevant rows in yellow."

Ray scanned the yellow rows, but the numbers meant nothing to him. Meanwhile, Elvin was standing behind the couch, leaning over him. His chin brushed against Ray's shoulder, his breath light against Ray's cheek. Ray squinted and forced himself to focus on the spreadsheet.

"I've been reconciling each entry with the matching purchase order or invoice." Ming scooted forward as he spoke, elbows on knees and excitement glinting in his eyes. "On the surface, everything looks fine. There's paperwork to support every entry. But what doesn't match up is the mill's efficiency."

"What do you mean by efficiency?" Elvin asked. His voice sounded so close to Ray's ear.

"If these numbers are accurate, the mill's output is way more than its inputs would suggest. They're producing more product than is possible with the amount of raw materials they're buying." Ming looked like he was about to jump out of his seat.

"So where is the extra production coming from?" Elvin asked.

"It's not," Ray replied. All the pieces were falling into place. "The extra purchase orders are fake. The customers aren't real and the products don't exist. They're laundering money."

"Yes!" Ming actually shot up, slapping his hands together as he did. He looked like he'd won the lottery and Ray had to admit, this was pretty close to it.

Ray pulled the laptop closer to him and scrolled through the spreadsheet. "The highlighted rows are the fake purchase orders?"

"Yep!" Ming strutted through Ray's office like it was his own. "Amounts to about twenty million this past year alone."

"Whoa," Elvin whispered.

Whoa was right. This wasn't some small operation they'd stumbled upon. It was looking more and more like Caron played a central role in the Rousopouloses' operations. That made Ray's job that much more difficult.

He closed Ming's laptop and stood. "Come on. Time to bring this to Joanna."

Chapter Twenty-Two

Elvin stood back as Ray and Ming explained what they'd discovered to Joanna. The drugs, the Rousopouloses, the money laundering. All of it.

She sat behind her desk, legs crossed, one finger tapping her chin as they spoke. If she was surprised at what they were telling her, she didn't show it. Not one muscle on her face twitched as they laid it all out.

She didn't even react when they finally finished. The whole convoluted story hung in the air as everyone absorbed just how much shit they were in. Not for the first time in his life did Elvin thank the gods that he didn't have Joanna's job. He'd never be able to make the decisions she did, and he certainly didn't envy the position she was in.

"Why the fuck am I only hearing about this now?" She sounded like she was inquiring about the weather.

All eyes turned on Ray, but if he was feeling the heat, he didn't show it. "I wanted to make sure we knew what we were dealing with before bringing you in."

Daggers shot out of Joanna's eyes as she reached for the phone. "Get Mike in here." She slammed the receiver down hard enough that Elvin jumped. Pissed was an understatement.

"I don't think that's a good idea." Ray must have had a death wish, objecting to Joanna like that.

"I didn't ask for your opinion."

Sometimes Ray didn't know when to stop. "It's better if I handle this alone—"

"Plausible deniability?" Joanna cut him off. "We're way past that."

Thank god Mike didn't take long getting to Joanna's office. "You asked for me?" he said as he let himself in.

She nodded toward Ray and Ming. "Tell him."

"Joanna—"

"Tell. Him."

Ray pressed his lips into a thin line and Elvin risked a quick touch on his arm to calm him down. Elvin didn't know what Ray was thinking, but he wasn't about to win this one with Joanna.

Ming took the lead. With each sentence, Mike's eyes grew wider, his shoulders got tenser and his face grew paler. "You've got to be kidding me."

"Nope." Ming chuckled. Nobody joined him.

"Loop in external counsel." Joanna directed the instructions at Mike. "No one is to take any action on this issue until Denise and her team are brought up to speed. However we choose to proceed, our top priority is to make sure our asses are covered."

Elvin glanced at Ray, who was still tight-lipped. Wasn't he going to mention the meeting his guy was setting up? But his expression was a cold hard mask, with anger seething underneath.

Joanna dismissed everyone with orders to regroup once external counsel had been brought in, and they filed out one by one.

"Ray," Joanna called out before he made it to the door.

He stopped and turned, blocking Elvin from leaving. When Elvin tried to sidestep him, Ray put a hand on his arm to keep him close.

"Listen, I know you're used to handling these things by yourself." Joanna's tone was only a fraction softer than before. "But this is different from anything we've faced in the past. I can't have you flying solo here."

Ray simply shook his head. "You're making a mistake."

Elvin suppressed a cringe. Only Ray could get away with talking that way to Joanna.

Ray took several steps forward. "The more people who know about this, the greater the risk we're taking. We don't even know Denise Washington and her people that well. What if they've got a leak?"

"I'm confident that they can maintain confidentiality."

Ray scoffed. "You know, I didn't have to come to you

with this. I could have taken care of it myself and you wouldn't have been any wiser."

Joanna's expression grew dark, her eyes so stormy and violent that Elvin wouldn't be surprised if she could strangle people just by looking at them. "This is my company. You work for me, Ray. Or have I given you so much leeway in the past that you've forgotten what your obligations are?"

"I haven't forgotten anything. I'm trying to protect you!"

Elvin rarely heard Ray raise his voice, and certainly not in this way, toward Joanna. "Ray," he whispered, trying to pull Ray back. "Easy."

"I don't need you to protect me. That's not your job." Joanna grew scarier by the moment. "Your job is to do what I say, when I say it. If you can't do that, then you know where the door is."

Oh shit. Elvin tugged on Ray's arm again. "Ray. Come on. Let it go."

Whether it was Elvin's urging or just that there was simply nothing else to say, Ray spun on his heel and marched out. Elvin hurried after him and quietly closed the door behind them. They walked back to Ray's office in silence and Elvin sent up a thanks that they didn't run into Ming along the way.

"Are you okay?" he asked once they were alone.

Ray was practically vibrating out of his skin as he paced back and forth. He tore off his jacket and loosened the tie around his neck, but even then he looked like he was suffocating.

"This is fucking bullshit!" He ripped off his tie and

whipped it across the room. "Everything I've done is for the good of this fucking company and this is how they repay me?"

Joanna had come down rather hard on Ray, but Elvin wasn't sure he entirely disagreed with her. Making sure their asses were covered was a smart move. But he wasn't about to tell Ray that.

"Should you reach out to your guy? Tell him to call off the meeting?" That would make Elvin feel a whole lot better. Having Joanna and legal counsel take the lead was a lot safer than Ray going rogue on all of them.

"No. I'm not calling off the meeting."

That didn't sound good. Not good at all. "What do you mean?"

"I'm still going to that meeting. I don't care what Joanna thinks she knows, that's the best option we've got." Ray stuck one hand in his hair, the other on his hip, and paused, his mind obviously racing even as his feet stopped moving.

"Best option for what?" Elvin went up to him and took both of Ray's hands in his own. "Best for who? Joanna's already made it clear she's calling the shots around here."

"She's calling the wrong ones," Ray spat out.

Elvin grimaced. He wanted to ask, *according to who*, but that would only set Ray off even more.

Ray wasn't used to being told he wasn't allowed to do something. Elvin could understand that. But it was the way the rest of the world worked, and Ray obviously bristled at the thought. Just another reminder that they came from two very different walks of life. Elvin wasn't sure he'd ever be fully comfortable in Ray's anything-goes lifestyle, and Ray certainly would never accept the limitations of Elvin's life.

He dropped Ray's hands and went to pick up the tie, which had landed on a shelf. "Maybe you should go home for a swim?"

Staying here wasn't going to do Ray any good, and there wasn't much Elvin could do to help him calm down.

Ray took the tie and stuffed it into his pocket. "Yeah, okay. Thank you." He gave Elvin a quick kiss that felt more perfunctory than anything else.

"Yeah, of course."

"You'll stop by later?"

Normally, Elvin wouldn't hesitate to agree. But with all that was happening, he had a sudden bout of doubt. "I think I need to go see my parents, actually."

Ray nodded, but didn't object. Then without a word, he left.

Elvin sighed and collapsed into an armchair. Everything was so fucked up and he didn't know how to fix any of it.

"He left?" Ming poked his head into Ray's office.

"Yeah." Elvin stood and led Ming out, closing Ray's door behind them. Better not to linger in there with Ming in case word got back to Ray.

"Whew, he didn't take that well, did he?" Ming hitched a hip on the edge of Elvin's desk.

He didn't, but Elvin wasn't about to betray Ray like that. "He's fine."

From the look he cast him, Ming didn't believe it for a second.

"Did you need something?" Elvin pushed his chair back to create some space between them. He wasn't in the mood to deal with whatever Ming had in mind.

"Yes, actually. You." Ming smiled smugly.

"Excuse me?" Ray's jealousy flashed through Elvin's mind.

"Look." Ming bent down, elbow on his raised knee. "You're good at your job and Ray?—" He glanced toward the empty office. "He's taking you for granted."

"Excuse me!" Who the fuck did Ming think he was to accuse Ray of something like that?

But Ming raised a hand to stop him. "Hear me out."

Elvin had no interest in hearing anything Ming had to say, but this was his desk and where else was he supposed to go?

"He's got you, what? Picking up dry cleaning, making breakfast for him, booking travel arrangements?" Ming shook his head. "You can do more than that. Don't you want to do more than that?"

Put that way, it did make him sound rather pathetic, but Elvin did more than that. He helped out in other ways that were less obvious—he made sure Ray stayed on track so *he* could do his job. Wasn't that what a good executive assistant did?

"You should come work for me," Ming continued, without waiting for a response. "You'd be doing a lot more than scheduling meetings and making photocopies, I can promise you that. You've got the right look. You're good with people. You're organized and you know the business inside and out. You'd make a first-rate investor relations associate."

Elvin's jaw hung open and he couldn't figure out how to close it. He must have heard wrong. Had Ming just offered him a job? A promotion? No way.

"You don't have to answer me now." Ming stood and adjusted his tie. "Think about it and let me know. The position's yours if you want it."

Elvin watched Ming stroll away like he hadn't dropped the biggest bombshell ever. Go work for Ming? No, he couldn't do that, could he? Ray would be furious, he would never allow it. Besides, Elvin liked his job. He'd been doing it for years and he was good at it.

No. He shook his head, at no one but himself. Leaving Ray to work for Ming was completely and utterly out of the question.

Chapter Twenty-Three

Ray had just stepped into his condo when his phone rang. The call display showed a Hong Kong country code—great.

"Hello?"

"Hello, Raymond?"

He didn't recognize the voice. "Yes?"

"Hello, I am Eliza, Chairman Chao's assistant. I am returning your call to arrange a meeting with Chairman Chao." The woman spoke with a thick Cantonese accent.

Ray switched to Cantonese. "Yes, I believe he's going to be in Toronto soon?"

"Yes, for your grandmother's birthday. There will be a party to celebrate and an invitation was sent to you," Eliza responded in English.

Ray rolled his eyes. If she insisted on English, he'd stick

to English. "I haven't received an invitation." It would be just like his parents to forget to invite him to his grand-mother's birthday party.

"It should arrive in the mail in the next couple days," Eliza insisted.

"Okay, fine." Ray couldn't be bothered to care. "So, the meeting?"

She offered some times, and he agreed to the first one without checking his calendar or with Ming. If Ming was so adamant about meeting with his father, then he could rearrange his schedule to make it.

He hung up with Eliza and tossed his phone onto the couch. It slid across the smooth leather, dropped off the seat and landed with a thud on the rug. Fuck. Was it only this morning when he'd woken up to Elvin wearing his clothes and making breakfast in the kitchen? It felt like a fucking lifetime ago.

Time to swim. Ray grabbed his Speedo, changed and dove in.

By the time he finished his laps and took a shower, it was mid-afternoon. His stomach grumbled, reminding him that he'd skipped lunch, though he didn't have much of an appetite. From the fridge, he grabbed the first box his hand landed on and stuck the whole thing into the mi-crowave to heat.

Joanna had threatened to fire him. He still couldn't be-lieve she'd done that. It wasn't about the job—he didn't need the money—but she'd always been on his side, no matter what kind of obstacles they'd run into in the past. Why had she turned on him all of a sudden?

Okay, yes, the situation with Caron might be a little more serious than anything they'd encountered before. But it was by no means too much for Ray to handle. He knew what he was fucking doing.

The microwave dinged and he yanked the door open to grab the box. Only to drop it on the floor when the container scalded his hand.

"Fuck!"

Bright red curry covered every surface within arm's reach—the counter, cabinet doors, the floor and a good portion of Ray's pants. "God fucking damn it."

Nothing was going his way today.

Ray stripped off his pants and left them on the kitchen floor. He'd deal with it all later. Fuck it. He'd get his housekeeper to come by and clean it up for him. Where the hell was his phone?

He found it on the floor, half tucked underneath the couch. There were dozens of messages waiting for him. He flopped onto the couch and scrolled through them, stopping at the one from Elvin. We need you back in the office.

We. Not just him, but everyone else too. That little word felt like a knife driving into the softest part of his belly. Not even Elvin stood by him on this. He hadn't said as much, but Ray could tell. Elvin had been pushing for them to go to the authorities from the beginning. He must be happy that Joanna and Mike agreed with him.

Then what the fuck did they need Ray for? If they

thought they knew what to do, then they could deal with this shit themselves. He had tried to do his part, his fucking job, but they obviously didn't think he could pull it off.

Fuck it. Elvin was right. He should call off the meeting with the Rousopouloses. If Joanna wanted to meet with them, she could figure out how to make contact without Ray's resources.

His phone rang in his hand. Unknown Caller. Perfect timing.

"Hello?"

"The meeting is set."

Fuck. *Tell the guy to cancel it.* Except his tongue wouldn't cooperate. This wasn't his problem anymore. They'd told him to stand down. But the words wouldn't come.

"Hello?"

"Yeah." Ray ran a hand over his face. "I'm still here."

"Do you want to know the details?"

No. He should say no. He should back away and save himself a whole lot of trouble. "Yeah, give them to me."

Ray didn't want to be here and he wasn't shy about letting everyone know. They were all seated around the small conference table in Joanna's office when he arrived. He took the last empty chair and pushed it away from the table, slumping as far down in it as he could go. Next to him, Elvin cast him a worried look, but Ray didn't bother returning it. As far as he was concerned, Elvin was on their side.

"Nice of you to join us." Joanna's voice held more venom

than humor. "Denise was just giving us her legal opinion of the situation."

Denise Washington looked as composed and unflappable as the last time Ray had seen her. If she'd been shocked by what they were discussing, it wasn't apparent in the way she held herself.

She nodded. "Unfortunately, we don't have many good options. Pleading ignorance would be the most obvious one, and from what I've been told, the closest to the truth. But that in no way protects you from criminal or reputational fallout."

Ray could have told them that without all the billable hours Denise was charging them.

"By pleading ignorance, you mean doing nothing?" Mike clarified.

"That's one way." Denise nodded. "And when the authorities come to you—*if* they come to you—we say we had no idea what was going on."

"That's not plausible," Joanna chimed in. "It's our job to know what's going on. Caron is our portfolio company."

"Or we can be proactive and self-report," Denise continued. "That might win us some goodwill with the prosecutor, and depending on the type of case they build, we could potentially negotiate a deal. But again, there's still a substantial risk that Jade Harbour would be held liable."

Joanna turned in her chair. That option wasn't going to fly with her. Ray had known all of this already. Joanna wasn't one to admit fault or raise the white flag. Joanna wanted to win, rules be damned.

"What are our other options?" Mike asked.

Denise hesitated. "I have to issue a disclaimer that I cannot condone any illegal activity."

Joanna's eyebrow twitched, the only sign that she wasn't impressed with Denise's statement.

"Your ultimate goal in this situation is to dispose of Caron quickly and quietly—"

"And at a profit," Ming cut in.

Denise chuckled. "And at a profit, if possible. Doing so in its current state is too risky. Dispositions draw a lot of attention, people poking around Caron, the chances that the truth comes out is high. The next logical step is to change Caron's current state so that there isn't anything to uncover."

"You mean get rid of the drug smuggling." Mike said what Denise wouldn't.

"That's correct."

"How do we do that?" Ming asked.

"Again, I cannot condone any illegal activity." Denise's words said one thing, but her eyes said something else entirely.

The table fell silent. Ray couldn't help but smirk. This was what he'd been planning on doing from the start, but would anyone listen to him? No. Apparently, they needed to hear the same goddamn thing from someone with a law degree.

From the corner of his eye, he could see Elvin watching him. Did he expect Ray to tell them about the meeting he'd set up with the Rousopouloses? The hell he was going to do that. They hadn't wanted his help then, he wasn't about to offer his help now.

"Guess we're at an impasse, huh?" Ming finally said what was on everyone's mind.

"I do think we have some things we need to discuss." Mike glanced at Joanna, who gave him a single nod. "Thanks for your time, Denise. We'll be in touch once we've determined a way forward."

She pushed her chair back. "I wouldn't wait too long. The sooner we can have a response plan in place, the better. We don't want to be caught unprepared."

"Understood." Mike stood to escort her out, leaving the rest of them sitting in silence.

Joanna was the first to speak. "I gather you have an idea for how to fix this." She stared at Ray.

"Perhaps." If she wanted to know, she'd have to ask directly.

Elvin shifted in his seat and shot a quick look in Ray's direction. It was fleeting, but Ray got the message. Tell Joanna about the meeting. What good would that do? She'd only try to take over, and it was clear that Ray worked better on his own.

"They're of the illegal variety?"

Ray gave her a subtle nod. There was nothing illegal about meeting with crime bosses, it was what they talked about that could get them into trouble. But that was nuance that Ray didn't feel like getting into.

Joanna considered him for a moment, long enough for Ray to wonder whether she'd try to question him again.

But then she pushed back from the table and stood. "We're done. Get out of here." She stalked back to her desk, leaving Ming and Elvin scrambling for the door.

Ray followed more slowly, pausing when he heard her softly call his name.

She was standing next to her desk, arms folded, staring out the window. "I've given you a lot of latitude in the past. You've never failed me before." She glanced at him over her shoulder. "Against my better judgement, perhaps I should trust you this time too."

Joanna was a proud woman and that was about as close to an apology as he was going to get. He'd take it. "I understand."

She turned back to the window and he slipped out.

Elvin was waiting for him a few feet away. "Why didn't you tell them about your guy?"

Ray shook his head and continued toward his own office. Elvin fell into step next to him. When they were safely alone, he answered. "They don't need to know."

"What do you mean?"

"You saw what happened back there." He pointed in the direction of Joanna's office. "They're too scared to do what's needed, but they don't want to suffer the consequences of coming clean. They can't have it both ways. Someone has to make the tough call."

"And that someone is you?" Elvin stood in the middle of his office, feet planted, arms folded across his chest.

Wasn't it obvious? "Yes."

"Why?"

"What?" Ray went to stand opposite him.

"Why does it have to be you who takes the risk? Why can't you let someone else do the dirty work?"

Ray blinked. Because it was his job. Because he was good at it. Because that's what he did—he was the fixer. He fixed problems no matter how big or messy they were. Elvin knew that. "I don't understand."

Elvin searched his face, looking for god knew what. "The meeting's been confirmed, hasn't it?"

He wasn't surprised that Elvin had guessed. He never could keep much from him anyway. "Tomorrow afternoon."

Elvin squeezed his eyes shut and bit his lip. He took a shaky breath like he was barely keeping himself in one piece.

Shit. "Hey." Ray pulled him into a hug, tucking Elvin's head against his shoulder. "I'm going to be okay. Everything's going to be okay. Have I ever let you down before?"

"It's not the same this time." Elvin's voice trembled.

"Maybe not, but it's not entirely different either." Ray ran his hand down Elvin's back in long, slow strokes. "It's a negotiation, and that's what I do best."

Elvin wound his arms around Ray's waist and squeezed. "I'm coming with you."

"Elvin—"

"Don't argue with me."

Ray sighed. He felt like he'd been arguing for ages, and arguing with Elvin was never fun. "Fine. But you're not coming to the meeting. You'll stay at the hotel."

"Ray—"

"That's the compromise."

It took a second for Elvin to snuggle in closer. "Fine."

The turbulence of the day calmed suddenly, and for the first time in hours Ray felt like he could breathe. Fighting with Elvin, even disagreements as small as this, didn't sit well with him. But now that they were on the same page again, Ray felt settled.

Everything would be okay. He'd hammer out an agreement with the Rousopouloses. Elvin would be waiting for him when he finished. And maybe they could celebrate with a night out in Montreal. Ray smiled and planted a kiss on Elvin's head. Yes, everything would be fine.

Chapter Twenty-Four

"Ray, can you..."

"Huh, what?" Ray spun around to pace back toward the other wall of the hotel room.

Elvin got up and stood in his way. "This. Can you stop, please?"

"Stop?"

"Stop pacing. You're driving me up the fucking wall." Elvin took him by the arm and directed him toward an armchair.

Ray sat, but his leg started bouncing involuntarily. He couldn't help it. He had too much pent-up energy with no way to burn it off.

They'd left Toronto early that morning to catch a flight to Montreal, and he'd been cooped up in the airport lounge, then the airplane, and now this room that was much smaller than he'd liked.

They hadn't said much to each other the whole trip. There hadn't been much to say. Elvin wasn't happy about what Ray wanted to do, but refused to let him do it alone. Ray didn't see any other option if Jade Harbour wanted to come out of this in one piece. Despite his disagreements with Joanna, this still felt like the right call.

Ray sat on the edge of the chair. "Promise me you won't leave the room."

They'd been over this before. Elvin had agreed to stay in the hotel room at all times, not even leaving to venture down to the hotel bar.

"I promise."

"Not even downstairs—"

"Because the Rousopouloses have ears everywhere in Montreal, I know." Elvin squatted down in front of him.

"I'll probably be gone for an hour."

"And if you're not back within the hour, I'm calling the police."

"An hour and a half."

Elvin pinned him with a disapproving look. "Don't try to negotiate with me. An hour. Whatever deal you're offering them, it's not going to take longer than that to present it."

"Fine." Ray huffed. "One hour."

"Not a minute more."

Ray nodded. "Not a minute more. Unless I text you that I'm fine, in which case you have to give me more time."

"No. What if they steal your phone to text me with it?"

"What if they want to take me somewhere else to talk?" He didn't like being limited like this. "Travel time could push me over the one-hour limit."

Elvin shook his head like he was reprimanding one of his siblings. "Then don't go with them. You talk at the café or you don't talk at all." He pointed a finger in Ray's face. "Okay?"

Ray wrapped his hand around Elvin's finger. "What if they send a junior guy to the café, someone who was tasked to bring me to the decision-makers? I can't talk to some gofer about something of this scale."

Elvin pulled his hand out and repointed it at him. "I don't care. You do not go anywhere else, because then I won't know where to send the police if something happens."

He was going to be fine, but nothing Ray said seemed to convince Elvin. "I'm not going to end up at the bottom of the Saint Lawrence River."

"You better fucking not because I'm not about to dive in looking for you."

Ray chuckled and after a second Elvin smiled too.

"You know I'm always on your side, right?" Elvin said softly.

Ray's heart did a double thump, like it'd been caught misbehaving. Logically, he knew Elvin was loyal, probably to a fault. But that hadn't stopped Ray from begrudging Elvin yesterday. Sure, he hadn't come right out and accused

Elvin of anything, but he wasn't surprised that Elvin had felt it anyway.

"Yeah, I know." He didn't know where the hell he'd be today if it weren't for Elvin. He always took care of him, anticipated every need, did the dirty work that Ray didn't want to do. He went above and beyond all the time and never voiced a single word of complaint.

He took Elvin's face in both hands and planted a kiss on his lips. It was a hard kiss, as much teeth and nose and forehead as anything else. Elvin kissed him right back, just as hard. If this was the last kiss they would ever share, he wanted the taste and feel of Elvin imprinted on him forever.

"You're amazing." Ray whispered it when they finally came up for air. He chuckled. "Past me was a genius when he hired you."

"Current you is pretty spectacular too."

Ray smoothed out Elvin's hair that he had ruffled. "What did I ever do to deserve you?"

Elvin took one of Ray's hands and planted a kiss on his palm. He folded Ray's fingers over the kiss and held it close.

Why the fuck did this feel like goodbye? He was going to be fine. He'd only be gone for an hour.

"I should go." Ray's voice cracked.

Elvin nodded and stood to give him room. "Be careful."

"I will. I promise." Ray went to the door and looked over his shoulder.

Elvin smiled at him and he smiled back.

Then he opened the door and slipped out.

He'd been adamant about Elvin not coming to Montreal

with him, but in truth, he felt better having Elvin close by. He was stronger and more focused when Elvin was around. And if he ever needed to be on the ball, today was the day.

He made his way out of the hotel and onto the cobbled streets of Old Montreal. The café wasn't far away, which was why Elvin had chosen this area for them to stay in. Ray turned to his right.

He'd come up with a couple options for dealing with the Rousopouloses, each depending on how the conversation went during the meeting. The easiest, but least likely to be accepted, was straight-up monetary compensation. Except Ray doubted that they could ever offer an amount that would cover the loss of a strategic logistical hub.

The other option was an offer to replace Caron with another non–Jade Harbour company. They could work together to find something suitable, with Jade Harbour covering the costs of moving their operation to a new location. Once completed, the two parties could go their separate ways.

The café was tucked away in a side street, with nothing more than a simple sign hanging off the side of the building to indicate it was even there. Ray pushed opened the door and a tiny bell rang overhead. Tables and chairs dotted most of the space, with the service counter at the back. It was small and quaint, nothing to indicate that it might be associated with one of the most notorious crime families in the city.

Ray spotted his contacts immediately—it was hard to miss Olivier's broad shoulders and orange-red hair. His beard, though, had been trimmed close, revealing a square jaw. And he'd traded in the plaid button-down for a silk one. In the midst of ruddy chest hair sat a thick gold chain with a crucifix dangling from the end. Next to him was Gilles, who looked exactly the same as the last time Ray had seen him. With eyeglasses and a sweater vest, he looked every part the accountant, especially next to Olivier's enforcer image.

Ray should have known it would be these two. Though, he never would have guessed that they had enough seniority to act on behalf of the Rousopouloses. Gilles maybe, but not Olivier.

He slipped into the one empty chair at the round table where they were seated. "Hello."

Gilles gave him a polite smile, but Olivier wore his typical scowl.

"Thanks for meeting with me."

Gilles nodded an acknowledgement. Olivier continued with his scowl.

Both men already had empty mugs in front of them, meaning they'd been there for a while.

"I hope I haven't kept you waiting." Nothing wrong with a little small talk before jumping into negotiations with the mob. In fact, it would be rude to take up space in the café without ordering anything, wouldn't it? "I'm going to get myself a coffee. Would either of you like refills?" He pointed to their empty mugs.

Olivier looked more pissed than he usually did, which was quite an achievement. Gilles, on the other hand, looked like he might want to take Ray up on the offer. But a quick glance in Olivier's direction had Gilles shaking his head.

"All right, then. I'll be right back." Ray took his time scanning the menu before making his choice. Then he stood at the counter while the barista made his order. Some might have called this a delay tactic, and they wouldn't be wrong. But keeping Gilles and Olivier waiting gave Ray a greater sense of control.

By the time he made it back to the table, Olivier had had enough. "You wanted to talk, so talk."

Ray took a sip of his cappuccino. Good. But it had nothing on Elvin's. "Mmm, yes, I did. Thanks for coming all the way down to Montreal. I hope you didn't come just for my sake."

He could almost see the smoke coming out of Olivier's ears. God, it was so satisfying getting on the big man's nerves.

"I've asked you here today to talk about the little side hustle you've got going at Caron."

Neither of them reacted.

"As you know—" Ray nodded at Olivier "—we at Jade Harbour are well aware of the movement of illicit goods through Caron's warehouses. What you might not know is that we've also found evidence of money laundering in Caron's bookkeeping."

This brought a pink hue to Gilles' pasty complexion. That was all the confirmation Ray needed that he was on the right track.

"Unfortunately, Caron is a Jade Harbour portfolio company and we have to be able to exit our investment. If your side hustle were to come to light during that process, that would be bad for everyone."

"There's no reason to think it *would* come to light," Gilles said.

Ray nodded. "True. But Caron would be under intense scrutiny. And if I was able to uncover your schemes, do you really think they'll go unnoticed by some entrepreneurial investigative journalist?"

Gilles had the nerve to look a little offended, his chin rising an inch in defiance. But he didn't object again.

"So I think it's in everyone's best interest that your operations be moved to somewhere less scrupulous." Ray left it at that and watched for Gilles' and Olivier's reactions.

Which weren't much.

Gilles spoke first. "I have to say that we don't have much incentive."

Olivier crossed his arms, which Ray took as a no.

"Fair enough. What kind of incentives are you looking for?" Rule number one of negotiating, never be the first person to put a number on the table.

Apparently Gilles knew about that rule too. "What are you willing to offer?"

Ray glanced from Gilles to Olivier. They had the upper hand here and they knew it. And short of threatening to go to the police, Ray couldn't see a way of changing those dynamics.

"A lump-sum payment." He could set the opening bid at what was most advantageous for Jade Harbour.

"How much?" Gilles countered.

That was the question, wasn't it? "We're open to suggestions."

Gilles eyebrows shot up and Olivier snorted.

"I understand Jade Harbour is quite successful, but even then, I'm not sure you'd be able to fully compensate us for our losses." Gilles was diplomatic, Ray had to give him that.

He took a sip of a cappuccino. A straight-up bribe didn't seem like it was going to go anywhere. On to the next strategy. "We can also help you move your operation. Find something equally—or more—suitable for your needs. If you plan on expanding your distribution network, you might require a larger facility."

That seemed to catch Gilles' attention. He cocked his head and nodded slowly before speaking. "Interesting proposition."

Ray pressed forward. "We're obviously well versed in diligencing companies." He chuckled. "Present case excluded. So I'm sure we can find something appropriate."

"Any changes to our current setup will be costly." Gilles clearly thought as quickly as Ray did.

"We can cover those costs."

Gilles nodded again and glanced at Olivier, who had yet to say more than a few words. But if Olivier had any opinions on his bosses' priorities, he wasn't making them known.

"The thing is—" Gilles winced dramatically "—it's not just monetary costs." He paused but Ray didn't take the bait.

Instead, Olivier jumped in, straight to the point. "What's in it for us?"

Ah yes. This proposal would allow the Rousopouloses to break even, but so would not making any changes at all. Ray needed to offer them something better than what they had now.

He wracked his brain for something that would entice the Rousopouloses, something that only Jade Harbour could give them.

"There is one more option." A fuzzy idea began forming in Ray's mind. The Rousopouloses wanted to make money, right? Well, Jade Harbour made a lot of money for their investors. What if...

"Yes?" Gilles looked skeptical, like Ray couldn't possibly have anything else of value to offer.

"We'll be starting a new round of fundraising soon." Ray's heart thumped so hard, his chest hurt. Was he really going to do this?

But Gilles' eyes brightened. He'd caught the Frenchman's interest. He couldn't stop now.

"*If* we can get Caron squared away, we *might* be able to reserve a small portion of the next fund for a strategic partner." *Come on...take the bait.*

Gilles grinned, an expression with a touch of viciousness. "That's a very interesting proposition."

Yes! That's it! Ray's heart picked up speed, circulating a sense of euphoria that was impossible to control. "Of course, we would need assurances that funds cannot be traced back to illicit sources. Government regulations and all that."

"Of course." Gilles still wore that grin and Ray found himself returning it.

This could actually work!

A sudden scrape of chair against floor made Ray nearly jump out of his seat. But it was only Olivier pushing away from the table. He stood without ceremony. "We're done here."

Gilles looked up at him, just as surprised as Ray felt, but still, he rose. Ray followed.

"Well, it was great chatting with you." He held out a hand, which Gilles accepted, but Olivier did not.

Instead, the big man headed straight for the door without even a goodbye.

"Please excuse my colleague," Gilles whispered. "He's... more of a doer than a talker."

Ray nodded, as the door swung closed behind Olivier. "I can see that."

"Yes, well, we will be in touch." He nodded once more before leaving.

Ray dropped back into his chair, his heart racing like he'd just sprinted to the pool wall. His fingers tingled, his skin was covered in goose bumps. He hadn't felt so exhilarated in a long time. Ray tried to finish off his cappuccino, but his hand shook so much, he put the cup back down. With his palms flat on the table, he took a deep breath. Then another. Than another until finally the adrenaline died down to a manageable level.

He'd done it. He'd actually fucking done it.

Wait—what exactly had he done? Offered to let a criminal organization invest in Jade Harbour? That wasn't even something he was authorized to do. Only Joanna could make a call like that, and the likelihood of her agreeing to his hare-brained, spur of the moment outburst was slim to none.

Even if she did somehow miraculously agree, they'd have to set up at least a dozen shell companies to hide the true source of the funds. And if government authorities ever found out they were taking drug money from the mob, Jade Harbour would be in so much fucking shit—to put it nicely. Hell, they'd be in violation of so many securities laws that Joanna would have to close up shop. They'd be fined until kingdom come and some of them might even end up in prison.

But they were in an impossible situation. If the Rousopouloses weren't amenable to anything else, what real choice did they have? He couldn't very well go back to Joanna empty handed.

No. This was risky, sure, but it was the best option they had—that Ray had. Besides, he was in too far. He couldn't turn back now even if he wanted to.

Ray stood, feeling like a different person than who he'd been when he'd walked into the café. Everything would work out in the end, he was sure of it. Nothing was set in stone yet. There was still time to find a way out.

Out on the street, he checked the time and sent a quick

message to Elvin letting him know he was alive and heading back to the hotel.

Elvin responded immediately.

Thank god. I'm waiting.

He set off, every step lighter and bouncier than the last. It really was a genius move, coming up with an offer like that on the fly. Joanna might be pissed when she found out, but she'd come around. The Rousopouloses had deep pockets and Jade Harbour was always looking for well-resourced investors. This could be a win-win situation!

He slipped his hands in his pants pockets and lifted his chin an inch. The air smelled of freshly baked bread and pigeons chirped in the background. The sky could not have been more blue.

The closer he got to the hotel, the more he was convinced that this was the best outcome for everyone involved. Ray swaggered the rest of the way back and took the stairs two steps at a time to Elvin waiting in their room.

Chapter Twenty-Five

Elvin pulled Ray into the hotel room and ran his hands over him. "You're okay? How did it go? What happened?"

Ray laughed and clasped Elvin's hands together. "I'm fine. Everything went great. Nothing to worry about."

"Worrying is my default state." If only Ray had seen him pacing a trail through the carpet, wringing his hands and nearly pulling out his hair, he wouldn't be so quick to dismiss Elvin.

"I know. But it's done and I'm alive." Ray flung himself onto the bed and stretched out. He held out a hand to Elvin. "Come here."

Elvin went, lying down next to him, head pillowed on Ray's shoulder, hand on Ray's chest. He could feel the beat of Ray's heart, thumping a little faster than normal, and a slight tremor in Ray's limbs. Ray's lips were curled into a self-satisfied grin.

He was enjoying this, Elvin realized. The bastard was having fun. He propped himself up on an elbow and poked Ray in the chest. "Tell me what happened," Elvin demanded again. He wanted every detail.

"It was Olivier and Gilles."

"What? Wait, who's Gilles?"

"Gilles is the CEO. Actually, more of an accountant than CEO, but that makes more sense now than it did when I first met him." He yawned and stretched, in the process rubbing his long body against Elvin's. His hand settled low on Elvin's hip, his fingers finding all the little dips and sensitive spots.

"Ray," Elvin warned. He wanted to know about the meeting and Ray was distracting him.

"Hmm?" Ray rolled so they were both on their sides, facing each other. He lifted one leg and hooked it around the back of Elvin's thighs, trapping them together.

"The meeting." The words came out more breathy than Elvin had anticipated. But Ray's flat stomach was pressed against his own, and the growing bulge in between Ray's legs was impossible to ignore.

"Oh, yes. Gilles. It was him and Olivier, which was kind of surprising. I was expecting more senior people." He bent his head to nibble on Elvin's neck.

Elvin sucked in a breath as shivers shot down his spine. The meeting. He needed to focus on the meeting.

"I have to say, Gilles is pretty shrewd. Didn't reveal his

hand at all." Ray snuck one hand into Elvin's pants and gave his ass a squeeze.

Elvin cried out as pleasure ran from his ass up to his neck and back again. Ray was doing this on purpose, the bastard, trying to avoid his questions. Well, Elvin wouldn't be so easily put off. He gave Ray a half-hearted push. "Ray." He meant it as an admonishment, but it came out as a plea.

Ray's lips curled into a sinful grin and he gave Elvin a nip on the chin. "Do you want to hear what happened? Or do you want to fuck?"

The last word, said slowly and in a whisper, rolled through Elvin like a speeding train. He dug his fingers into Ray's defined chest muscles and his hips bucked against Ray's.

Fuck. He wanted to fuck. They could get to the rest of the details later.

Elvin let Ray capture his mouth in a searing kiss, tongue twirling and teeth sliding across wet lips. Kissing Ray was an aphrodisiac, ramping up Elvin's desire in ways he'd never experienced before. Who knew it could be so all powerful and consuming?

Ray flipped them so that Elvin was on his back and Ray above him. He slid his hands under Elvin's shirt, trailing two tickling paths up to Elvin's nipples. He pinched them, bringing Elvin off the bed as he arched. Ray licked his way down Elvin's throat, sucking at the delicate skin before soothing it with a lap of his tongue.

His neck, his nipples, his dick, the flurry of sensation up and down his body was confusing and intoxicating at the same time. Elvin didn't know what he wanted more. All he could do was cling to Ray and beg for something he couldn't put a name to. "Please, Ray. Oh, god."

"Please what?" Ray ran his teeth lightly across Elvin's collarbone. "What do you want?"

The devious asshole. He knew full well that Elvin didn't know what he wanted. Frustration forced a growl from Elvin as he grasped the back of Ray's neck and pulled him up for a kiss. Elvin plunged his tongue inside Ray's mouth, seeking the source of that sweet, sweet pleasure. He bucked his hips against Ray's, the friction shooting through him as his dick hardened.

"Please, Ray. Fuck me."

Ray froze. Elvin whined. Why had he stopped?

Ray raised himself up onto his elbows. "Are you sure?" His hair was disheveled, pupils dilated, lips red and swollen. But there was clear concern in his voice.

"Yes, Ray, please." He tried to pull Ray down for another kiss.

"Wait, Elvin." Ray held him still with one hand on his cheek. "Do you know what you're asking for?"

Elvin blinked, slowly sobering to what Ray was asking him. *Did* he know what he was asking for? Yes, he did. He wanted it. Now. With Ray.

"I do."

"Anal sex." Ray enunciated each syllable. "With you on the bottom." He said it so matter-of-factly that it effectively killed the mood.

"Um, yes?" Did Ray *not* want to do that? Was it wrong or inappropriate somehow? "Is that okay?"

Ray flung his head back and laughed out loud. "Of course it is. I just wanted to make sure. It's a big step and I don't want to pressure you into something you're not ready for."

Elvin gazed into Ray's eyes, his heart bursting at the care Ray showed him. There was no doubt in his mind that he wanted to do this with Ray, and no one else but Ray. "I'm ready."

Ray blinked and he sucked in a sharp breath. "Okay. In that case…" He rolled off Elvin and straight off the bed.

"Hey, where are you going?" Elvin sat up. This felt like the opposite of getting naked and fucking.

"I didn't bring supplies!" Ray scrambled for the shoes he'd toed off when he got back.

Supplies? Elvin's half-addled brain took a second to catch up. "Don't you carry them with you?" With Ray's sexual history, he would have expected Ray to keep a stash of condoms in his wallet.

Ray paused in his search of the room. "No, I don't. Who do you think I am?"

Elvin raised one eyebrow and cocked his head. "Eh…"

"Never mind. Don't answer that." He grabbed his phone and wallet from the nightstand and went to the door. Pointing back at Elvin, he said, "Don't move. I'll be right back."

Then he slipped out and shut the door behind him.

Elvin huffed and plopped back on the bed. So much for the heat of the moment. Who knew sex required so much preplanning? Wait a minute... Elvin sat up again. Should *he* be preparing for this too? It couldn't hurt, right?

He hopped off the bed and stripped on his way to the bathroom. He wasn't sure exactly how to do this, but it couldn't be that hard. He turned on the shower and stepped in to clean himself up.

By the time Ray got back, Elvin had toweled himself off and was back on the bed, naked. Ray's cheeks were flushed and he was breathing hard, like he'd run the entire way. In his hand, he clutched a small plastic bag.

"Got everything?" Elvin asked.

"Mmm-hmm." Ray nodded as he approached, eyes glued to Elvin's body. Everywhere his gaze landed, Elvin's skin heated, until he was breathing hard too. "You took a shower?"

"Mmm-hmm."

Ray swallowed visibly. He put the bag on the nightstand and sat on the bed. He reached out with one hand, hovering it right above Elvin's chest. "God, you're beautiful."

Elvin could say the same thing about him. He took Ray's hand and brought it up to kiss his palm.

"Damn, I'm lucky."

Elvin's heart skipped a beat. "I'm the lucky one." He pulled Ray down to him, still fully clothed, to plant a kiss on his mouth. Slow and leisurely, it stirred the embers of passion that had been left glowing while Ray was gone.

Ray gently broke the kiss and flipped them over so he was on his back with Elvin on top of him. "Undress me?"

he asked, and the two simple words sent a surge of power through Elvin.

He'd done it before, but it felt different this time. Like Ray was a gift who was all his to unwrap. He started with the buttons down the front of Ray's shirt, bending forward to taste every inch of skin he revealed. Elvin lapped at Ray's nipples, luxuriating in how they hardened into pebbles under his ministrations. Then the subtle ridges of Ray's stomach and the creases right above each hip. Every spot tasted delicious, warm, salty, heady.

Elvin ran a finger along Ray's belt and slowly pulled the end through the metal loop. There was something about undoing another man's belt that hit Elvin deep in the spot where his desires usually hid. The strip of leather, the metal warmed by proximity to skin, wrapped tightly around the narrow waist of a man, so close to the most vulnerable parts of him. Elvin tugged and Ray's hips came off the bed. Ray sucked in a breath and let it out in a series of shudders. A surge of pure power rushed through Elvin.

He unbuckled Ray's belt, but left it in the belt loops, going instead for the clasp on his pants. He inched the zipper down and pried apart the two sides to reveal black underwear, pulled taut over a hard and bulging cock.

Then Elvin sat back to admire his handiwork. Wrapped in tight cotton, Ray's cock was framed by two rows of zipper teeth and the leather and buckle of his belt. It was the treasure hidden securely behind a vault and Elvin alone had the combination to open it.

He reached out to pull the waistband of Ray's underwear down. Ray's cock popped out, veins engorged and oozing pre-come, his balls already high and tight. Elvin hooked the band under Ray's balls and ran his finger lightly up Ray's length.

It was scalding to the touch. And soon it would be inside him. Elvin's asshole clenched in anticipation.

"Fuck," Ray bit out through a tight jaw. His hands were fisting in the sheets and he looked like he was being unmercifully tortured.

Elvin grinned. To think, this inexperienced virgin holding the city's most eligible bachelor captive with a simple touch. What would happen if he went a step further? Elvin wrapped his fingers around Ray's dick and gave it an experimental stroke.

Ray cried out, his stomach muscles engaging. "Fuck."

"You okay?" Elvin chuckled.

"Mmm-hmm."

Elvin stroked Ray's dick again and, thrillingly, got the same response.

"Fuck, Elvin. I'm not going to last long if you keep that up."

"Hmm, we wouldn't want that, would we?"

Ray made an incomprehensible sound while taking rapid breaths though his teeth. Elvin gave Ray's dick one last squeeze before letting go and reaching for the bag of supplies. He dumped the contents out on the bed to find a bag of condoms and a bottle of water-based lube.

He opened the bottle and squirted some onto his hand. It was a cold, slippery gel and he rubbed it between his fingers until they were well coated. Then he reached for Ray's cock again.

"Oh, dear fucking god." Ray squeezed his eyes shut as Elvin glided his hand up and down, twisting as he went. He could see how lube made a hand job that much easier and from Ray's reaction, a whole lot more pleasurable too.

But before he got far along, Ray grabbed his wrist and held him still. "Elvin, you're killing me." His chest rose and fell as he took several deep breaths. When he finally let Elvin go, he sat up to take his shirt off.

"No." Elvin pushed him back down. "Keep your clothes on."

Ray's eyes glazed over and his mouth hung open. "What?"

Elvin leaned forward and repeated himself into Ray's ear. "Keep. Your. Clothes. On."

Ray sucked in another breath. "Elvin, Jesus Christ, motherfucking god."

Elvin grinned. He loved seeing Ray like this, strung out and barely hanging on, and knowing that he was the one responsible for it. Elvin lifted one leg and straddled Ray. He gave Ray's pants and underwear a little tug, but otherwise left them snug around Ray's hips.

"Fuck." Ray ran his hands up and down Elvin's thighs, reaching around to tickle those sensitive strips of skin where his glutes met his hamstrings. "You're so fucking beautiful."

Elvin ducked his head and reached for the packet of condoms. He managed to pull one free but when he went to put it on Ray, he faltered. The last time he'd tried to put a condom on a penis was in high school sex ed. And that had been a banana.

"Um…"

"Here, let me." Ray took it from him and deftly rolled it on.

Then Elvin rose to his knees and shuffled forward to position himself on top of Ray.

"Wait." Ray stopped him with a frown. "You're not prepped."

Elvin bit his lip and flushed at the thought of what he'd done in the shower. "Actually, I am."

"Are you sure?" A crease formed on Ray's brow.

"Probably not as much as I could be," Elvin admitted. After all, he hadn't been entirely sure what he was doing. But he'd felt pretty good about it, and his asshole definitely felt…different.

Ray narrowed his eyes in suspicion. "Let me check."

Elvin forgot to breathe. Check? Did that mean? Ray's fingers? In his ass?

Of course, his own fingers had been in there not long ago, but this was different. And sexy and mind-blowing and…

Elvin shut his eyes as Ray lubed up his fingers and reached between his legs. The touch was soft at first, a single finger right behind his balls, searching and probing until it found the wrinkly skin of Elvin's hole. Elvin braced himself with hands on Ray's thighs as that single finger pressed, firm and insistent, seeking entrance into his body.

"Push out." Ray had sat up to give himself better access, and he whispered against Elvin's chest.

Elvin did as he was told and the finger slid in—all the way in.

"Ahhhh." There was a finger in his ass. Ray's finger was in his ass. Then Ray started moving, pulling out and pushing in, setting off sparks of pleasure that radiated through Elvin's body. God, if this was what a finger felt like, what would Ray's cock do to him?

Then there was more pressure as Ray inserted a second finger. Stretch and fullness and the need for more. Elvin latched onto Ray's shoulder and dug his fingernails in. "Ray, please."

Ray lifted his chin and Elvin bent down to kiss him. This phenomenal man, gorgeous, genius, caring, was showing him pleasure beyond reason.

That hour sitting alone in the hotel room while Ray embarked on such a dangerous venture had been the most terrifying of Elvin's life. Ray had repeatedly assured him that everything would be fine, but Elvin couldn't help dwelling on all the worst-case scenarios his imagination concocted. What would he do if Ray didn't come back? How would he be able to go on?

Elvin had silently loved this man for so long, hiding his true emotions behind a veil of duty and obligation. He might have been able to ignore his feelings before, but those days were long gone. Love like he didn't understand bubbled up from the deepest part of him, overwhelmed him, consumed him.

He needed Ray like he needed oxygen. He couldn't fathom a life without him. No matter what happened with this Caron business, or if Ray grew tired of him down the line, Elvin would always be devoted to him. It was a promise he made to himself.

Ray slowly extricated his fingers from Elvin's body and lay back down on the bed. On shaky limbs, Elvin positioned himself and took Ray's cock in hand.

"Ready?" Ray held on to Elvin's hips and rubbed tiny circles on Elvin's skin with his thumbs.

Elvin nodded. "Ready."

Chapter Twenty-Six

At first nothing happened. But Elvin was persistent and Ray willed himself to stay still.

Then all of a sudden, Elvin's body gave way and the head of Ray's cock popped inside. It sent shock waves through Ray. He dug his fingers into Elvin's hips and forced himself to keep his eyes open. The view above him was better than anything he could have imagined and he didn't want to miss a single second of it. Elvin's face was the epitome of ecstasy. Furrowed brow, mouth open, eyes wild with want. An angel hovered above him and Ray would take every blessing he offered.

"Breathe," Ray whispered after the initial shock died down to rolling waves of sensation.

Elvin sucked in a breath and lowered himself an inch.

More shocks of pleasure that bordered on pain. Ray had experimented with some pretty out-there stuff in the sex world, but nothing had ever been as erotic as this and his dick had never felt as tortured as it did now. Another inch and another shock, again and again until Elvin was seated in his lap.

They paused to catch their breath. But really, how was Ray supposed to breathe when his cock was being held in bondage by Elvin's ass? So tight and hot that it was a wonder it remained attached to his body.

"Oh fuck, Elvin, baby." Ray wasn't even sure what he was saying. "God, you feel so good. So fucking good. Jesus Christ." Words poured out of him, overflowing from the emotions filling the hollowness he carried inside. Elvin was everything he needed, everything he wanted. Elvin made him complete.

With his head thrown back, and steadying himself with hands on Ray's chest, Elvin rocked back and forth like he'd been doing this for years. He rose to his knees until Ray almost slid out of him, then ground himself into Ray's groin, burying him deep. Over and over, Elvin moved like he was dancing to a silent rhythm that thrummed through their connection.

Sex had never felt this way before. This all-consuming, this transcendent. They weren't merely communing with their bodies; it felt like Ray's very soul was being lifted out of him to be knitted with Elvin's. It shouldn't be possible for sex to feel this good, to feel so completely satisfying.

Who knew how long they went on for. All Ray knew

was it wasn't long enough. Soon, Elvin's movements became more jerky, more urgent. He clamped down around Ray and brought one hand to his dick. Creamy white come spewed across Ray's chest, hot and wet, filling the air with the pungent smell of sex.

It triggered Ray's own orgasm, pulsing through him as if his very essence was being emptied through his cock. He was no more, he had nothing of himself left. Everything he was and everything he had was Elvin's now, and Ray wouldn't have it any other way.

As Elvin came down from his orgasmic high, Ray gathered him close. Sticky chest against sticky chest. Ray's clothes soaked through with sweat.

He loved Elvin. That much was clear. More than a cherished colleague or a close friend. He loved Elvin and he was in love with Elvin and he had no idea when or how that had happened.

Ray pressed a kiss to Elvin's temple and squeezed his eyes shut. Elvin deserved the best the world had to offer and he was going to give it to him.

Elvin stirred against his chest.

"You okay?" Ray asked, running his hands up and down Elvin's back.

"Mmm-hmm." Elvin yawned. "You still need to tell me about the meeting."

"You were saying something about Gilles before we, uh, got distracted," Elvin said as he set the tray of room service down on the coffee table.

"I was?" Ray couldn't remember much from before the orgasm that changed his life.

"Yes, something about Gilles making sense." Elvin stood in the fuzzy white hotel bathrobe, hands plunged into the deep pockets.

Hmm, he'd have to get one of those for home. Maybe he'd institute a rule that Elvin wasn't allowed to wear anything but the bathrobe when he was over. Ray gave his wet hair one last tousle and tossed the towel on the floor.

"You're supposed to hang those up again." Elvin looked pointedly at him.

"They have to wash them anyway. They're not going to leave used towels for the next guest." But he still bent down and picked the towel up. Putting on his own matching bathrobe, Ray went to Elvin and pulled him into his arms. "You're wonderful, you know that?"

Elvin chuckled and leaned in for a kiss.

Ray obliged, kissing Elvin like he was drinking from the fountain of youth. By the time he let go, they were both breathless and Ray's cock was raring to go again.

But Elvin pushed him toward the couch and handed him a plate. They'd stayed in bed until both of their stomachs grumbled with complaint, but neither of them were interested in venturing out of their room. So they'd ordered two types of burgers and asked the kitchen to cut the burgers in half. Elvin settled next to Ray and they made the exchange. Half of Ray's blue cheese and mushrooms for half of Elvin's French onion and beer.

Ray took a bite and sighed at the pungent taste of cheese

on his tongue. So good with the medium-rare patty and perfectly toasted bun.

On the coffee table, Elvin's phone started buzzing so fast it almost fell onto the floor. He grabbed it. "It's Janice. Sorry, I'll send it to voicemail."

"No, go ahead and answer it." Ray bit into his burger again. It'd give him a chance to enjoy his meal.

Elvin cast him an apologetic smile and brought the phone to his ear. "Janice? What's wrong?" Elvin squinted as a high-pitched voice rambled on the line, loud enough that Ray could hear the odd word.

Elvin dropped his head into his hands. "Okay, okay, calm down. I'll figure something out. Just tell him it's a surprise or something." A moment later, he hung up. "Sorry about that."

"What did Janice want?" Ray dipped a fry in some sriracha mayonnaise and popped it into his mouth.

"It's Eason. His birthday was last week and he's not happy with the cake my parents got him." Elvin put his phone down and grabbed his burger.

"Oh? What was wrong with it?"

Elvin swallowed the huge bite he'd taken. "Nothing. But he wanted a big-ass party to go along with it. We don't really do parties in my family. We never have. My parents don't have time to plan that kind of thing." Elvin sighed. "Eason does this every year."

Ray felt for the little guy. When he was young, his birthday parties were both out of this world and not at all what he wanted. His parents spent a shit ton of money to send

him and some friends to amusement parks or hired enter-
tainment staff. But once he'd gotten old enough to understand what was going on, those "parties" had been more
of a chore than anything else.

"Are you going to plan one for him?" Ray asked.

Elvin shrugged. "I think I'll have to do something. He's
throwing temper tantrums and generally being a terror
around the house. I don't think anything else is going to
get him to calm down. Got any ideas?" Elvin chuckled as
he polished off one half of a burger.

Ray cocked his head as an idea came to him. "Why don't
you all come over to my place? We can throw him a pool
party." Now that he'd said it out loud, it made so much
sense. Here he was, one person with a huge pool. Meanwhile, the Gohs had seven people squeezed into a single
house. The juxtaposition was so stark it was comical. He
should have had them over long ago.

"What?" Elvin laughed like Ray was joking. "No.
Thanks, but no."

"Why not?" The more he thought about it, the more he
liked the idea. He swam regularly, sure, but he hardly ever
used the hot tub or the combined sauna and steam room.
"I'll get some pool toys and order food. All you have to do
is show up. It won't cost your parents a thing."

Elvin looked dumbfounded. "Seriously?"

Ray leaned over for a quick kiss. "Seriously. It'll be
great!"

Still, Elvin shook his head. "If we do this, we'll pay for
it. It's only fair."

"No, absolutely not." The very suggestion was offensive. "I'm not taking a penny from you or your parents. Who do you think I am?"

"Ray, no. It's too much!"

Ray put an arm on Elvin's shoulder. "Elvin, it's not too much, not by a long shot." Ray had promised himself that he'd give Elvin the best the world had to offer and that extended to Elvin's family too. He could take care of all of them and damn it, that's what he was going to do.

Elvin's shoulder relaxed under his hand and Ray knew he'd won. "If you're sure…"

"I'm sure."

"Okay, fine. Thank you." Elvin picked up the other half burger and jabbed Ray in the side in one swift movement. "Don't think I've forgotten about the meeting."

Ray groaned. Fuck. He'd almost gotten away with it.

"Gilles. Tell me. Now." Elvin bit into his burger.

"Right." Ray put his burger down and thought back to the conversation earlier that day. Olivier's permanent scowl. Gilles' quiet shrewdness. They'd come knowing they had the upper hand and not once had they shown their cards.

Hell, Gilles had had Ray fooled from the very beginning when they'd met at Caron's offices in Montreal weeks ago. He'd played into a stereotype and Ray hadn't even thought to question it. "The first time I met him, it struck me as odd that Caron would have an accountant at the helm. That's what I thought Gilles was, a glorified accountant, not a management executive. I didn't think to dig into him; he seemed harmless."

"But?" Elvin had put down his burger too.

"Now we know that he's a plant put there by the Rousopouloses. They don't need someone to run the business. They need someone to falsify their books."

"Is he going to be a problem?"

Ray shrugged. "I don't know." One thing was for sure: Gilles knew what he was doing. Whether that translated into something beneficial for Ray, only time could tell.

"So what did you talk about?"

Ray looked at Elvin, who stared back at him expectantly. Ray wanted to tell him, to share all the nitty-gritty details and show off the extent to which he'd go to protect Jade Harbour. But something warned him that Elvin wouldn't take it quite the way Ray wanted him to.

"Well?"

"I don't think I should tell you."

"Why not? And don't say plausible deniability. That wasn't good enough for Joanna and it won't be good enough for me."

Ray chuckled. That was exactly the excuse he was going to use. That or something similar, to justify not telling Elvin the truth. But even as he searched for another lie, the prospect of misleading Elvin left a rock in the pit of his stomach.

"Come on, Ray." Elvin gave him another elbow jab. "Why won't you tell me?"

"Because..." Ray braced himself. "I don't think you'll approve."

Elvin's carefree expression faded to something somber. "Why wouldn't I approve? What did you do?"

Ray shook his head. He couldn't tell Elvin. Not now. Not after he'd made that promise to himself to give Elvin the best the world had to offer. Telling him now would only expose him to undue risks. He'd be complicit, an accomplice. Ray couldn't let that happen.

"Ray." Elvin set his plate on the coffee table and shifted away from him on the couch. "What did you do?" There was a note of fear in Elvin's voice, a hint of disbelief.

"Nothing!" Ray set his plate aside too and stood to shake off the unease that found its way onto his shoulders. "You don't have to worry about it."

"But I am worried about it! And I will continue worrying about it until you tell me what's going on."

Ray paced away, running his fingers through his hair. He couldn't protect Elvin if he insisted on knowing all the gruesome details.

"Ray. Please." Elvin sat sideways on the couch, one hand gripping the back cushions so hard his knuckles were a little white. His eyes were pleading, his voice insistent. "Whatever it is, let me do this with you."

Ray swallowed. He didn't want to tell Elvin and yet he did. How the hell was it possible to feel two completely contradictory emotions and have no idea which one he should follow? He shook his head, squeezed his eyes shut and blurted it out. "I told them they could invest in Jade Harbour."

Silence.

So quiet Ray could hear the blood rushing past his ears. A steady litany of all the ways his little stunt could go wrong.

"Isn't that illegal?" Elvin asked quietly.

Committing Jade Harbour to taking drug money from a criminal organization? Especially since he had zero authority to make such an offer. If it wasn't fucking illegal, it was certainly a fire-able offense.

But it wouldn't have to come to that. He could fix things before it did. "We'll be fine as long as the authorities don't find out."

Elvin's eyebrows shot up. "You didn't just say that. Of course the authorities are going to find out!"

"Not necessarily. Who's going to tell them?"

Elvin's jaw dropped. "Have you forgotten that we're subject to annual government audits?"

He hadn't, but that was far from a deal breaker. There were tons of loopholes they could exploit. "If we set up the accounting right, they won't find it in their audits."

"Like we didn't find sketchy accounting in Caron's books?" Elvin massaged his temple. "I can't believe we're having this conversation."

He *knew* Elvin wouldn't approve. But a hypothetical government auditor finding fraud in a hypothetical audit was so far from where they were at. Ray would deal with that if and when the time came. Right now, he had to find a way to get the Rousopouloses to cooperate, and he'd done what he'd had to do to achieve the best outcome possible. Why couldn't Elvin understand that?

"I need some air." Elvin started pulling on clothes.

"What are you doing?" The rock in Ray's stomach cracked, letting out wisps of panic.

Elvin shrugged out of the bathrobe and pulled on a T-shirt. "I'm going for a walk. I can't be here right now."

"Wait. Don't go." Ray planted his feet in front of the door. He had to explain. He had to get Elvin to see things from his perspective.

But Elvin wouldn't even meet his gaze. "Let me through."

"No."

Elvin sighed heavily. "Ray, please. I won't be gone long. I just need to clear my head. A couple times around the block and I'll be back."

Ray took hold of Elvin's shoulders. He was so tempted to tie Elvin up and keep him close. He'd just found him, Ray couldn't risk losing him now. "You promise?"

"I promise."

Against his better judgement, Ray stepped aside and let Elvin go.

Chapter Twenty-Seven

Ming was going to owe him. Big time. Ray stood by the window in the library of his grandmother's house, working his way through his second whiskey in half an hour. He gazed out onto the back lawn, a massive rolling green pasture that extended to the row of trees in the distance. From his vantage point, he could see the man-made pond, complete with a waterfall and mini lazy river. Next to it was a bar and an industrial-sized barbecue. He doubted his grandmother ever used it.

He'd arrived an hour late to the party and had still managed to get there before his parents. They were yet to be seen. Plenty of other people were there, though. Some of them were MaaMaa's mahjong friends, a group of seniors that got together on a weekly basis to play mahjong. Others were business associates of Ray's father. The rest? Ray had no clue.

The only people he knew were a couple cousins who had made the trip to Toronto for the occasion. But even then, he wasn't close enough to them to actually want to talk to them.

He'd tried convincing Elvin to come with him, but that had gone as well as trying to boil an egg in ice water.

He'd never forget the look on Elvin's face when he'd left their hotel room. Sadness, anger and, most of all, disappointment. Like Ray was a stranger. Like all of their years together and the intimacy they'd shared meant nothing. The remainder of their time in Montreal had been downright painful.

Elvin had come back from his walk a different person. He had put on a mask that Ray had never seen before—cool, calm and polite to a fault. Any attempt Ray made to restart their conversation was met by a firm rebuttal. Then Elvin had pleaded a headache and gone to bed early.

Ray didn't sleep a wink that night. He doubted Elvin had either.

Since then, they'd been walking on eggshells around each other. Elvin still came over first thing in the morning. Ray still went to work like nothing had happened. But their easy comradery was gone, never mind the romantic relationship they'd embarked on.

If Elvin was anyone else, Ray would've said his goodbyes and moved on already. But this was Elvin, and Ray wasn't giving up. Elvin just needed time to process and get over things. He'd come around. He had to.

The chatter outside the library rose in volume, which meant his parents must have arrived. Despite not being the guest of honor, his father always managed to be the center of attention.

Ray went out to the hallway and hung back as his parents made the rounds. They stopped to shake hands and chat with everyone there. A young woman shadowed them, whispering to his father when they moved from one guest to the next. Ray shook his head. His father had someone reminding him who the fuck he was talking to.

The woman didn't whisper anything when his parents got to him. At least they hadn't forgotten who he was. "Father, Mother." Ray bowed slightly to show respect.

"Raymond, you came." His father sounded neither happy to see him nor sad. It was merely a statement of fact.

"Yes, I received the invitation." It showed up the day after his call with Eliza, his father's assistant.

"Good." His mother put a soft hand on his elbow. "I'm sure your grandmother is very glad to see you."

They moved on to the next guest before he could respond. Well, that was half of his duty done. He tossed back the remainder of his drink and made his way to the bar.

"Another whiskey, please?" Ray set his empty glass down and the bartender exchanged it for a clean one.

"Coming right up." The guy was older than Ray and already graying at the temples. He looked like he worked out and managed to fill his bartending uniform enough for Ray to notice.

"What's your name?" The question slipped out without Ray really thinking about it.

The man met his gaze with soft brown eyes. One corner of his mouth curled like he knew exactly what Ray was asking. "I'm Bradley. And you are?"

"Ray."

Bradley nodded as he put the whiskey bottle back on the shelf. "Grandson, right?"

"How did you know?"

"People talk. Bartenders listen."

Ray chuckled for the first time in days. It felt good. Casual banter. Zero expectations. It would take absolutely nothing for him to get Bradley's number and arrange to meet him after the party. Not too long ago, he wouldn't have given a second thought to bringing Bradley home with him for the night. But now, the prospect held no appeal.

Ray picked up his drink and raised it in salute. "Thanks, Bradley. I'll be sure to remember that."

He walked away, weaving through the guests and sipping on his whiskey. He didn't feel a single ounce of regret. With Elvin, Ray had experienced a connection the likes of which Bradley could never live up to. He just needed to find a way to get Elvin to forgive him.

"Raymond!" His grandmother waved at him from her chair. Standing next to her was a slightly younger woman with a head of white hair tied back in a severe bun.

"MaaMaa." Ray bent down to give her a quick hug. She

was the only family member he ever remembered hugging when he was a child. Even then, they were short and to the point rather than a source of comfort. He turned to the other woman. "Auntie Sherry."

Auntie Sherry had been MaaMaa's companion for as long as Ray could remember. He didn't know the full extent of their relationship, but he had his suspicions. It wasn't something the family talked about and it wasn't something that was appropriate to ask.

Auntie Sherry patted his cheek. "Look at you. More and more handsome every time I see you."

Ray laughed politely. "No, no. I still look the same."

"Raymond, you must be working too hard." MaaMaa scowled. "Otherwise you would come see me more often."

She had a point. Living in King City, MaaMaa was only an hour north of Toronto. Yet Ray only managed to visit her a handful of times a year. "Sorry, I'm always so busy."

"Aiya, I know. You're just like your father. Always working, working, working." MaaMaa shook her head. "It's about time you started a family."

Ray took a long sip of his whiskey. The same old thing, every time. No wonder he didn't come by more often.

"MaaMaa." Auntie Sherry called her mother in Cantonese as an endearment. "Don't start on that again. Raymond will start a family when he's ready." She winked at him. "Or maybe no children at all. I have no children and I'm very happy."

MaaMaa cast a sidelong look at Auntie Sherry. "That's

because you spent all your time raising my children and grandchildren."

Auntie Sherry scoffed in mock offense. "As if I had a choice."

Ray glanced back and forth between them. They'd always had this kind of banter that was somehow familiar and heartwarming. It took a moment for him to place it and when he did, his heart lurched. They reminded him of him and Elvin. He took another sip of his drink.

"Raymond, what's the matter?" Auntie Sherry stepped close and put a comforting hand on his arm.

"Huh? Oh, nothing. I'm fine."

MaaMaa tsked disapprovingly. "You are not fine."

What the fuck? Was he really so transparent? Ray prided himself in always being poised and polished. Yet these two old women took one look at him and could immediately tell something was wrong.

"It must be heartache." MaaMaa nodded. "That expression is always heartache."

What expression? He wasn't wearing any expression.

"Yes, I agree. Who broke your heart, Raymond?" Auntie Sherry looked at him like he was actually going to answer the question.

Ray laughed louder than was natural. "No one. No one broke my heart. I told you, I'm fine."

Auntie Sherry and MaaMaa exchanged a quick glance, but neither of them said another word. Whatever. What did they know? They spent all their time watching Chinese dramas and playing mahjong.

"Anyway, happy birthday, MaaMaa."

"Thank you, Raymond. You were always such an obedient child." MaaMaa gestured him to come closer. "Oh, and don't let your father get the better of you."

"What do you mean?"

She smiled like she'd just given him the riddle of a lifetime, then turned to greet another guest.

Ray slipped away. Don't let his father get the better of him? He wasn't planning on it. But then, who knew how that upcoming meeting would turn out.

Ming had roped in every senior partner at Jade Harbour and they'd gotten confirmation that his father would be accompanied by three others from Phoenix Family Trust. They were going to serve lunch catered by one of the hottest Asian fusion chefs in the city. Then Ming had prepared a twenty-minute presentation touting the glories of Jade Harbour.

The office had been abuzz about it for days now. Ray didn't share their excitement.

"Ray!"

He turned at his name to find Ginny making her way toward him. She had a phone to her ear and was still talking into it when she got close enough to give him a quick side hug.

"Sorry about that." Ginny hung up but kept her phone in her hand. "It's always something, you know."

"I didn't know you were going to be here." Ray hadn't seen her in person in so long, he barely recognized her.

"I didn't know either!" She threw her hands in the air as

if her whole life was chaos. "It was last-minute, but your father asked me to come. I had to cancel a trip to Thailand and push back the renovations on our house." She rolled her eyes.

Ray chuckled. Somehow he suspected she wasn't really that inconvenienced. "I'm sorry to hear that."

"Yes, well, I'm glad I could be here for MaaMaa."

"Have you said hello yet?" Ray pointed in MaaMaa's direction.

"Not yet. I'll do that later. I wanted to talk to you about something." Ginny grabbed his arm and pulled him into the library where he'd hidden earlier.

"What is it?"

"Oh, it's nothing to worry about." She waved a hand as if to dismiss his nonexistent concerns. "I heard that Jade Harbour has a paper factory in your portfolio."

Paper factory? The only paper-related portfolio company was Caron. Fuck. Shit. How did Ginny know about Caron? "Yes, we do."

"How is the investment doing?" Ginny wore a pleasantly neutral expression, one Ray was sure she'd acquired through many years of practice. She gave nothing away, no hints whatsoever.

He put on his best mask too. "It's fine as far I know. I haven't heard anything otherwise."

Ginny nodded as if Ray's comment was actually substantial. "Do you have plans to exit it?"

Why the fuck was she asking these questions? "I'm not sure. Why do you ask?"

She chuckled like Ray had told the funniest joke. "No reason. It's not important." She patted him on the arm and moved toward the door. "We're all looking forward to the meeting at your office. Are you really getting Sammy Lee to cater lunch?"

Figures that Ginny would be more interested in what was for lunch. "Yes, we are. Only the best for Phoenix Family Trust."

Ginny laughed again. "Oh, you're too funny. I'm going to say hello to MaaMaa. I'll see you later."

She disappeared as quickly as she had arrived.

Ray set his glass on a nearby table and made a beeline for the front door. He'd done his duty: put in some face time, wished MaaMaa a happy birthday, and dropped his red envelope full of cash into the collection box. There was no reason to stick around for another minute.

Outside, he handed his ticket to the hired valet. As he waited for his car to be brought around, Ray replayed Ginny's questions. How was Caron doing? What were their exit plans? What did she know about Caron that she wasn't telling him?

He pulled out his phone and tapped a quick message to Elvin. Meet me at my place. We need to talk.

His thumb hovered over the send button. Should he? Elvin had made it clear that he was upset about how Ray had handled Caron. This would only give him more reason to disapprove of Ray. Maybe it was better he keep Ginny's questions to himself. What good would it do to share them with Elvin?

Ray moved his thumb to the delete button and held it down until the message cleared. He slid his phone back into his pocket and jogged down the steps to his waiting car. He'd handle this himself.

Chapter Twenty-Eight

He'd told Ray repeatedly that they didn't have to have the pool party, but Ray wouldn't take no for an answer. And despite the awkwardness between them, Elvin was grateful. Eason was ecstatic and the rest of his family was pretty thrilled too.

He didn't know how Ray did it. Elvin was usually the one who handled things like this. But Ray had managed to bring in a catered lunch filled with all the foods the kids loved but that Elvin's parents would never feed them. He'd also ordered a massive cake that oozed glowing green slime when they cut it down the middle. The pool was full of noodles and other floaties that Elvin swore Ray hadn't owned before. He had to admit, he was impressed.

Elvin's brothers and sisters were splashing and laughing

in the water while his parents relaxed in the hot tub. At least they were having a good time.

"Why don't you go in?" Ray came to sit on the lounge chair next to Elvin's.

Elvin shrugged. It didn't feel right to have fun in Ray's pool with everything that was going on between them. Ray had crossed a line back in Montreal and Elvin was still trying to figure out how he felt about it. Angry, sure, but what's done was done and there was no point punishing Ray for something that he couldn't take back.

The problem was, Ray didn't seem to think he'd done anything wrong. And if Elvin had been in his shoes, he'd probably feel the same way.

"You know, this party is for you too."

"How am I supposed to enjoy it when—" This wasn't the time or the place to rehash the argument. Ray had been raised in a life of few boundaries, where the word *no* was like a foreign language. After the initial shock, Elvin wasn't surprised at all that he would take things as far as he had.

Ray huffed, frustration etched in every single line on his face. For the sake of the party, Elvin kept his mouth shut. He wouldn't be able to relax while the fate of Caron was still in limbo. Hell, they still hadn't told Joanna about the Montreal meeting and Elvin did not want to be in the same building as her when she found out.

Ray pulled his phone out of his pocket. "Yeah?" he almost shouted into the microphone. "Okay, send them up. Thanks." He put his phone away and stood. "The massage therapists are here."

"You didn't have to do that."

"Stop it," Ray said softly, almost defeated. "I wanted to do this. What's so wrong about that?" He sulked off in the direction of the hot tub.

Elvin watched Ray talk to his parents, a pleasant smile plastered to his face. To anyone else, he probably looked like he was enjoying himself, but Elvin could see the tension in his shoulders and the strain in his expression. Ray grabbed a couple towels and helped his parents out of the hot tub. Then he led them out of the pool area to the sauna and steam room area to meet the massage therapists.

He was a good man. A kind and caring man who didn't hesitate to provide for the people around him. That was fundamental to who Ray was and so much a part of why Elvin had fallen in love with him. That much would never change.

But he couldn't pretend that Ray hadn't crossed a line. He'd aligned himself with a criminal organization and despite his good intentions, it was a step too far.

"DaaiGo!" Jessie shouted from the shallow pool steps. "Come play!"

"Come play!" A chorus echoed off the high ceilings and Elvin gave in. This party was a rare opportunity to have fun with his siblings and he'd be a fool to give it up so easily.

He made his way to the steps and sat down next to Jessie. After the initial shock of being wet, the water wasn't nearly as cold as he'd expected. God, how much must it cost to maintain this thing? To keep the water so warm?

Jessie had little floatation rings threaded over both arms,

and she splashed her hands on the surface of the water. Her feet kicked wildly underneath, but she never made it far.

"Want to go into the deep end?" Elvin asked.

Jessie's eyes grew wide. "Can I? Is it scary?"

Elvin got in deeper and took hold of Jessie under her arms. "It's not scary. I'll be with you the whole time."

"Okay!"

Slowly, Elvin pulled her toward the deep end. Along the way, he passed Janice lounging on a floating hippo, tapping on her phone.

"Hey, why do you have your phone in the pool?" Elvin shouted at her. "You're going to get it wet!"

"Relax." Janice didn't even look up. "Phones are waterproof these days."

"I don't care if it's waterproof. If it dies, I'm not buying you another one."

Janice rolled her eyes. "I'll be careful."

Elvin shook his head, but continued on.

"She's always on her phone," Jessie whispered. "Because of a girl." Her voice rose and fell to say that it wasn't just any other girl.

"Oh yeah? How do you know?" Elvin had had no idea Janice was dating, never mind another girl.

Jessie shrugged as best she could with the floaties. "Everyone knows."

"I didn't know."

"You're not everyone."

Elvin scoffed. "How am I not everyone? Everyone is... everyone."

"Her name is Cory."

Elvin narrowed his eyes. Was he going to have to big brother this Cory person?

"She's older than her."

"Older?" Elvin's hackles rose. "How much older?"

"I don't know." Jessie turned toward the wall and splashed. "I want to jump in! You can catch me!"

"Okay, okay. Hold on." He swam to the wall and helped her climb up. "Wait!" he shouted as he got into position and held out his hands. "Ready!"

Jessie shrieked at the top of her lungs and cannonballed into Elvin's arms, nearly kneeing him in the jaw. When he finally surfaced and got the water out of his eyes, Jessie was laughing out loud and kicking her way back to the wall. "Again!"

Joyce and Eason quickly caught on, and soon all three of them were hurtling themselves into the deep end. "Catch us, DaaiGo!"

They tested Elvin's water treading skills as he caught one after another. When he felt like his legs were going to give out, he shouted at Edwin. "Get over here and help me!"

The two of them caught and tickled the younger kids and then each other until it turned into an all-out water fight. They each hoisted a kid onto their shoulders to battle it out and see which pair got knocked down first.

Elvin was so caught up in making sure no one drowned that he didn't notice when Ray returned and took a seat at the edge of the pool. When he finally called a time-out, Janice was sitting next to Ray, their heads bent together as they chatted quietly. Were they talking about Cory? Ray should be the last person giving dating advice.

Elvin hoisted himself out of the pool and went over to them. "What are you talking about?"

"Nothing," Janice was quick to respond.

Elvin turned to Ray, but he only shrugged. So that's how it was going to be, huh? Janice rose and went to the food table, leaving Elvin alone with Ray again.

"Teenagers," Ray said.

Elvin scoffed. "Yeah, right." He sat down and braced his elbows on his knees. Who knew playing in the water would leave him out of breath?

"I'm sorry."

Elvin snapped his head around. "What?"

"I'm sorry." It wasn't just the word. Elvin could see the apology in Ray's eyes. "I know you're upset with me about...you know. And I hate that you think less of me because of it."

Elvin opened his mouth, but he had no idea what to say. Where the hell was this coming from?

His siblings were being noisy as they fed their sugar high and his parents were still getting their massages. It was unlikely that they'd be overheard, but even then, they shouldn't be talking about this here.

"Please, Elvin. These past few days have been killing me." The angst in Ray's voice was palpable and it tore at Elvin's heart.

Their distance had been killing him too. Elvin had done his best to reestablish the dynamic they'd had before getting intimate, but he was beginning to think it wasn't possible. He couldn't unlearn what it felt like to be held by Ray, to kiss Ray, to fall asleep in each other's arms.

"What can I do to show you how sorry I am? Just tell me. I'll do anything."

Elvin shook his head. "Stop." It wasn't that simple, and the fact that Ray didn't quite get it was at the heart of the problem. "I'm not upset at you. Not anymore."

Ray frowned. "Then why the silent treatment?"

"I'm not—" Elvin cut himself off. He *was* giving Ray the silent treatment, but only because he didn't know what else to do. "Listen, we come from different worlds and I'm not sure how we bridge that."

"What do you mean?"

"Like this!" Elvin gestured to the pool. "And the New York trip. All the fancy events you go to, and the one-night stands."

"I haven't slept with anyone else since you," Ray was quick to object.

Elvin believed him, but again, that wasn't the issue. "I know."

"What's wrong with throwing a party for a friend? Or taking someone I like on a date?" Ray sounded exasperated and Elvin didn't blame him. To Ray, this was all he'd ever known. How could he fathom anything else?

"Ray, it's not the party or the date. It's the type of party and type of date. It's over the top. It's extravagant. And I..." The words caught in Elvin's throat. The truth that had kept him in check all these years. The fear that constricted his chest and made it difficult to breathe.

"What is it?"

He had to tell Ray. If they were ever going to have a future together—no matter what that future looked like— he had to be honest. The words came out in a sob. "I can't keep up with it."

Ray looked stunned. Elvin couldn't help but notice it was kind of adorable.

"I don't know what you mean."

Elvin burst out laughing. So loud that it caught the attention of his siblings on the other side of the room. He had to laugh. What else was there to do? Of course Ray didn't know what he meant. Elvin sighed. "Yeah, I know you don't."

"Then explain it to me!" Ray threw his hands in the air and let them drop onto his thighs with a thud.

He was trying. Elvin had to give him that much. If he was willing to listen, then Elvin had an obligation to explain.

Elvin shifted on his lounge chair so he faced Ray. This was far from the ideal environment for this conversation, but it was too late to walk it back now. "You're rich, right? Like, filthy rich."

Ray looked taken aback. "I don't know about the filthy part."

Elvin cocked his head and raised his eyebrows.

"Okay, okay. I'm pretty wealthy. Go on."

"That opens a lot of doors for you. Doors that are closed to most people, including me."

Ray blinked and Elvin could see the wheels turning in his head. "Okay."

"So we're not starting out from the same place. We're not on the same playing field. You've got an advantage over me."

Ray huffed and folded his arms across his chest. Elvin had lost him.

"Why is it always about money? You have advantages over me too. Look at your family."

Elvin glanced back toward his siblings. Sometimes he was hard-pressed to consider them advantages, but he got what Ray was trying to say. "Sure, they're great. Whatever. But the fact is, it *is* about money. If not all the time, then almost all the time. You know this. Money dictates so much about who we are and how we live our lives. We can't ignore it."

Ray didn't look convinced at all. In fact, Elvin didn't think he agreed with anything Elvin was saying. "So because I'm rich and you're not, we can't be together?"

Elvin dropped his head into his hands. It was just like Ray to reduce something complicated and nuanced to such simple terms. "No, that's not it."

"Then what is it?"

Maybe this conversation was beyond him. Maybe they'd never be able to understand each other on that level.

Ray laid a hand on his shoulder and gave him a gentle shake. "Don't give up on me. Explain it to me again."

Elvin sighed. "Fine. Let's try this again. It's not about the money."

"Not the money. Got it."

"It's what the money allows you to do. It gives you status in society. It makes people listen to you. You can get away with things that people who don't have money—people like me—can't get away with." Elvin held up a hand when he saw Ray about to object. "Just, take my word for it."

Ray took a deep breath. "Okay."

"What you did in Montreal?"

Ray frowned and Elvin could see he was having difficulty making the connection. "Stay with me. It'll make sense. I hope."

"Okay."

"You went off the rails in Montreal." He paused to get Ray's reaction: a mix of indignation and acquiescence. "You did it because you knew you could get away with it."

Ray winced. Maybe Elvin was finally getting through.

"You knew you could get away with it, because you've *always* gotten away with the wildest shit. And *that's* because you're filthy rich."

Ray shot to his feet and paced a circle around the lounge chairs before dropping back down. He looked confused, like the world had suddenly shifted and he couldn't tell up from down. "Wha—I..." He ran a hand over his face and sighed. "What you're saying is I'm entitled."

"Yes!" Elvin threw his arms in the air like he'd won. "Entitled. That's precisely it. Why didn't I think of that word?"

"That's not really a flattering attribute."

"But it's accurate." Elvin took a deep breath and let it out slowly. This conversation was exactly what he'd needed. The tightness he'd been carrying around for days fell away and he could finally breathe normally again.

He'd needed to call Ray out on his bullshit. And he'd needed Ray to take him seriously. What happened next was anyone's call, but getting this far was a milestone that Elvin wouldn't take for granted.

"So I'm a filthy rich, entitled bastard." Ray cocked his head as if he was considering the description. "I guess I can't really argue with that."

Elvin chuckled as relief flowed through him. Maybe they'd be able to find their way back to normal after all.

Chapter Twenty-Nine

He was here, but he wasn't happy about it.

Two people from Phoenix Family Trust had shown up twenty minutes ago, neither of whom Ray had ever met before. From the way they conducted themselves, they were probably quite junior, and unfortunately Ming could tell. He'd stashed them in a conference room until the real guests arrived. Meanwhile, Ming was directing all his ire at Ray.

"I don't know where he is," Ray said for the millionth time. "He's always late."

Ming's face was so red, he looked like he was about to explode. He stalked back and forth between the three elevators, waiting for one of them to discharge Ray's father. But they kept skipping their floor.

"Maybe you should sit down, have some water." Ray glanced over his shoulder at the receptionist. "You have any water back there?"

The receptionist pulled two bottles from a mini fridge and set them on the counter.

"Ming, come on." Ray held a bottle out to him. "Before you pass out."

Ming sent him a death glare and ignored his offering. Ray shrugged. He might be a filthy rich, entitled bastard, but never let it be said that he wasn't generous. He cracked open the bottle and took a swig himself.

Janice had been right, smart young woman. Ray had been sulking on the lounge chair, watching Elvin play with his siblings when she'd walked right up to him and asked if he and her DaaiGo were having a fight. He'd been moody for days, she said. Ray should apologize, she said. When he asked what made her think he was the one at fault, she'd pinned him with a look that was identical to Elvin's, and he'd let the question drop.

Since his conversation with Elvin, things had slowly gotten better. They weren't quite where Ray wanted them—Elvin still hadn't stayed overnight. But at least he'd stopped giving Ray the cold-shoulder silent treatment. And Ray hadn't given up yet. He'd figure out Elvin's objection to their relationship soon enough.

The elevator dinged and the door slid open to reveal Ray's father and his entourage. Ming near fell over himself trying to welcome them. Chairman Chao looked more startled than impressed. Ginny, who was barely containing her laugher, was half a step behind his father, as was that young woman who had trailed his father around at MaaMaa's birthday party. Two very large security guards brought up the rear.

"Father." Ray greeted the older man with a slight bow. "Welcome to Jade Harbour."

"Raymond." Chairman Chao surveyed the simple reception area like he wasn't sure he'd made the right decision to come.

"Chairman," Ming spoke a little too loudly. "Right this way, we've prepared a room for you." He gestured down the hall before proceeding with an awkward sideways walk, trying to face the Chairman while walking in the opposite direction.

Ray fell into step with Ginny behind his father. "Nice of you to join us," he whispered.

"We were held up at our previous engagement," she said with a touch of haughtiness.

Ray smiled. "Mmm-hmm." Damn was he glad Ginny was here.

When they reached the conference room, the two junior PFT staff shot to their feet and bowed deep. "Chairman Chao," they greeted their boss with deference.

The Chairman nodded at them and they quickly moved out of the way to let him have the seat of honor at the head of the table.

Joanna appeared a second later, with a few of the other senior partners behind her. She stood tall and proud in her stilettos and walked right up to the Chairman.

"Chairman Chao." She greeted him with a handshake, like they were equals. "I'm Joanna Chiang, CEO of Jade Harbour. I'm so glad you made the time to visit us."

Way to go, Joanna. Show him who's boss.

"Thank you, Ms. Chiang. I've always wanted to see where my son worked." The Chairman said this without even sparing a glance in Ray's direction.

Though Ginny did cast Ray a smirk. Ray barely stopped himself from rolling his eyes. His father didn't care about where he worked. He'd be surprised if the Chairman even knew the name of the company before this meeting was scheduled.

When Ray first announced that he wasn't joining Phoenix Family Trust right out of grad school, the Chairman had been furious. There'd been years of threats to disown him and cut off his inheritance. But since Ray was an only child, those threats had ended up meaningless. The Chairman couldn't very well let his wealth go to some stranger when he died. Eventually, they had come to a kind of truce—the Chairman stopped pestering Ray to return to the family fold as long as Ray didn't do anything to embarrass the family further. It'd always amused Ray to think that his desire to forge his own career path could be viewed as a blight on the family name.

"Would you like a beverage?" Joanna offered. "Tea? Water?"

"Tea."

Joanna shot Ming a quick look and Ming scrambled to oblige. It took another fifteen minutes before the requisite small talk was completed and they were all settled around the conference table.

Ming started the presentation and Ray had to admit that it lived up to his hype. Ming sufficiently praised PFT for its renowned history and success and painted Jade Harbour as a humble little venture that diligently aspired to the same level of greatness. Along the way, he peppered in actual facts about Jade Harbour's track record as the leading private equity firm in Canada.

Just as Ming was finishing up, Ginny interrupted him. "I understand you have some investments in the paper and pulp industry."

Ming paled ever so slightly and sent Ray a knowing look. Ray gave him a hard stare back. *Keep it together, Ming.*

"Uh, yes, we do." Ming fidgeted with the presentation's remote control.

"What are your projections for the investment? We're seeing a decline in the industry given the global move toward digital. Do you have plans to exit?"

Ray couldn't tell if Ginny's questions were a harmless coincidence or if she knew something about Caron. But the fact that she'd already asked him at MaaMaa's birthday party made him suspect it was the latter.

He snuck a glance in Joanna's direction. She was not pleased. God damn it, Ginny. Maybe it would have been better if she weren't here.

Ming nodded, then nodded again. For a second, it looked like he wouldn't be able to answer Ginny's question. But then something clicked and Ming launched into full sales mode.

"Yes, we do have investments in paper and pulp. If you turn to page fifty-six in the presentation deck, you'll find all the pertinent information on Caron Paper." He paused as everyone flipped to the page he indicated.

At the top of the page was Caron's logo, followed by several pictures of the mill they'd visited. How Ming had managed to get the photos, Ray had no idea. He quickly scanned the description of the company and the summary of Jade Harbour's investment. No mention of drugs, thank fucking god.

Ming dove into a high-level analysis of Caron's performance and Ray had to hand it to him, he made the port-folio company sound like a golden child. Key performance indicators were stellar. Sales were up. Expenses were down. If they exited today, they'd make a healthy profit.

But Ray had to wonder, how much of Caron's success was real and how much was due to inflated numbers from laundering drug money?

Out of the corner of his eye, Ray watched Ginny study-ing the presentation deck, her expression giving nothing away. Farther down the table, the Chairman looked un-impressed. But that didn't necessarily mean anything; the Chairman always looked unimpressed.

Ginny sat back in her chair when she finished and tapped her chin. "Interesting." She cast a smile in the Chairman's direction. "We may have to hire them, Uncle. They seem to know the secret to running a paper company."

For a moment, no one spoke. They could hear a telephone ringing from down the hall.

Then the Chairman chuckled and everyone broke into quiet, nervous laughter. Ray exchanged a look with Ming—close call.

"Well, I believe it is time for lunch," Joanna announced, pushing her chair away from the table. Not a minute too soon.

She led the way to Jade Harbour's dining room, chatting with the Chairman along the way. Ray waited until everyone else had filed out before stopping next to Ming.

"Nice save." He had to give credit where credit was due.

Ming let out a shaky breath and nodded. "Yeah, thanks."

The in-house dining room was usually where Jade Harbour employees came to eat their meals. Today, it'd been converted in an attempt to impress their guests. A formal round dining table that could seat twelve was set up in the middle of the room. Liveried waiters stood behind each chair to help the guests into their seats.

Once they were all seated with their glasses filled with water and teacups filled with tea, Chef Sammy Lee came out to announce the first course: an Asian-ingredients-inspired coleslaw with salted plum dressing, topped with tuna sashimi. Everyone waited for the Chairman to pick up his chopsticks and take the first bite. Only after he nodded his approval did the rest of the table join in.

Sitting between Ray and Ming, Ginny dug in with gusto.

"Mmm, I've heard such good things about Sammy Lee,"

she said between bites. "I figured his food must be good if he's well-known even in Hong Kong."

Ming preened. "I'm good friends with Sammy. When he heard that the Chairman was going to be in town, he didn't hesitate to cook for us."

Ray smothered a scoff. To call Ming a friend of Sammy's was a stretch. Ray happened to know that Ming had invoked *his* name in order to get Sammy to agree to come. But whatever. Today was Ming's day, and who was he to steal the guy's glory?

"So, Ginny." Ming leaned in close. "What's your interest in the paper and pulp industry?"

Fuck, Ming, Ray could have throttled him. They'd made it through Ginny's questioning, why the hell was he bringing it up now?

"Mmm." Ginny nodded as she dabbed her mouth with the cloth napkin. "We have some related investments in Asia. But like I said, with the move toward digital, they aren't doing as well as we would like. Frankly, I'm surprised your portfolio company is performing as well as it is. I haven't seen numbers like that in the industry in a long time."

Ray caught Ming's eye and gave him a sharp shake of the head. *Enough already. Let it go.* But Ming either didn't get the message or didn't care.

"We are blessed with low cost of inputs here in Canada," Ming continued, as if they weren't playing with fire.

"Ah yes, so many forests with so many trees."

The waitstaff interrupted Ginny before she could finish. After they cleared the table, Chef Lee came out again to announce the next course of caramelized Atlantic black cod with miso mustard, preserved vegetables and turnip cake, topped with crunchy noodles.

Ginny helped herself to several bites before picking up where she left off. "You see, the problem in Asia is infrastructure. There are plenty of trees, but no way to get them to the processing facilities."

Ming nodded sagely, as if he could understand her frustration.

Ray shook his head and tuned out. There was only so much of Ming's posturing he could take. Around the table, conversation hummed over the clicking of ivory chopsticks on ceramic tableware. The Chairman sat opposite him, next to Joanna, and the two of them had their heads bowed together like they were sharing secrets. Hopefully not about him.

Suddenly, from outside the dining room came faint cries. "Wait! Stop! You can't go back there!"

The doors burst open with a bang, and in stormed a gang of men all dressed in black.

"What the hell?" Ray pushed his chair back and stood. Most others at the table stood too.

The Chairman's bodyguards, who were seated at their own table, rushed forward, but the armed men simply went around them.

"Raymond Chao." One of the men marched up to Ray.

It took a split second for him to process what was going on, but by then it was too late. He was being turned around, his arms pulled behind his back and cold steel clipped around his wrists.

"What the fuck is this?" He tugged at his restraints, but they only dug painfully into his skin. It was only then that he saw the word "Police" printed in block letters across the bulletproof vests.

Police? His world spun as the chaos around him got louder and farther away at the same time. They'd found him. They'd figured out what he'd done. It was over. It was finally over.

As Ray got passed from one set of hands to another, a strange sense of calm came over him. The weeks of wondering, of uncertainty, had come to an end and no matter what the outcome would be, he wouldn't have Caron hanging over his head anymore. In a twisted way, it was freeing.

The relief was bittersweet. He'd spent his career testing the limits, seeing how far he could go before someone stopped him. A part of him was surprised he'd gotten this far—or rather, gotten this far off the straight and narrow. He wasn't looking forward to suffering the consequences, but at least he could finally pay his penance.

"Ray!"

The sound of his name on Elvin's lips pulled him from his thoughts and back to the pandemonium around him. "Elvin!"

Elvin rushed over and managed to squeeze himself between Ray and the officer who held him. "Oh my god, Ray, are you okay? Get these things off him!"

"Step back, sir." The officer pushed Elvin away.

"Hey! Don't touch him!" Ray shouted in the guy's face. *He* was the one under arrest. They didn't have any right to lay hands on Elvin.

The officer passed him along to someone else and Ray stumbled over his own feet. "Elvin!" Ray lost sight of him in the mix-up.

"Ray!"

Ray twisted against his captor, trying to catch one last glimpse of Elvin. He just needed one more moment, one more chance to say how sorry he was about the whole thing. He needed Elvin's strength and confidence that together they could achieve anything.

Ray shouted and wrenched himself away from the hands that held him. But instead of Elvin, he caught sight of his father. The Chairman stood with his hands clasped behind his back, chin raised and brow furrowed. He looked stern, disapproving, disappointed. Like he'd known something like this was bound to happen one day.

It'd been a long time since Ray had cared what his parents thought of him. He'd assumed he was immune to the Chairman's opinions by now. But seeing his father standing there, stoic, unmoved, it hit like a baton in his gut.

Ray withered and collapsed into the hands that grabbed him and pulled him away. He staggered forward, unseeing, going where he was directed. When the elevator doors closed, cutting him off from Elvin, Jade Harbour and his father, Ray had never felt more alone.

Chapter Thirty

"Mike, do something!" Elvin grabbed Mike's arm and he wasn't going to let go until they had a plan for getting Ray out.

The initial squad of police officers had left with Ray, but there were dozens of uniformed men and women filling the hallways. They'd demanded to know where Ray's office was and had started tossing the place, confiscating every piece of paper and technology they could get their hands on.

Elvin's desk wasn't off-limits, either, and it was such a violation to have strangers going through a space he considered his own.

"I *am* doing something. You need to calm down and let

me work." Mike extricated himself from Elvin's grasp and walked away.

But Elvin had no intention of letting Mike out of his sight. They wove through the crowd of officers and rubberneckers until they reached Joanna's office. She was already there with Ming.

"Mike, talk to me."

"I've already called Denise Washington. We need to figure out what Ray's being charged with and get him out on bail."

Joanna turned to Elvin. "Do you know of any reason why Ray might have gotten arrested?"

Elvin gulped. Ray hadn't told Joanna about Montreal. He was going to, Elvin had made him promise. But with his father coming to the office and everything, he must not have gotten around to it.

"Um."

All eyes zeroed in on him and Elvin took a step back.

"Elvin, what is it?" Joanna pinned him with a look that warned him not to move another inch.

"Um, Ray and I went to Montreal last week."

Mike slapped a hand over his face. "I'm going to need to sit down for this."

Ming joined Mike on the couch, but put his feet up on the coffee table like he was settling in for a movie.

"Ray met with a couple people from Caron, or rather, um, the Rousopoulos crime family."

"What?" If looks could kill, Joanna would have murdered him by now.

"Damn," Ming whispered.

"Wait. Stop." Mike pulled out a notebook and started jotting down notes. "Start from the beginning. What crime family?"

Oh god. How the hell did they end up in this fucking mess? Elvin told them everything. Ray's military intelligence guy who'd discovered the connection to the Greek mob in Montreal. The meeting with Olivier and Gilles—that got a laugh from Ming. And finally the deal Ray had tried to strike, offering the Rousopouloses a spot on Jade Harbour's investor list.

By the time he was done, Ming's jaw was on the floor, Mike's face was sickly gray, and Joanna looked like she was going to drag Ray out of prison and strangle him herself.

"You didn't think it prudent to tell us yourself?" Joanna spat out the question.

It was a fair one. "Ray thought it best that no one else knew."

"Ray doesn't know fucking shit! If he thinks I'm going to bail him out now, he's got another think coming. Putting himself at risk is his prerogative, but he had no right jeopardizing Jade Harbour."

Elvin cringed at Joanna's outburst, but she was right. Ray had gone too far and Elvin wasn't about to defend his actions.

Mike raised a hand like he was asking permission to speak.

"What?" Joanna nearly shouted.

"Okay, so Ray broke the law, but how did the police find out?"

Everyone turned to him again like he had all the answers. Shit, if he had the answers, Ray wouldn't be in jail right now, would he? Elvin shook his head. "I don't know."

"Think, Elvin," Mike implored him. "Is there anything else you haven't told us?"

He wracked his brain. He'd told them everything he knew. Ray's guy found out about the Rousopouloses, which was bad news because the police could never touch them. "Wait." It came back to him. "There's some sort of investigation and an undercover cop had infiltrated them. That has to be it."

"Oh shit," Ming whispered before covering his mouth with a hand.

Joanna glared at him. "Shut up, Ming."

"Okay, okay. This is good." Mike scribbled furiously in his notebook. "I'm going to tell Denise to go straight to the police station. We'll meet her there."

"When I said I didn't condone any illegal activities, I didn't think you'd actually get caught doing them." Denise was already waiting for them when Elvin, Mike and Joanna arrived at the station. Ming offered to stay behind and keep an eye on the officers still going through Ray's office.

Mike winced. "This was unsanctioned. Ray went rogue."

"I'm not surprised." She turned to Joanna and sobered.

"I'm sorry things turned out this way. I'm going to do everything I can to get it sorted."

"Don't try too hard. I wouldn't be opposed to Ray spending a couple nights in there." Joanna stalked past her and into the station.

Elvin really hoped she was joking. Ray wouldn't last one night in a jail cell, never mind a couple.

Denise and Mike went up to the front desk as Elvin hung back with Joanna. The station buzzed with activity. Some uniformed officers hurried past them while others stood in groups chatting. Most of them wore bulletproof vests and all of them had guns on their hips. Elvin had never been in a police station before and he hoped to god that this would be his last time. None of the people in there looked the least bit friendly.

Next to him, Joanna stood stone-faced, hands on her hips like she was about to take someone down. Elvin swallowed. He might not go back to Jade Harbour after this either. He'd be lucky if he still had a job.

He took a breath and braced himself. "Um, Joanna, I'm really sorry about this. I tried to talk Ray out of it. I really did."

Joanna scowled at him for so long that he almost slinked away. But then she softened her expression. "I've known Ray for a long time. We're lucky he hasn't gotten arrested before. This isn't on you."

Elvin wasn't sure he agreed with her exoneration, but he wasn't about to argue with her either.

Mike came back to them. "They've got him down in

holding. Only Denise and I will be allowed to see him. She's arranging that now."

"What?" Elvin grabbed Mike's arm. "Why only you and Denise? Why can't I see him?"

Mike put a hand on Elvin's and squeezed reassuringly. "Because we're his lawyers. Don't worry. We'll tell him you're here."

It wasn't fair. Elvin needed to see him. He needed to tell Ray that he'd forgiven him for all the harebrained absurd things he did. Yeah, he was a filthy rich, entitled bastard, but that was what made him endearing. And oh god, he needed to tell Ray he loved him with every fiber of his being. He sucked in a shaky breath as his head spun.

"Whoa." Mike grabbed hold of him and led him to a chair. "Here. Sit. Breathe."

Elvin did as he was told. "I'm okay. I'm fine. I just—"

"It's okay." Mike rubbed his back. "I know it's hard, but we're going to get through this. You've got to hang in there."

"Joanna."

They all looked up to find an impeccably dressed Asian woman approaching.

Joanna stepped forward. "Ginny, what are you doing here?"

Ginny—Ray's cousin. She'd been at the office earlier with the Phoenix Family Trust team, but Elvin hadn't noticed when they'd left.

He stood and hovered behind Joanna.

"Chairman Chao sent me." She hooked a very expensive-looking handbag on her arm. "Ray should be brought here shortly."

"You bailed him out?" Elvin moved from behind Joanna.

Ginny gave him the once-over. "And who are you?"

Crap. "I'm, uh, Elvin. Ray's assistant." It was nothing to be ashamed of, but in front of someone from Ray's family, it suddenly sounded silly.

But Ginny gave him a friendly smile. "I'm glad he has someone looking out for him." She turned back to Joanna. "Now that you're here, I feel better about going."

"You're not staying until Ray's out?" Elvin blurted out again.

Joanna cast him an admonishing look, but Ginny chuckled. "No, unfortunately. Uncle and I have more engagements to attend. Please give Ray my best."

She gave them a delicate wave of the fingers and floated out the front doors.

"Who was that?" Denise asked as she approached.

"Ginny Chao," Joanna answered. "Ray's cousin."

"She's the one who posted bail," Denise said.

Mike frowned. "How did you know?"

Denise pointed behind her. "They just told me someone posted an astronomical bail on the condition that Ray is released immediately." She shook her head. "Whoever she is, she must have some serious sway with someone high up on the food chain."

"No kidding," Mike agreed. "We'd normally need a separate court date for the bail hearing."

"You said Ray is going to be released immediately?"

Elvin didn't care about bail hearings or court dates. All he cared about was being able to take Ray home.

Denise nodded. "They're bringing him up now." She turned toward a set of doors that led to a stairwell.

Right at that moment, Ray appeared, escorted by a uniformed officer. Elvin rushed to him and pulled him into the tightest hug he'd ever given. He was never, *never* going to let Ray go.

"Sir." A firm hand on his shoulder peeled him away. "You can't do that here."

"It's okay, Elvin." Ray steadied him before Elvin could launch himself at the officer. "I'm okay."

"Are you sure?"

"Yes, I'm fine." Ray smiled and it was like the sun shining down on him. "Come on. Let's get out of here."

Chapter Thirty-One

Ray hadn't been in the cell for more than a couple hours, but when he walked through the front door of the police station, it felt like his first breath of fresh air in ages. He gripped Elvin's hand and followed Mike to a waiting car.

"You two take this one." Mike held the door open for them. "I've called for another car."

"Thanks, Mike." Elvin gave Ray a gentle push and he climbed in.

"We'll meet you back at Ray's place," Mike said before he shut the door.

Ray pulled Elvin close. God, it felt so good to hold him, to breathe in his scent and melt into his body. There'd been several moments when he'd been alone in the basement of the police station when he wasn't sure he'd ever see Elvin again.

"Are you sure you're okay?" Elvin asked.

"Now I am."

Elvin poked him in the stomach. "You scared me."

"I know. I'm sorry." Hell, he'd fucking scared himself. Sitting on the cold hard metal bench with nothing and no one else but his thoughts, it'd been hard to keep them from spiraling out of control. Joanna had done so much for his career and this was how he repaid her? He'd put all the people at Jade Harbour at risk of losing their livelihoods. He'd betrayed Elvin's confidence in him and might not ever have the chance to win it back.

"Don't ever do that again."

Not if he could help it. He was going to do everything in his power to be the person Elvin deserved, even if it took him the rest of his life to get there. "I won't."

They rode the rest of the way in silence, leaning into each other's presence, relearning how it felt to be in each other's arms. Eventually, the car slowed.

"Um, excuse me," the driver called from the front seat.

"What is it?" Elvin pulled away and leaned forward.

"There's a crowd of people milling about the front of the building. Do you still want to be dropped there?"

Ray leaned over to peer out the window. There was a mob all right. Complete with cameras and microphones. "Fuck."

"Do you want to use the garage entrance?" Elvin asked.

It was tempting, but it would only put off the inevitable. Better to get it over with now. "No, let's face the firing squad."

The driver pulled up slowly and put the car into park right in front of Ray's condo building. Elvin opened the door and led the way out. The second Ray's foot hit the pavement, they were on him, lobbing question after question.

"Ray! Did you really conspire with the Rousopoulos mob family?"

"Ray! What do you have to say about the police allegations?"

"Ray! Do you think it's fair that your father used his money and clout to get you released?"

They had been pushing their way through the mob, but now Ray froze.

"What?" He searched the group of reporters around them for the person who had asked the question.

"Your father, Chairman Chao, is friends with the Chief Justice of Canada. He posted a ten-million-dollar bond to get you released immediately and without conditions. Do you have any comments?"

His father was friends with who? He did what?

"No, we do not have any comments regarding today's events." Mike appeared out of nowhere, stepping in front of Ray, and spoke into the microphone. "Jade Harbour will release a statement on behalf of itself and Raymond Chao shortly. Until then, we are not taking any questions."

Mike nodded to Elvin and together they forged a path to the front door.

"You okay?" Mike asked once they were safely inside.

"What was that about my father?"

Mike exchanged a look with Elvin.

"What is it?"

"He posted your bail. We ran into Ginny at the station."

Ray spun around to find Joanna stalking up to him. Furious didn't begin to describe the look in her eyes. "Joanna, I am so sorry."

She held up one hand. "Save it."

He'd find a way to make it up to her.

The four of them, plus Denise, rode the elevator up to his condo. It'd been less than twelve hours since he last set foot in this place, and yet it felt utterly foreign. All the goddamn white, stone-cold floors and reflective windows. It had never felt less like a home.

"Do you want to go rest?" Elvin asked, with a hand on Ray's lower back.

He did, but that wouldn't help them figure out what their next steps were going to be. Ray shook his head. He'd manage for another couple hours.

He let Elvin lead him to a spot on the couch and sank down into it. Mike, Denise and Joanna joined him in the living room while Elvin went to fuss in the kitchen.

"You're sure you're okay, Ray?" Denise reached over and put a comforting hand on his shoulder.

"Yeah, thanks."

She cast him a sympathetic smile before turning to Mike. "Okay, what do we have?"

Mike flipped open his notebook. "Ray's being charged

with conspiracy to commit fraud. They claim to have a recording of Ray working with the Rousopoulos crime family to conceal a drug trafficking and money laundering operation."

Ray sagged in his seat, dropping his head against the back of the couch.

"Is it true?" Joanna directed the question at Ray.

"Yes."

Joanna closed her eyes like she was desperately trying to maintain her cool. "Guess it was too much to hope that Elvin had been wrong."

Denise picked up where Mike left off. "We haven't heard the recording, obviously, so we don't know how damning it is yet. I'm not about to take their word that the recording is conclusive."

"So there's a chance this could all get dropped?" Elvin asked. He'd returned with a tray of drinks and started handing them out.

"Not quite." Denise shook her head. "The charges will most likely go through, but their case might not be as strong as they're making it out to be."

"Is that all they have? A recording?" Joanna sounded skeptical. "Where did they get it?"

Mike shot Ray an apologetic look. "The meeting Ray had recently in Montreal. One of them was an undercover cop. He was wearing a wire."

Elvin's jaw dropped. "Which one?"

Denise shook her head. "We don't know."

"Olivier." It all made sense now. Olivier's warning that

nothing would happen as long as they didn't tell anyone. Olivier calling all the mill workers away so they could make a clean break. Olivier's attempt at intimidation at the meeting.

"Are you sure?" Elvin asked as he took the spot next to Ray. He put a hand on Ray's and they intertwined their fingers.

"It has to be." Ray squeezed his eyes shut and shook his head. "I should have known."

Elvin gave his hand a squeeze. "How could you have known? Ming and I were there too and we didn't piece it together either."

"It's not the same thing." It was his job to know these things. He should have suspected it from the very beginning.

"Anyway." Mike went on. "At least now we know what we're dealing with. Denise and I will take it from here."

Denise nodded. "But before we go, I want to prepare you for what is probably coming next." She glanced around the room, making eye contact with each one of them before continuing. "We've most likely got two options: going to trial or agreeing to a settlement. I always advise against trials because the media scrutiny is relentless. Trials are basically public spectacles where all your dirty laundry gets aired for the world to see. No one wants that. Plus, trials are notoriously unpredictable. Even with the strongest case, the chances of winning are about the same as a coin toss."

Joanna pressed her lips into a straight, flat line. It was

clear what her opinion about that was and Ray had to agree, the less media involvement the better.

"But with a settlement, we'll have to admit to some wrongdoing. What kind and how much will depend on the strength of the prosecution's evidence."

"Is there a chance Ray could go to prison?" Elvin asked with a frown.

Denise didn't mince words. "Yes, there is."

"Then no. We can't do that."

"Elvin." Ray appreciated how quickly Elvin jumped to his defense, but someone had to take the fall and that someone had to be him.

"What? You're not seriously okay with going to prison, are you? We have to fight this."

Elvin's insistence tore at Ray. Of course he didn't want to go to prison, who did? But it was the right thing to do, and Elvin had to know that. Wasn't that why they'd gotten into such a drawn-out argument in the first place?

"That's not something we have to decide now," Mike jumped in. "Let me and Denise talk to the Crown Attorney's office first and then we can go from there."

Elvin nodded but he obviously wasn't satisfied.

"In that case, you should get some rest." Denise stood and went to Ray. "Try not to worry too much. We'll let you know as soon as we've made progress."

"Thanks, Denise." Ray walked with them to the front door. "Joanna."

She stopped in the doorway.

"You have no idea how sorry I am. I shouldn't have kept

all this from you. You have to know, I'm going to do everything in my power to make this right."

Joanna sighed and for the first time all day her expression softened. "Raymond Chao, you are a pain in my ass." She patted him on the shoulder and left.

"What is that supposed to mean?" Elvin asked from behind him.

Ray shut the door and pulled Elvin into his arms. "I think that means I'm forgiven?"

"Are you sure?"

"I don't know. I don't know anything anymore."

Chapter Thirty Two

Elvin's phone beeped on the nightstand and Ray reached over to turn it off.

"You're awake?" Elvin's voice was groggy.

Ray turned to face him, scooting in so they shared the same pillow. "Yeah."

"Did you sleep at all?"

"No."

Elvin caressed his cheek with soft fingers, the tenderness of the touch reaching deep into Ray's heart. He took Elvin's hand and held it against his chest.

There were so many things he wanted to say. He'd stared at the ceiling all night, carefully crafting every sentence, but now that it was time, the words escaped him.

"What is it?" Elvin whispered.

He'd wanted to apologize, to explain himself, to comfort Elvin and reassure him. But all of that paled in comparison to the single most important realization of his life.

"I love you."

Elvin didn't react. He didn't smile or frown or move a single muscle. It was like he hadn't heard Ray at all.

"Elvin?"

"Yeah?"

"I said, I love you."

"I heard you."

So...did that mean he didn't feel the same way? Pain shot through Ray's chest like a knife had pierced his heart. But that was okay. Elvin didn't have to love him back. Ray wouldn't force that on him. God knew, he hadn't given Elvin much reason to love him. He was arrogant, pretentious—oh, and don't forget filthy rich and entitled.

Ray let go of Elvin's hand and pushed the duvet away to sit up.

"Where are you going?"

Ray glanced back. He didn't know where he was going, just away from here.

Elvin sat up with him. "You can't say something like that and then leave."

What? Ray opened his mouth and shut it again. If he wasn't allowed to leave, then what did Elvin want him to do?

"We need to talk."

A minute ago, Ray would have agreed. But now? "About what?"

"Jesus Christ," Elvin muttered.

"What? What did I do?"

Elvin took Ray's face with both hands. "Ray, sometimes I think my siblings have more sense than you do."

Ray wasn't about to argue with that—he'd met Elvin's siblings.

Elvin dropped his hands and crossed his legs. He pulled a pillow onto his lap and played with the hem of the pillow-case. "I love you too, you dumbass," he said, eyes down-cast. "But that's not enough."

Ray rubbed his eyes. He was pretty sure he'd heard Elvin correctly, but maybe his lack of sleep was playing tricks on him. "If I love you and you love me, why wouldn't that be enough?"

"Because we come from two different worlds—"

Ray dropped his head into his hands. Oh god, not this again.

"Hey." Elvin pulled Ray's hands down. "Listen to me."

"I'm listening." Though with having stayed up all night and now the roller coaster of Elvin's declarations, he wasn't sure he'd be able to follow.

"We talked about this before, remember?"

"Yes, I remember very clearly. I have too much money. Would you like me to denounce my inheritance? I can do that. No problem. Just say the word." Because if his wealth was the obstacle between him and Elvin, he'd gladly give it up a hundredfold.

"No, I don't want you to give up your inheritance."

"Then what do you want from me?" Ray flopped back

onto the bed. He was trying, he really was. But for the life of him, he couldn't understand what Elvin was so hung up about.

Before his arrest, it wouldn't have bothered him so much. They would have had plenty of time to find their way to each other. But the clock was ticking now—who knew how long they had until he had to go away? And who knew how long he'd be away for?

Elvin hung his head. His eyes were closed and his hands were curled into fists on the pillow. God, he was so fucking beautiful and Ray was so fucking lucky to have known him. If that was all he got, then he'd count his blessings and be happy about it. Elvin deserved someone who could make him happy. All Ray had managed to do was bring upheaval into his life.

A single tear dropped from Elvin's eyelashes and landed on the pillow.

Great, now he'd made Elvin cry. Ray sat up again and lifted Elvin's head.

"Hey, don't cry. I'm sorry." He wiped away the tears that stuck to Elvin's cheeks. "I'm so sorry. Please, Elvin." His chest hurt like someone had twisted the knife in his heart.

Elvin shook his head. "It's not you."

It had to be him. Who else was there to blame?

"Ray, I'm scared."

A million more daggers jabbed him right where it hurt the most. He pulled Elvin to him and cradled him close. "Oh god, Elvin. I'm so sorry."

They rocked back and forth as Elvin's tears soaked Ray's

T-shirt. Ray ran his fingers through Elvin's hair and stroked his back. What had he done? How had he managed to do this to the one person he loved most in the world?

Elvin sniffled. "What's going to happen if they send you to prison?"

Then he'd go to prison. But something told him that wasn't what Elvin was asking. "What do you mean?"

"Will you still love me?"

The words were so quiet Ray almost didn't hear them. But they thundered through his soul and left whatever remained in pieces. He squeezed Elvin tight. "I will always love you. Whether or not I'm in prison. You can count on that."

"Are you sure?"

Ray couldn't believe Elvin was asking this. "Of course I'm sure." He shifted his hold on Elvin so he could look the man right in the face. "Elvin, you are the love of my life and I will never stop loving you. Do you understand me? Never."

Elvin blinked some stray tears away. "But…why?"

"Why?" Now who didn't have any sense? "Because! You're gorgeous and sweet and charming. You're devoted to your family. You take care of everyone around you. And you know me better than anyone else in the world. Why wouldn't I love you?"

Elvin peered at him through damp lashes. "You won't get tired of me?"

He was making less and less sense with every question. "Why would I get tired of you?"

Elvin bit his lip like he was too afraid to ask.

"Elvin, why would I get tired of you?"

He squeezed his eyes shut. "Because you've had so many lovers before and maybe you'll get bored with me."

Oh god, he was the worst human being in the goddamn world. "Is that why you think I brought home a different person every night? Because I wanted, what, variety?"

"Isn't it?"

"No!" Jesus Christ, if he could go back and redo life, he would do things so differently. He was a fool. "None of them wanted to stay more than one night. Not really. Not because they actually knew who I was and liked me."

Elvin looked at him like he couldn't possibly be telling the truth.

"Think about it. Not a single person I've ever dated or slept with stuck around long enough to really get to know me." Ray shrugged. "Maybe I didn't want them to stay. But the end result is the same."

Elvin nodded. Maybe he was finally getting through.

"So if I give up my inheritance and promise never to look at anyone else but you, will that be enough?"

Elvin rolled his eyes and slapped Ray on the shoulder hard enough that it actually hurt. "Ow!"

"Serves you right." Elvin glared at him, but Ray would take that over the tears any day.

"Seriously, though." Ray rubbed his shoulder. "Is that enough for you to love me?" He held his breath, hoping against all hope that the answer was yes.

"I love you regardless of all that." Elvin smiled, but his

bottom lip trembled like more tears were about to fall. "I've loved you for so long that I can't remember a time I didn't love you."

The words were a balm to Ray's soul. "Tell me more."

"I love you because you're an entitled bastard and in spite of it."

Ray cringed. "I'm not sure that's a good thing."

Elvin laughed, but kept going. "I love that you're the most generous person I know. You go out of your way to help people. You have an incredible sense of loyalty and obligation, so much so that it often gets you in trouble."

"Again, not that great." But Ray would take it if it meant Elvin loved him. He would take all of it and anything else the world threw at him if he could call Elvin his.

"I love you," Elvin whispered.

"I love you too."

"We'll get through this, right?"

"We always do."

It was well past dinner by the time Mike and Denise made it back. Good thing too, because Ray wasn't sure he'd be able to eat with the things they had to discuss.

"How are you feeling?" Denise asked, genuine concern in her eyes.

"Good." Ray caught Elvin's gaze from across the room. "Better."

Denise followed his line of sight and smiled when she realized what he was looking at. "I'm happy for you."

"Thanks."

"So your father is friends with the Chief Justice of Canada." Mike helped Elvin bring over a tray of wineglasses and a couple bottles from Ray's personal collection.

"Is he?" Ray didn't even know who the Chief Justice of Canada was. "I'm not familiar with my father's acquaintances."

"Apparently, they're golf buddies," Mike added.

"Sure." That didn't surprise Ray. The Chairman knew people all over the place.

"Mike and I went to see the Crown Attorney handling your case." Denise accepted a glass from Elvin before taking her seat.

"The good news is he's willing to negotiate a settlement." Mike handed Ray a glass. "Especially since we told him that you'd give a full statement against the Rousopouloses. That's really going to help their other case."

Ray held out a hand to Elvin and pulled him to his side. "What's the bad news?"

"You're most likely looking at jail time." Mike winced. "Sorry."

Ray nodded. He'd been expecting that.

"There's another thing." Mike sat down and clasped his hands together.

Ray didn't know Mike that well, but even he could tell that was probably Mike's stoic lawyer face.

"I talked to Joanna. You have to understand she doesn't wish you any personal harm, but you've left Jade Harbour in a difficult position."

"What do you mean?" Elvin asked. "The Rousopouloses didn't invest in Jade Harbour. And didn't you just say the police were going to shut them down?"

"It's not that, is it?" Ray knew what Mike was talking about. "It's our other investors."

Mike nodded. "They want to know what went wrong, and they want assurances that something like this won't happen again."

"They need someone to blame." Ray said the words Mike didn't.

"You mean, they want a scapegoat." Elvin put it even more bluntly. "I can't believe this."

Ray appreciated the anger in Elvin's voice, but it was unfounded. "We were expecting this, remember?"

"We were expecting jail time!" Elvin's volume rose. "This is another thing entirely. We're talking about throwing you under the bus for the sake of Jade Harbour's reputation with investors. As if you haven't saved the company dozens of times in the past."

"Investors have short memories," Mike said.

"I would do the same thing in Joanna's shoes." Ray turned to Mike. "What did she have in mind, exactly?"

"Formal apology. Take full responsibility for anything connected to Caron. Resignation."

"Anything connected to Caron?" Elvin shook his head. "Ray wasn't responsible for the drugs being there in the first place."

Mike sighed. "Someone has to own it."

"This is so fucked up," Elvin spat out.

"Elvin, it's okay." Ray tried to calm him down. He didn't

like it any more than Elvin did. Throughout his career, he'd built a reputation for getting things done, quietly and effectively. Owning up to a failure of this magnitude was a hard pill to swallow. Not to mention what his father might say—the biggest *I told you so* in the history of the Chao family. Look what happens when he doesn't do what he's told.

"I don't fucking like it."

Ray pulled Elvin close to plant a kiss on his temple. If there was any other way, Ray would have gladly opted not to have his name publicly smeared. But if someone had to be sacrificed, better him than anyone else. "I don't like it either. But if Jade Harbour has any hope of surviving, I have to do this."

It took a moment for Elvin to be able to nod and respond. "Fine."

"The Crown Attorney made a preliminary offer," Denise jumped in. "It's a lesser charge than the original allegation of conspiracy to commit fraud."

"What is it?" Ray asked.

"Obstruction of a police investigation." She let that sink in before continuing. "Six months in a minimum-security facility, with the option for parole after three. Then two hundred hours of community service."

Ray blinked. Six months. In an actual prison facility. Put in those terms, it sounded scarier than he'd originally anticipated.

"I can't believe this is happening," Elvin muttered.

Neither could Ray.

"And one more thing."

Elvin huffed. "What else is there?"

"Once you plead guilty, it'll go on your record forever," Denise added quietly.

"So I'll be a convicted criminal."

Elvin took Ray's hand in both of his. "But you'll be *my* convicted criminal."

It was so fucking surreal that Ray couldn't help laughing out loud. Maybe he was a little hysterical, or maybe he just had nothing else to lose. Laughing was the only thing that made sense. He glanced around the room. Elvin was smiling at him like he'd lost his mind. Mike was chuckling along, and Denise looked like she was sitting with a group of clowns.

Denise and Mike stood to leave, and Ray walked them to the door.

"I'll hammer out the details with the Crown Attorney and let you know if there are any substantial changes to what we've discussed tonight. You'll also have to appear before a judge to make it official. The whole process will take a while, so you won't be shipping off tomorrow. You have time."

"Thanks, Denise." Ray pulled her in for a quick hug. "I really appreciate it."

"Remember that art fundraiser?" Denise laughed. "Who would have thought this is where we'd end up?"

Mike came over and shook his hand. "I'll let you know how Joanna wants to proceed."

Ray nodded. "Thanks."

Then it was just the two of them again. Ray found Elvin in the kitchen digging through the fridge.

"What are you looking for?" He took his usual seat at the island.

Elvin sighed. "I don't know. I'm not hungry. I just needed something to do with my hands."

"Come here."

Elvin came around the island to sit next to him.

"I've been thinking—"

"Uh-oh. Aren't you in enough trouble already?"

Ray rolled his eyes. "Funny." He shifted so he could catch both of Elvin's knees between his. "Seriously, I want to make sure you and your family are taken care of while I'm away."

"Ray, you don't—"

"No, hear me out." Ray had spent all afternoon planning, on the off chance he would have to go prison and leave Elvin on his own. Now that that was a certainty, it was time to put his plans into action. "I want you to move in here while I'm gone."

"What? I have my own place."

"Elvin," he scolded. And Elvin thought he was the one who wouldn't listen.

"Okay, okay. Go on."

"If I'm not here, this place will sit empty. Rather than paying your rent, you might as well live here for free."

Elvin narrowed his eyes but didn't object. Ray knew appealing to Elvin's sense of frugality would be the way to go. His other ideas would be tougher sells.

"I want to send your dad to a specialist for his back."

Elvin snorted. "Good luck with that. I've been trying to do that for ages."

"Yeah, but you're not me, and I can be very persuasive." Ray wiggled his eyebrows.

Elvin raised both hands, palms out. "Hey, if you can get him to go, I won't object to it."

"Good. Done. I want to hire a caretaker for your family. Someone to look after the kids, drive the teenagers where they need to go, help your mom cook meals and clean the house." Ray couldn't believe that the Gohs had gone this long without an extra pair of hands to help them out.

"No, that's too much. They'll never go for that."

"Which is why I need you to help me convince them." Ray gave Elvin a gentle shake. "Please. Let me do this. It'll make me feel like I'm still a part of things out here."

Elvin sighed and Ray knew he'd won. "I can't believe you're using that card."

Ray grinned. He'd use whatever card he needed to if it meant he could give Elvin everything he deserved. "So that's a yes?"

"It's a grudging yes."

"Good. Now, one last thing." This part Ray hadn't quite figured out a solution to. "Since I'll be in jail, I won't need a personal assistant."

Elvin's eyes grew wide. "Right."

"But that doesn't mean you should be out of a job," Ray hastened to add. "I'm going to talk to Joanna. Don't worry."

"Actually, about that." Elvin suddenly grew sheepish.

"What is it?"

"Ming offered me a job a while back."

Ray narrowed his eyes. "Ming? What job? When?" Had Ming been trying to poach Elvin all this time?

Elvin shrugged. "A while ago. It doesn't matter. I'm pretty sure the offer still stands."

"What offer is it, exactly?" Ray wasn't going to like it, no matter what it was.

"Investor relations associate." Elvin sounded unsure. "I've never done that type of work before, obviously. But Ming said I'd pick it up quickly. And it might be nice to try something new?"

Elvin wanted this, Ray could tell from his nervous babbling. He had no reason or right to stand in his way. "It sounds like a great opportunity."

Elvin looked at him suspiciously. "You really think so? Even if I'm working with Ming?"

Ray rolled his eyes. He didn't love the idea of Elvin working so closely with Ming every day, but what was he going to do about it? Ming had proven he was good at his job and Elvin deserved this. "I think you'll be the best investor relations associate the company has ever seen."

Elvin quirked his lips into a shy smile. "Thanks."

Ray pulled him in for a kiss. "I love you."

Elvin returned his kiss enthusiastically. "I love you too."

Epilogue

Elvin leaned against the side of the car as he tapped away on his phone. Ming didn't need help with his inbox, but now that he was working in investor relations, Elvin's inbox was obscenely full.

It turned out that working for Ming wasn't all that bad. Yes, Ming was sometimes obnoxious and annoying, but he was also really good at his job. Elvin was learning a lot about how to court and manage relationships with Jade Harbour's investors, and he liked to think he was good at it too.

It hadn't been easy after news about Caron broke out. Any plans to exit the company were put on hold, so Jade Harbour still had Caron on its books. Despite Ray taking full responsibility for the whole debacle, several investors still pulled their money out. The past four months had been a daily grind to convince their investors that Jade Harbour had truly cleaned up shop.

When Elvin wasn't working with Ming or at his parents' house, he was on the phone with Ray or planning visits to see Ray. They'd done a few day trips where Ray was allowed to leave the minimum-security compound as long as he was back before curfew. They'd even had a few conjugal visits, much to Ray's delight. He wanted the "full experience," he claimed, even though his living arrangements were more like a college dorm room than a real prison.

Elvin had thought it was a joke when he first found out. Rather than cells, Ray had been assigned to a four-bedroom apartment unit where he had his own room and shared a bathroom with one other inmate. The unit even had its own living room and kitchen. With a tennis court and community center on-site, Ray's prison sentence was more like an extended stay in a country club. Hardship, his ass.

The door of the compound's main administrative building opened. Elvin pushed himself to standing and put his phone away. He didn't want any distractions for the rest of the day.

Ray stood just outside the doors, his hair a little too long, his jaw and cheeks covered in stubble. He'd buffed up a bit, stretching the sleeves of his T-shirt more than he used to. But his waist and hips were still slim, perfectly clad in old, worn jeans. He looked the role of the ex-convict to a tee, and even Elvin could see how that could be appealing.

Ray strutted toward him, one hand in his jeans pocket, the other pulling his suitcase. The closer he got, the harder Elvin's heart thumped until it felt like it was going to burst out of his chest. This man had walked through highs and lows and had survived it all. This man was strong, courageous and brave.

Ray stopped about a foot away, close enough for Elvin to touch.

"Hey, stranger." Ray's voice carried only as far as Elvin's ears.

"Hey to you too." Elvin nodded to the car. "I heard you might need a ride?"

Ray nodded. "Yeah, you heard right."

Elvin inched forward, no longer able to maintain the distance between them. Ray met him halfway until they were chest to chest and nose to nose. Carefully, like Ray might disappear if he moved too fast, Elvin put both palms on Ray's chest.

Ray sucked in a breath and let it out shakily. He squeezed his eyes shut and put his hands on top of Elvin's. One by one, he brought Elvin's hands to his mouth to press a kiss into Elvin's palms. Searing, hot kisses that felt like brands Elvin would gladly wear.

Elvin leaned in, replacing his hands with his mouth. Ray's lips were soft and his chin was scratchy and the conflicting sensations ricocheted through Elvin until he couldn't hold back anymore. He wrapped his arms around Ray's shoulders, pressing himself close until not one molecule of air could get in between them. Ray held him back just as tightly.

It felt so, so good to be able to hug Ray, to kiss him and touch him with no conditions and no time limits. They could do as they pleased, act however they wanted. They were free.

Elvin pulled back to get a better look at Ray. He ran his fingers through Ray's hair, tugging lightly at the strands at the nape of his neck. He traced the line of Ray's jaw, the curve of his nose and his bottom lip.

"You're crying," Ray whispered, raising a hand to wipe the tears away from Elvin's cheeks.

"I'm happy." Elvin sniffled.

"I'm happy too."

"You want to get out of here?" Elvin asked.

"Absolutely."

They stashed Ray's suitcase in the trunk and got in the car.

"Joanna wanted to send a whole entourage," Elvin said as he drove them away from the correctional facility. He glanced over at Ray, who was staring at the side mirror through his window. "I told her it might be too over-whelming."

"Mmm." Ray made a sound of agreement.

"My parents also want to see you."

"How are they doing?" Ray was still staring at the side mirror.

"They're fine. They want to thank you for the weekly

massage appointment you made for them on top of every-thing else."

"How's your dad's back?"

"Better. The doctor's got him on some pain medications and the physio is helping him regain his strength."

"I'm glad to hear it."

They stopped at a red light and Elvin held out a hand. "Hey."

Ray turned to him, finally, and slipped his hand into Elvin's.

"You okay?"

"I'm fine."

"You keep staring back at that place."

Ray smiled sheepishly. "I want to remember it."

"You do?" Elvin stepped lightly on the gas, keeping Ray's hand in his.

"Yeah, as a reminder of what not to do in the future." He lifted Elvin's hand to kiss the back.

Elvin couldn't imagine a scenario where Ray would have to cross into morally gray territory again. His job at Jade Harbour was forfeited and with his record, he wouldn't get hired by any other financial company. Not that money had ever been a problem for Ray. What he needed now was some other way to occupy his time and give meaning to his life. Elvin had a few ideas, but they would discuss them in time.

Today, they were going home. It didn't take long to get to Ray's downtown condo with Toronto's notorious traffic somehow cooperating. Elvin pulled into the underground parking and they rode the elevator up to the penthouse.

"You ready?" Elvin asked before the doors opened.

"Do I need to prepare myself?" Ray asked in return.

Elvin shrugged and stepped back to let Ray through first. He made it two strides before stopping short. "Whoa."

"Do you like it?" Gone was the all-white living space. Elvin had donated most of the furniture to charities and then painted the walls rich, warm colors. He'd recruited Janice—who had an eye for design—to go shopping with him and they'd picked out pieces that looked a little bohemian and purposely mismatched.

A giant red and orange area rug covered most of the space. Multicolored blankets and pillows decorated the couches. The glass coffee table had been swapped out for an upholstered ottoman. The kitchen's long, white island was now dotted with vases of fresh flowers, and the white stools had been replaced with industrial-looking ones.

Ray shuffled through the space, touching everything he passed. His eyes were wide and his jaw hung open like he couldn't believe what he was seeing.

"I know I went a little overboard. I hope it's okay."

"Are you kidding?" Ray turned in a circle and laughed out loud. "This is amazing!"

"Yeah?"

Ray came rushing over, grabbed Elvin by the waist and spun him around. By the time he set Elvin down, they were both laughing and dizzy, collapsing into a pile on the floor.

"You're amazing." Ray kissed him hard and desperate,

igniting an answering call within Elvin. "I love you. So much."

"I love you too. So much."

"I should have asked you to decorate this place ages ago."

Elvin pressed another kiss to Ray's mouth. "Wait till you see the bedroom."

★ ★ ★ ★ ★

Acknowledgments

A big thank-you to my beloved writing group and especially Edie for being my cheerleader; Tanya for being my cube boss; Nazri and Sadie for being my Zoom writing buddies; Jenn for critical emotional support during my darkest days; and Allison, Sam, Delphina, HL and Roberta for being generally wonderful human beings.

Thank you to Allie, Annabeth, Andie, Katy, Jennie and Piper for understanding and commiserating when things felt impossible.

My undying gratitude to Margrit for always having my back, knowing exactly what to say and keeping me grounded when life is spinning out of control.

Lastly, thanks as always to Stephanie Doig, my editor, for her understanding and patience and for helping me make this book better.

All Mason wants to do is fall in love, get married, and live happily ever after...but it turns out the traditional life he expected has some surprises in store.

Keep reading for an excerpt from The Life Revamp
by Kris Ripper.

Chapter One

Tim was perfect. He was everything I looked for in a partner: employed (hello, *doctor*), stable (no crazy exes lined up around the block or stories about how he wanted to punch people), and kind. He didn't drink too much or spend all night fighting with strangers on the internet or say passive-aggressive things and then gaslight me when I called him out about it. He had a retirement fund. He always found interesting things to talk about.

He was *perfect*.

We'd been dating for almost six months and it seemed like now was the appropriate time to Get More Serious. To be honest, at this point in my not-quite-disastrous but also not-quite-fruitful dating life I wasn't even sure what getting more serious was supposed to look like. I guess we'd go exclusive and, having done that, we'd make more of an effort to see each other? Move in together eventually, get married, combine our finances, buy a house, adopt a kid or two?

It was a little heteronormative and cookie-cutter, but that didn't trouble me much; whoever it was who said that thing about no battle plan surviving contact with the enemy could have said it about relationships. All of my friends had fallen in love and paired off, and their relationships took whatever shape made sense to the people involved—not necessarily the shapes they would have predicted.

Tim and I would find our way. That's how it worked, at least judging from observational data.

Which is why, when he said, "Should we discuss where this is heading?" over wine at a fancy restaurant, smiling at me with all the assurance in the world, I should have been elated.

Wasn't this what I'd been waiting for? Wasn't this exactly what committed adult dating looked like? Two grown-ups, fancy restaurant, having a Serious Conversation About Their Relationship?

So why was there a heavy sensation in my gut, a weight that held me back from all the excitement I'd expected to feel in this moment?

"Yes," I said, or forced myself to say, pushing down that feeling and willing it to disappear. "Let's do that."

"Well, Mason." Tim lifted his glass. "I really enjoy what we've been doing and I'd like to do more of it."

"Me too," I echoed, clinking my glass against his. He

was a busy doctor, I was a less-busy-but-still-working-full-time-with-a-solid-social-life bank sales associate. We saw each other once a week. It's not like he was going to give up his doctoring to see me more—and I wouldn't want him to—so I guess that meant... I'd be giving up things in my life?

But no, I was just being paranoid about this after the many, *many* times I'd dated people who expected me to make all the allowances for them without getting anything in return. Tim wasn't like that.

Tim was the perfect guy. Who was now looking a little uncertain.

I was officially screwing this up. "Sorry, a lot on my mind. Let's definitely do more of this, um, of everything." I smiled at him, which wasn't hard, because Tim was the guy you smile at. We'd met through a dating app and from the first texts back and forth he was always easy to smile at, even when he was just words on a screen.

He shook his head slightly. "I'm doing this all wrong. I was so caught up in having this conversation I skipped over all the usual catch-up things. How was your week? Is everything all right?"

"Yeah, everything is all right, sorry. Just having an off night, I think?" I wasn't going to compound my weirdness by inventing a crisis. That was a thing younger Mason might have done, and while I slightly envied his willingness to make something up when he didn't know what to say, I was no longer that careless with the truth. At least that's what I told myself as the silence grew awkward.

"My timing is terrible," Tim said. "I apologize. Let's table this for right now and revisit it when we're both fully present. But for the sake of my future reference, this *is* something you want to revisit, isn't it? It's completely okay if it's not! Only I would appreciate knowing that now."

"Definitely." The relief of being let off the hook made my voice firm. "Very definitely."

"Okay, good. Now let's pretend I never brought it up." Self-conscious laugh. "I just signed up for a training I thought you might find interesting. If you want to hear about it?"

I did want to hear about it. More than that, I wanted the conversation to return to something completely neutral, which didn't demand I have or think about my feelings.

We went back to my place after and had exceptional sex—Tim wasn't just a pretty face, let's be clear, he had the skills to back it up—and then he went home because he had early appointments the following day.

And I nominally went to bed. By which I mean I stared at the ceiling for a long time. And then sent a snap to my best friend. I was too lazy to turn on the lights so it was just a shifting pattern of darkness and less darkness while I spoke, though I turned on a sparkle filter to give Declan something to watch.

"Okay, date recap, I fucked everything up? He wanted to talk about our relationship and I froze like—" I paused, trying to come up with a really good metaphor. And failing. "Like a freaking deer in headlights, Dec, what is *wrong* with me? He's perfect. He wants all the things I want. He's a doctor. He's nice. He's stable. Why am I not over the moon right now with an exclusive boyfriend, picking out table toppers for my wedding Pinterest board?"

And send. That's how I'd pictured this moment, when I'd imagined it, but now that it was here I couldn't even be happy about it.

I expected Dec to be asleep and get back to me in the morning, but a few minutes later my phone buzzed.

He was using a filter that gave him a cowboy hat, which was a funny juxtaposition against the rainbow shower curtains in what was clearly his partner Sidney's tiny apartment bathroom. "Wait, what happened? I'm confused. Also oh my god, make Sid stop editing, I'm sooooooo tirrrrrrrrred. But tell me what happened, because I don't know what you fucked up and I want to be supportive." He pointed. "Supportive face, now tell me how I'm supporting you."

I was just about to reply when a new series of snaps came through.

"Also, nothing's wrong with you. You say he's perfect when you know there's no such thing. If I'd drawn a picture of who I thought was perfect for me it'd be a picture of you, which is obviously not true, and I'd have never been open to Sid, and then we'd all be super sad. Romance is not a formula in a spreadsheet, Mase!"

One more snap, this time no cowboy hat, just Dec with his hair mussed in front of a plastic rainbow.

"This is me not apologizing *again* for leaving you at the

altar. Please note my emotional growth." Then he stuck his tongue out at me and added, "I haven't grown *that* much."

I flipped on my lamp and said very solemnly, "I see your emotional growth and I appreciate it." I left a long pause where I did not stick my tongue out in return even though he'd be waiting for it, just to mess with him. And I really didn't need him to apologize again for leaving me at the altar when we were twenty-two. "But seriously, why am I like this? I've been hoping that dating Tim—or anyone— would get to this point and now it has and I can't even be happy about it? Am I self-sabotaging? Should I call him right now and propose? Ahhhhh."

Snapchat is like a super-sped-up version of the telegraph, where you send a message and then wait for the other person to watch it and record their own, then they wait while you do the same. Sometimes I kind of like all those pauses. The lack of immediacy can be perfect and allow me to virtually chat with my friends throughout the day while actually hearing their voices.

Right now the lack of immediacy was super annoying because I wanted Declan to tell me how to fix this thing with Tim.

Which he didn't. He did send four entire series of snaps, this time from Sid's kitchen, with a chicken on his head. Not an actual chicken, a filter of a chicken, which was one of his favorites and also let me know that he was trying to reassure me with a calm, meditative chicken filter, even though he himself was pacing and gesturing and couldn't stay still.

"Okay, first, you are *amazing.* You are an amazing human being, there is *nothing* wrong with you, you're wonderful, and of *course* Dr. Tim NoLastName wants to lock that down, because you're a fucking catch, Mase, okay? So stop acting like he deserves better than you! He doesn't. Literally *no one* deserves better than you, you're the fucking best, and I say that as an authority on the subject."

New snap. "Second, you should definitely not call him up and propose, oh my god, don't even *say* that." He shook his head violently and the chicken filter glitched trying to keep up. "Seriously, take it from me, that is the exact wrong thing to do. I know ambivalence is scary when you think you have everything you want, but *listen to it.* You're not doing anyone any favors if you pretend you're more into something than you are."

New snap. "And Sid totally backs me up on that, FYI, but anyway, I don't think it's self-sabotage. You just need some time to think about it, and you're allowed to need that. Just because a guy seems 'perfect'—" aggressive air quotes "—doesn't mean he's perfect *for you.* Like maybe he is? But you don't have to decide that tonight."

New snap, with his face closer to the screen. "Ummmm also Sid's done editing so we're kind of on our way to bed—or going to do something bed-related anyway—but I'm totally here for you—both of us are here for you—but don't propose to Tim, just take a bath and read a book or something, okay? I love you sooooooo much! There is *nothing* wrong with you." He got even closer, his eyes slightly out of focus. "Mase, you're incredible. I'm so lucky you're my bestie." He blew me a kiss.

By the time I'd seen all the snaps I had a text that read, *Also if you need me, we can phone?*

In other words, he'd put off having sexy times with his partner if I was freaking out. Which was sweet, but no. *I'm fine, you two kids go have a good time*, I sent back.

And I was fine. Mostly. Just confused.

Ambivalence? Was that what this was? This…this feeling of *meh* when I expected feelings of *yay*? But I liked Tim. We had fun. I respected him. He respected me. Sure, it wasn't a formula in a spreadsheet, but when you added up all the good things, shouldn't that still equal *hell yes, let's take this to the next level, baby, I'm totally in?*

Chapter Two

The night after Unnatural Disaster Ambivalence hit, I went out on a blind date. Not, like, *because* of the ambivalence. The blind date had been scheduled two weeks earlier when I finally caved and told my friend Claris I'd go out with her and her husband. Not in a threesome way. (I'd checked.) In a "my friend Claris is in an open marriage with her polyamorous husband and she thinks he and I would hit it off, which I know because she's mentioned it no fewer than every other time I've talked to her in the last year" way. They had tickets to an art gallery opening and I said I'd come along. No pressure, plenty of things to talk about, no big deal.

I really liked Claris. I'd liked her ever since the first time she showed up at the bank where I worked to sell us on supporting some incredibly wholesome community improvement event she was planning for some incredibly wholesome community organization. Claris was an organizer and grant writer for local nonprofits, the kind of person who could juggle a dozen projects at once and never show up without all of her notes in perfect order. It was admirable as hell, to be honest. And beyond that, she had a whole *way* about her, like one of those old movie stars, a sprinkling of Mae West attitude—flirty and funny and clever, but always like she was bringing you in on the joke. It went without saying that her husband would also be interesting and smart, since those things tended to run in couples. But since I'd always pictured getting married as part of my own future, which I couldn't very well do if the dude was already married, I'd said no to her attempts to set us up. Until either she wore me down (likely), I got increasingly desperate (somewhat likely), or she came up with a meet-up that was so low pressure it actually sounded kind of fun (pretty likely).

And okay, maybe I was a *little* bit curious. Diego—the husband—was a fashion designer. He was one of Claris's favorite conversation topics, and even after running what she'd said through a filter of *is married to him and therefore not objective*, I was still left with a pretty intriguing set of characteristics. He was Claris's age, so only a few years older than me. He'd gotten a degree in fashion design and then went out into the world and worked at an entry-level customer service job like the rest of us. But he'd never stopped designing clothes, and had been designing his own clothes since childhood. (Which, not gonna lie, was charming AF.) He apparently specialized in tailored suits and casual "menswear," though Claris had said it with the air quotes and clarified that Diego didn't believe in gendered clothes.

Diego Flores, she'd said, in that tone that meant someone else might recognize his name, though I hadn't. And I didn't go digging around for info. Because I was not a creeper. Even though when someone tells you her husband is a rising star in the local fashion scene, every neuron in your head is screaming to google. I am a man made of self-control, so I hadn't.

Which, in retrospect, was kind of dumb because if I'd googled I might at least know what the guy looked like, instead of standing outside the gallery scanning everyone who approached, waiting to see Claris and A Husband-Like Figure, whose clothes would probably be unique and on point, who'd probably be handsome and have a good laugh. I couldn't imagine Claris with anyone who didn't have a good laugh. Maybe I'd at least make a friend out of this deal. Not that anything was technically stopping me from going out with other people. Tim and I weren't exclusive—yet. At least not until we revisited that getting-serious conversation.

I refocused on the present instead of some imaginary potential future. No couples in sight. I checked my phone again. Where the hell was Claris? I'd just started to text her when I was jolted rudely out of my huff by a dude staring down at his phone as he walked and bumping into me.

There's this moment when something like that could

go a few different ways. Was I going to be a dick about it? Was he? Were we going to launch into dueling apologies until one of us abashedly walked away? I was already annoyed that I'd been standing there like a dunce looking for Claris, so at the slightest hint of aggression I probably would have taken this random klutz down.

But he didn't give me aggression. He gave me a wide-eyed blink, from under long eyelashes. "Oh no, was that my fault? That was my fault, wasn't it? I'm so sorry, I was distracted and—"

I waited, but he didn't follow it up. Just kind of stood there, brows slightly tilted down, like a kid had been playing with an avatar designer and matched the "mad" eyebrows with the "slightly embarrassed" mouth. "No problem," I said. "I'm actually just waiting for people." I wasn't totally sure why I felt the need to justify standing outside the gallery, but there it was.

"Are you?"

Something about his tone—curious? dubious?—made me want to further justify myself. "Blind date, to be honest. I have fewer than zero hopes, if that's possible." *Liar. You wish you had fewer than zero hopes.*

"Oh no, one of those? Let me guess—you were set up by someone you didn't feel you could refuse, but it's obvious to you that it will never work so you've resigned yourself to wasting your evening?"

"Exactly. I did *try* to refuse, but my friend is very persuasive." I made a show of sighing so it would be clear I was mocking myself more than anyone else. "This sort of thing happens more and more as I age out of 'attractive and unattached' territory and into 'destined to die a spinster' territory. I used to have to fight the rakes off with a stick, but sadly even they've stopped paying attention to me."

He smiled, lighting up exactly one dimple, on the right. The asymmetry was oddly compelling. "Oh dear. You'll end up living with a poor relation out in the countryside somewhere, a topic of pity and derision, unable to manage your own affairs unless someone very rich dies and leaves you their fortune."

"And *then* I'd have to fend off the fortune hunters," I agreed solemnly. "It's really a terrible life, so you can see why I'm on another blind date, despite my track record of not being good at blind dates."

"Indeed. As a matter of fact—"

But whatever he was about to say was cut off by the flurry of Claris arriving, her curly hair having broken free of its severe braid to form something of a mane around her face, her voice slightly panicked. "Oh thank god, you found each other. I'm so sorry I'm late! The freeway was a parking lot, I swear I could have gotten out of the car at University and walked here faster. Hello, darling," she said to the man beside me, kissing him. "You've met Mason, then?"

"Not exactly." He turned to me, his smile a little mischievous now, and held out his hand. "I promise I'm neither a fortune hunter nor a rake. Diego."

"That is cold, man. Seriously cold." I shook my head and took his hand. "Mason, as you apparently already knew."

"I had an inkling."

"So you *didn't* meet?" Claris frowned at each of us in turn. "Leave it to two people on a blind date to fail at basic introductions."

"To be clear, I figured out who I was talking to when he mentioned becoming a spinster." Diego paused before adding, "I hope it isn't *too* cold? I couldn't find a good place to interject. And we were kind of…riffing."

My desire to remain disgruntled was at war with my desire to find him charming. "You're on probation," I told him. "And you, Claris, are fifteen freaking minutes late to a date you've been haranguing me about for months. What the hell."

"I know, I'm sorry. It was the damn traffic. And the fundraising meeting ran long, which I did warn you it was likely to do, but I honestly did not expect it to run over by forty-five minutes. Who on earth does that? Plus, I had no idea I could have called in, and there people were, on the little spaceship speakerphone." Her hands strayed to her hair and she turned back to Diego. "Oh dear god. Tell me it's not as bad as it feels like it is."

"I promised I would never lie to you, so…" He let the thought trail off, lips still curved, humor in his eyes.

"Damn. Let's get inside so I can find a bathroom. Today has been a mess." She started resolutely marching toward the doors.

We followed after her. Diego called, "Yes, but did you get the money?"

Claris turned and beamed at him, hair forgotten. "Of

course we did, silly boy. You know I always get my way."
Then off she went.

"She's going to get there first and she has the tickets," he
observed. "She'll just end up having to wait for us anyway."

"It would be undignified to run," I said primly.

He laughed. "I am sorry about before. I didn't mean to
deceive you, kind sir."

I couldn't help playing along. In any other circum-
stance—like if I was out on a real blind date, with a person
who wasn't married, whose wife wasn't also on our date—I
probably would have held back. People tend to be attracted
to my Cool, Calm, Have It All Together persona, which
doesn't leave a lot of room for romance novel banter. But
this was Claris's husband, so I had literally nothing to lose.
"Intentionally deceiving me would be fiendish indeed."

"Fiendish! Perish the thought."

Claris was gesturing madly to us as she held out her
phone to the person scanning tickets. "I'm so tempted to
slow down just to see what happens," I confessed. "It would
serve her right if they made her wait."

"They won't. She really does get her way most of the
time."

And sure enough, with a glance at us, the ticket-scanner
waved her through.

I sighed. "There's no justice in the world when rude
people are rewarded for their behavior."

"But she's so *charming* with it is the problem. Have you
ever tried to be mad at her? It doesn't take."

"Only once, and not mad so much as disgruntled because

she'd written the bank's participation into a grant before we'd had a chance to actually finalize our contribution. So I read her the riot act about professionalism and responsibility and blah blah blah."

He smiled, pushing his hair behind his ear. "You lectured *Claris* about professionalism? That can't have gone well."

"Oh, but see, that's how she got me. I was sure she'd be pissed but instead she apologized and told me I was right, and she wouldn't do it again, but she just *knew* I'd want the opportunity to support a queer youth center, wouldn't I? She could hardly send out the grant without acknowledging the bank's support, could she? And somehow by the end of it I was *thanking* her." We'd only known each other a short time at that point, but I remembered walking away from that meeting knowing that A) I'd been played and B) I admired the hell out of the play.

Which… "All right, I grant your point. I cannot be mad at that woman, even when she's clearly in the wrong. But you're married to her. Aren't you supposed to be bemoaning the chore split and crying about how the sex is boring?" Not that I was prying exactly. But not that I wasn't.

Ticket-scanner waved us through and we entered the gallery together, making our way through the small crowd toward the back. "Oh, the sex is never boring with Claris," he said, when we'd wandered to stand before a display of photographs, black and white, all mounted in black frames with wide mats. I was still thinking about sex with Claris, but Diego had apparently moved on, because his next comment was, "This is a bit…on point."

They were all forced-perspective pieces with humans looming over what I could only describe dryly as "the effects of climate change"—acres of burnt forest with looming blackened trunks, eddies of trash overwhelming a shoreline, an actual garbage dump site. Which, you know, yes, humans are responsible for the collapsing global climate. I agreed. But there was something a little annoying about the photos.

"I think the problem I'm having," I said after a minute of study, "is that the voice my brain has assigned the photographer is basically the voice of the person who holds up the line at Starbucks to ask about the origin and pasteurization process of the milk."

"Exactly. It's not quite to my taste, to be honest. I suppose I like my art like I like my sex partners."

Hard as I tried, I couldn't pick up the thread. "Um. Not looming over you looking terrifying?"

He grinned, the dimple flashing again. "In the right mood I might not mind that in a sex partner, but no, I meant *subversive*. The last thing you want in sex or in art is to be bored." He tilted his head to the side. "Do you think we're missing something? It can't be this obvious. Can it?"

"Missing something. Hmm." I stepped back. Then to the side. Then to the other side, shifting around him and appreciating how his hair brushed the top of his collar. Just the kind of hair you'd want to run your hands through if you were kissing...

Begone, random, unwelcome thought.

I viewed the nearest photo from the other side, up close,

looking for…well, okay, I wasn't looking for anything really. But it did give me a moment to realize just how aware of Diego I was, his body, his attention, which was confusing since if I hadn't choked on my date with Tim I'd be standing here in an exclusive relationship with a doctor I already knew I liked. Yet… Diego was not a doctor. But I did seem to, uh, like him. If that's what this was.

"You look like a spy," Diego whispered. "Are you trying to find a secret code embedded in the surface of the image?"

"Maybe I am." I leaned in closer. "You never know. There could be a microchip for me to scan with my spy tech. Or a tiny bar code or something."

"Bar codes are so nineties, it's all QR codes now."

I shot him a raised eyebrow. "Now who's the spy, my dear sir?"

He moved slightly closer to me and lowered his voice. "Don't shout about it. But yes, if you must know, I'm a trained agent with the Art and Espionage Service."

I also lowered my voice. "I've never heard of it."

"Well, *obviously*. If you'd heard of us we'd have a much harder time doing our job, now wouldn't we?"

"And what is your job? I mean, in broad strokes."

"To ensure hostile forces are not transmitting state secrets via the visual arts. That's my department, of course. There are other departments for music and film and…" He paused to flesh out the story. "Um. Podcasts? Maybe they're embedding things in podcasts."

I nodded very seriously. "Verbal triggers, right?"

"Yes, that's exactly it. Trying to take control of the populace via verbal triggers implanted in seemingly mundane podcasts."

"It's probably *The Moth*," I said. "I've always been suspicious of *The Moth*."

He tilted his head closer confidentially. "Our technicians have gone over every millisecond of that show and so far detected nothing. But the analysts agree there's something fishy about it."

"This is cozy," Claris said, stepping up beside Diego.

I suddenly realized we were basically two grown men playing make-believe and felt myself flush.

But Diego, without changing his tone, said, "I've had to bring Mason in on the secret nature of my intelligence work, but you did say he was trustworthy."

"Ah. Yes. Your...intelligence work." She nodded. "I am comfortable vouching for Mason in this capacity."

"You don't believe he'll be a liability to my work investigating art and its use by spies to buy and sell vital intelligence data?"

She bit her lip as if trying to control a rogue smile. "Oh, no, in fact I think Mason could be an, er, asset. To your important work. He's *very* observant." She winked at me. "I'll leave you two gentlemen to it. I have some contacts of my own to develop." And away she whisked.

I let out a breath I didn't realize I'd been holding.

"You okay?" he asked.

"Sure. I just had a meta moment of thinking that playing pretend wasn't exactly normal behavior for a blind date."

Diego reached for my hand, clasping it between both of his. "Mason. If you can't play pretend with your date, then why are you dating them?"

The question, teasing as it was, knocked me back a moment. I would never have talked like this with Tim. It wasn't that he didn't have a sense of humor, just that he wouldn't have understood *art gallery* as an appropriate venue for pretending to be spies. I didn't allow myself to be bothered by the fact that I couldn't think of any venue Tim would find appropriate for playing spies.

I brought myself back to the moment. "According to my friends I'm usually *fixing* them more than dating them, so maybe that's your answer."

"Oh no, that's not good. Fixing never works out well in the long run, though I suppose it does form the basis of a lot of marriages. Let's go find some other possible security exploits." And then, as natural as anything, we were holding hands. Walking through the gallery, looking at the next display, fingers loosely intertwined.

It didn't last long. Maybe two minutes. Four or five at the most. But since most of the people I'd dated expected me to initiate all the contact, it stood out to me as A Thing. Not forced, not entirely casual.

Since we weren't on a serious date, I wasn't exactly running my usual program of balancing my outgoing appearance with an internal checklist of ways Diego did and didn't meet up with the kind of person I saw myself with. Still, without The Usual First Date Questions, we ended up just…talking. A little about our jobs, but since Claris had told him that I worked in marketing and sales at the bank, and she'd told me that he designed clothes, we were robbed of/saved from the general chitchat.

And honestly? It was fun. If I didn't have a well-established friend group already, or if we'd been younger when we met, Claris and I would have probably had a non-work friendship from the beginning. But something about being in our thirties made that kind of thing more complicated than it used to be, so it had never exactly shaken out until now, and if this semi-sham of a blind date was the thing that made it happen, I wasn't complaining.

It might have been easier if I liked them just a little bit *less*. They were obviously so into each other, so delightful together, so damn #relationshipgoals. It was almost intimidating to watch, except each time I started feeling slightly alienated, one or the other of them would find a way to pull me in again. And Diego didn't take my hand after the first time, but he did find other ways to touch me, brush against me, stand close beside me to study the crooked beak on a painted parrot and quietly debate whether the hooked end of it might in fact be a disguised arrow, and if so, was it pointing to the location of a hidden microchip lower in the painting?

I left them outside the gallery at the end of the night, exchanging cheek kisses. Claris teased Diego about how she'd really just set us up to encourage him to finally separate his business and personal finances, adding to me that creatives were notoriously bad at doing so. Diego promised to come by the bank where I worked to set up a business account. Claris promised he would have all the necessary information to do so, with the kind of sidelong couple-look that should have made me feel excluded, and would have, except she followed it by saying, "We don't want Mason thinking you keep poor records, darling, so we'll try to hide that from him as long as possible."

"I don't keep *poor* records," he told me in his defense. "I just don't keep a picture of every single receipt in a data-base cross-referenced by purchase, company, tax year—"

"That's hot," I interrupted.

He groaned. "Oh no, not another one."

Claris laughed. We said goodnight.

I sent my post-date recap to Dec, as usual. This time it took me longer than ten seconds to figure out how to summarize. *NGL, I really liked him. Too bad he's super married and I'm sorta taken.* True statements. I added, *Also we pretended to be conducting a counter-espionage investigation. So FYI, you're covered if you need any help with that.*

He sent back a toothy emoji—the happy one, not the eek one—and *That sounds amazeballs. You liked him?*

Me: *Yeah. Like I said. But I'm in the market for a serious boo and he's already got one.*

Declan: *I'm just glad you liked him! At least it sounds like you had way more fun than you usually do!*

Me: *I've definitely never gone out on a date and had my date's wife along for the ride before. Look at me, trying new things. :P*

He replied with an entire rainbow of hearts. I sent the same back and put my phone away, trying not to take it too personally that Dec didn't think I sounded happy after dates with the guy I was actually dating. I couldn't worry about that, not tonight, not while I was still thinking of things Diego had said and smiling. And the way he'd held my hand, just for a minute or two, the warmth of his palm in mine.

I'd been right, by the way. He had a great laugh.

Don't miss The Life Revamp *by Kris Ripper, available wherever Carina Adores books are sold.*

www.CarinaPress.com

Also available from Hudson Lin
Three Months to Forever

Ben is looking for an adventure when he accepts a temporary assignment in Hong Kong, but he never anticipated how his life might change when he meets a sophisticated older man named Sai. Their initial attraction is sizzling and soon grows into more as Sai takes Ben on a tour of the city's famous landmarks and introduces him to the local cuisine. Sai stimulates Ben's intellect and curiosity, and for jaded corporate lawyer Sai, Ben's innocent eagerness is a breath of fresh air. It would be so easy to fall in love…

But nothing is that simple. Sai's job forces him to do things that violate his morals, and his relationship with his family is a major obstacle to any lasting relationship with Ben. For Ben, he misses his family back in Toronto. Can he really leave behind his home for a man he's only known for a short time? With the clock ticking, they must decide whether to risk it all and turn three months into forever.

To purchase this and other books by Hudson Lin, please visit www.hudsonlin.com/books.

Discover another great contemporary romance from Carina Adores

There are three things you need to know about Preston "PK" Kingsley.

1. *He's a writer, toiling in obscurity as an editorial assistant.*

2. *He is not a cliché.*

3. *He's been secretly in love with his best friend, Art, since college.*

When Art moves in with PK following a bad breakup, PK hopes Art will finally see him as more than a friend. But Art laughs off the very idea of them in a relationship, so PK returns to his writing roots—in his book, PK can be the perfect boyfriend.

Before long, seemingly the whole world has a crush on the fictionalized version of him. Including Art. But when his brilliant plan to win Art over backfires, PK might lose not just his fantasy book boyfriend, but his best friend.

Don't miss
Book Boyfriend by Kris Ripper,
available wherever Carina Press books are sold.

CarinaAdores.com

CARBB0422TR